After Moondog

After

New York   San Diego   London

Jane Shapiro

Moondog

Harcourt
Brace
Jovanovich

Sha

"Down In Florida," "Volpone," "Mousetrap," and "Poltergeists"
originally appeared, in somewhat different form, in *The New Yorker*.
"Commedia dell' Arte" appeared, under the title "The Summer Visitor,"
in *The Ladies Home Journal*.

The author wishes to thank the Corporation of Yaddo,
the MacDowell Colony, and The New Jersey State Council
on the Arts for their generous support.

Library of Congress Cataloging-in-Publication Data
Shapiro, Jane, 1942–
After Moondog/Jane Shapiro.—1st ed.
p.   cm.
ISBN 0-15-193096-1
I. Title.
PS3569.H34118A697   1992
813'.54—dc20   91-43142

Designed by Camilla Filancia
Printed in the United States of America
First edition   B C D E

MAY 0 4 1998

For Peter and Amy

After Moondog

Prologue

In July 1965, wearing new sandals, blind to life's possibilities, I met the boy who would immediately become my husband, while we were standing at 54th and Sixth talking to Moondog. It was early evening and the sky was full of light. I was twenty—still easily, routinely stunned by the beauty of the known world. Moondog was glistening, sweating in his leather helmet.

William, the boy, was skinny and white-faced and urgent, twenty-three, young enough still to act precocious. He had ridden the subway down from Columbia expressly to talk to Moondog about Oscar Peterson: as a child, his parents' amazing lone child, he had been taken to Copenhagen and there heard Oscar, with Pettiford on bass and J. J. Johnson and Kai Winding sharing the bill. This had changed him, he told us: it gave him jazz. Although we were in a dazzling, record-breaking heat wave and standing in exhaust fumes with taxis going crazy and light flashing and hot dust swirling around us, Moondog and I were all ears.

I stood and listened to my future husband talking while I thought about Moondog's life at home—I assumed he had an apartment and at night he went home to it. It was 1965—there were Bowery bums, smoke drinkers, and lost men, but Moondog was the only well-known street person. If you were young and thinking of giving a party, you might for a few minutes consider inviting Moondog: you knew him as well as half the people on your list. These ideas I rehearsed now, and said to William an hour later while we were inclining toward each other in a coffee shop during a daylight supper. We talked about Moondog's blurry voice and, boldly, about his blind eyes. My husband and I would be storytellers together from this moment. We produced our first story: How Moondog Dreams Away His Nights.

Some paratroopers at a place called Bien Hoa had just been guaranteed a regular beer ration. President Johnson was steadily predicting dark days and planning new moves; by late summer, he had told the paper, the military buildup could reach 100,000 men, or boys. William was in law school, uptown, to avoid being among the 100,000, and I was in summer school, downtown. In a year I'd graduate, and then, I'd begun to wonder, where would I go? What would I do? Get a leather headdress? Stand next to Moondog? I was preoccupied, trying to blink my eyes open and shiver my feathers dry. William looked good to me.

William had spent half the day seeing *Cat Ballou* and *Help*, which he now, like a boy following his mother around the kitchen, described exhaustively. On the way out of the coffee shop, passing the register, he held my forearm, too tight; I tugged it away and he looked injured: already we were a couple, with problems. In the wedding pictures, two months later, we're staring, falling into each other's faces, telling each other the story of our supervening, inordinate love.

2

A few years later I was surprised to read an article about Moondog, saying he had been adopted and taken to Germany by somebody—a countess!: on reflection, that part seemed unsurprising, that's the kind of "homeless" guy he was. But by the time I read this, Willie and I had married and had babies and long since moved out of the city so as to deepen our sense of stability and own a small green lawn.

Part I

1. Calamities Befalling the Previously Normal

Nora was six, interested in justice and safety and holiness. She started to cry. She said, "How could God let the man fall, when he only wanted to go to a safer place?" The photograph was going to become famous—the man trying to hang from a wheel of one of the last American planes leaving Saigon, his picture taken as he drops into the South China Sea.

Zack went to his room and brought back his new globe, a seventh-birthday present. We sat with our hands on the cool surface and looked at the ocean lying beside yellow curving Vietnam, pale matte blue with lavender depths. If you fell into deepest purple, you would sink 3,000 feet, then lower, dropping like Alice down the rabbit hole, monsoons far above you, fish flying by. The waters growing dark, tuna and mackerel and anchovies and croakers and shrimps calling out in the blackness as you sank. Zack took his father's hand. We sat close together, squeezed into the couch, as if we figured our staying together, and close, might help.

In September, back in the neighborhood, in the middle of New Jersey, where William's college years had been happy, fog hung in the branches and it was eighty degrees. The war had been over four months. The Vietnam vets were back among us, though we couldn't see them. Other families were still at the beach, jumping through the waves, feeding each other sandwiches and fruit, riding together in their campers. I could almost see the tiny perfect groups—each family member inextricably, intentionally linked with every other, the steady mother keeping the little boat afloat.

An hour into the day after Labor Day, my husband left for work and I was immediately pained at our separation; we had just enjoyed two weeks of surprising truce. William was a lawyer now, with his own practice; he had a meticulously appointed office, in decor slightly reminiscent of a ski-resort condominium, five miles from our house, a world away. I dialed him at the office. We talked loudly and self-consciously, as in the early days of telephoning.

William had taken on a new, equally young, very calm partner, and he was terrified about whether the money aspect would smooth out and the wildly different personalities would mesh. This made him a new man every day—enraged, exhilarated, or doomed. Now he cried, "Immersed three hours and just finishing the mail!" His voice cracked.

"You're not making sentences," I said.

"What's wrong?"

"Nothing." It was something ordinary. It was this: I'm young, my children are young, my husband and I have become estranged while we were looking the other way. I have no plans. It seems, obscurely but certainly, to be all Willie's fault; then all mine. He feels the same way, he just won't say so. If I try to recall the start of our troubles, lengthy reflection carries me back to the wedding.

We had been married in my mother's house in Wellfleet ten years before, on the dune above the Atlantic, during a September week so warm and damp that the guests were like the bridal couple—shiny-faced, exhausted, confused. Every important thing Willie and I ever did seemed to take place during a heat wave. A decade later, I remember my sister, Rhoda, eighteen years old, standing in a blue satin dress near some pots of mums, whispering, *"Don't get married. You'll die."* I remember so well the rabbi, imported by my mother from Boston, a man I had never met before and would never see again; he was large, with a deep, resonant voice, and he was excited about being near so much sand and water. I can barely remember the groom—I think he was a febrile boy, heedlessly sweating in a summer suit. Everybody was so recently arrived from the fifties, washed up on this shore. Nobody cried, "What! You're children! Get back into your playsuits!" After the wedding, we drove off in our Volkswagen Beetle, zooming and bucking, my hand under his as he shifted. Exiting the Cape, the first thing we did was leave the highway fast and drive twenty miles in the wrong direction.

We were still on the phone. Papers rustled. Willie said absently, "Why did you call?"

It occurred to me to say, Don't go to the office anymore. I need you with me. The new partner was David Grieves, so the name of the law firm was Green and Grieves. I said I'd called to say the new name sounded like a London shirtmaker, and we hung up gaily.

Zack and Nora were in the upstairs hall, lying as if dead on the rug. They were waiting for grammar school to open. Nora fanned herself with newspaper clippings she had been reading with the whole family's assistance. We were six months into our current events reports, and both children were specializing in calamities befalling the previously normal. Unfortunately, one of Nora's main subjects, Patty Hearst, had recently done nothing but continue to hide. Nora kept her clippings in a drawer set into the base of her bed, along with Lambie and her barrettes, and at night she could lean over and slide the drawer open and, had she been able to read better, follow once again Patty's abduction, brainwashing, and apparent, though actually completely implausible, conversion to a new political position, before dropping quickly into a placid sleep.

It had been the eighty-ninth Labor Day, the safest on the road in fourteen years—this from Zack's traffic-accident and freak-of-nature report of the night before. Only 407 people had died in their cars. The National Safety Council had no immediate explanation: they had expected more dead.

Nora was six, Zack was seven, and they had lived their entire lives side by side. They lay with their eyes closed and fluttering, in dim light, reminiscing about their even younger days. Nora felt for Kibbie's front paws and dragged him onto her chest, and, Kibbie wildly purring and kneading, the kids lay in silence for a while.

I sat down on the rug next to them. Sand was falling out of their hair, and they smelled as if they had been rolling in dirt.

Finally Nora said, "Sometimes I feel like a kernel of corn."

The next day, I went back to teaching the bad boys who couldn't read. They lived at the Training School, where they had been incarcerated for breaking and entering, armed robbery, arson, occasional murder. They were antic and depressed. Being in the halls with them was like being with hundreds of troubled young drama students—theater keeping them from going crazy— while they constantly rehearsed a single scenario of dominance and submission. Standing in lines, they would pass the time showing each other how to strangle and stick people between the ribs. One would grasp another deliberately from behind, as if demonstrating lifesaving holds. The victim was often incapable of portraying a person physically without recourse—he'd just have to make an effort, sink to his knees gaily choking, suffocating, then dying.

I started to work again with Arden, aggravated assault, mother alcoholic, father gone, sixteen years old, white, recognizes small words. His face was shrewd, impassive, pale. He had broad, smooth fingernails, deeply curved, with satiny pink showing through—I was falling in love with his big hands and their strange, elegant nails. We sat together, flipped flash cards, avoided reaching for each other and having sex. Sitting next to Arden was always a strong experience, feeling him near and not undressing him. Like many of the boys, he had an air of carrying himself carefully, as if trying not to give up and rape or slaughter the nearest person out of a natural desire to get his true story out.

As usual I wanted to say, what's your address? I'll send you a card, we'll go to the theater, you can come home with me. Let's meet.

I'll save you. We'll save each other.

After the lesson, there was the short personal discussion. In his wing the night before, Arden said, they'd watched a program on educational TV, a history of public executions. The blood inside the brain starts to boil. The body reaches 140 degrees and they have a fan in the room to blow out the smell.

"Burning flesh?" I said.

"Right. *Burning flesh* smell." He grinned. Arden heard the clock hand move, stood, and, grinning, turned and walked.

I got paid very little for trying to teach the boys, and they learned very little; as though we were all doing it for love.

Most of the summer of Patty Hearst's seclusion, at my suggestion and with my constant help Nora had been filling in with the lackluster and overprotected but at least dependably visible Susan Ford. Susan had danced with the French ambassador and received a muskrat coat. This week Nora and I had been momentarily engrossed by Squeaky Fromme pointing a .45-caliber semiautomatic pistol at President Ford at close range in Sacramento, California, and secret service agent Larry M. Buendorf leaping for the gun. When Nora reported about Squeaky, Zack said: "The guy who *saved* the president is Larry? Then you should tell about *Larry.*"

Nora said, "Mom and me are reading about *girls* more!"

In fact, Zack alone among us was an appreciator of ordinary heroes and a disinterested observer of broad events. William and I, the initiators and insistent perpetuators of the current events project, were in the grip of powerful personalities. Through our quiet, steady attention, we were developing intimate connections with the truly violent and the larger than life. All last year I had followed Kissinger's resistance as the last Americans departed from Vietnam plane by plane. William was watching Ali; he was ten years into it, since two months before we met, when Cassius Clay had battered Sonny Liston in the head in the first round, up in the deprived city of Lewiston, Maine: in May 1965 the shortest bout in heavyweight history. Giving our reports, Willie and I sometimes held hands.

A week into September, Muhammad Ali appeared at a rally in Newark in support of Rubin "Hurricane" Carter, and four black kids at school managed to almost strangle a big, vicious white kid who thought Hurricane Carter didn't deserve a new trial. They leaned on his windpipe, and he came to class the next morning with the whites of his eyes blackish red, full of blood. I had to stay late at work for a long meeting— the need for increased discipline and vigilance on the part of the already exhausted, overly realistic staff.

I got home just before Willie, and remembered things were bad again between us. Five minutes later he stood in the door, his briefcase hanging, on his face a white, disgusted look. He stared into the house before stepping into it. Our relationship depressed him.

At dinner I explained my day to the kids. Willie was uncharacteristically silent. At last he said one thing: "Do you actually seem to be intimating that Hurricane Carter is more likely to be innocent because Ali appears at a rally?"

As at a tennis match, Nora and Zack looked at him, then me. "Do they need this?" I said to Willie.

"Excellent," he said. "Grab the moral high ground."

"Pardon me," I said, "I forgot: It's your Muhammad Ali."

Nora said quickly, "If I was President Ford, I would make aerosol cans against the law."

Willie, eyeing her proudly: *"That's very intelligent, Norie."*

As the evening wore on, Willie's spirits picked up and he strolled through the house full of hostility. He sat in front of a police drama as if he were a frantic invalid parked in his chair, his body stiff, his leg jiggling, reserves of adrenaline triggered and coursing. Through the commercials he hunched with a sandwich, holding it out and violently bending, to avoid dropping drips on himself. He bit off chunks, stuffed his mouth. His eyes and nose ran. He breathed quietly after each bite, letting his pulse rate drop, and looked at the pickle.

The police lieutenant grasped the shirtfront of a pockmarked, life-hating drug pusher and smashed him against a wall. He was sickened by what he had seen in the world, the child molesters, muggers of old people, girls on the street, sociopaths of every stripe, even corruption in his own precinct. His teeth flashed, he spat, spit flew from his lips, he turned his beefy back. Off duty, he could be avuncular, even tender.

William was furious too. He would not speak.

Willie stared in flickering light. He struggled with big bites, chewing and swallowing, gazing inward, already a divorced man.

The second week after Labor Day, a Volkswagen pulled up and a young man crossed the lawn. He stood on the porch looking at me through the screen while I talked on the phone. Then he moved out of view to ring the bell. "Come in," I said. The guy was three feet away but remained hidden. "Come in, come in!"

He entered, staring through the sudden darkness. He introduced himself as Mr. Randall-Black, someone who had once lived on our street but had grown up and moved away. He was quite pretty—slender, with lots of soft, dark hair. Through his eyeglasses, our gazes locked. He advanced a step, searched my face. Would I prove to be a caring person about education?

I'm already putting in my time, I thought, caring and caring. Arden would break your face for you.

He was offering materials to help my children with reading skills, history, the vagaries of social science, so relevant to our place and time. He quickly mentioned the Komsomol, Sputnik, Sherman's march to the sea: could my husband and I discuss such things with our young children at dinner, secure that no family member was underinformed?

"You don't seem to have a clear picture of our dinner hour," I said. I laughed.

He looked hurt.

I said into the phone, "Could you hold on another minute?" I had been talking with my friend Annie about our confusions, and a tear was in my eye. "Seriously, no thanks," I said pleasantly.

"I don't think you understand."

"Thanks for stopping," I said. "I'm not interested right now." Perhaps earlier than necessary, I was speaking in that contrived, steady tone which seeks to avoid the extremes of cowardliness and rage.

I had been telling Annie that the first time I saw William he had looked adorable to me—oddly delicious, like a complicated dessert—and she had laughed frantically in support. She was still barking in the phone.

Mr. Randall-Black drew back, then advanced. Clearly I had insulted him, but he refused to yield even to his own discomfort. He peered into my face, as if reading something off my nose. "When would be a more convenient time?" he said, with vivid, quiet interest.

"Thanks! Not interested at all!" I said jovially.

"Then you have a fine reference library," he concluded. "Because surely you'd want—"

"Please! Please!" I cried. "Not today! *That's it!* I'm not buying encyclopedias!"

He cast his eyes down, bowed slightly, eased back out the door, slunk to his Beetle across the grass. I watched him go—he looked nice, out there in the bright light and the green.

As soon as William walked in, I told him about it,

acting the parts. I said, "He was religious. He was the bearer of the joyous news in educational materials." Willie was stepping around the kitchen in his suit, looking into the refrigerator, pawing the bills. He turned and cast me a smile. Things were improved. Our grievances were set aside, preparatory to being forgotten, as if mislaid.

Late at night, sometimes we did impersonations. Our favorites were discussions between President Ford and Willie's father, in which Pep reviewed for the president the news of the day while William's mother, Lainie, corrected his phrasing. Pep would say, "If I might interject," and advise Ford on foreign policy and cold cuts, two favorite subjects.

Then maybe we'd bring in Mrs. Curran from the drugstore, who arrives at the White House wearing Earth Shoes and wild with irritation about being called away from the register. William would nuzzle my neck. We'd plan a week in Paris for Jules and Annie and the Rosemans, two couples who disliked each other for reasons only he and I could see.

"Peep peep!" William cried. "Peep peep eep eep!" Deenie Roseman has brought her bird to Paris, to the Tour d'Argent, up in the elevator. She sets the cage on the table high above the curving Seine, the bird cries out from under its drape. "Lala la la!" William threatened to sing. He hummed "Under Paris Skies" and threw his body around the mattress.

We did this often. We'd laugh and thump the pillows. We'd push each other's shoulders, the night would wear on; we'd be rolling in our sheets, tangled in bedding, our bodies damply touching.

David Grieves, William's law partner, was a tall mournful-looking man with lots of fuzzy, reddish hair—people were always calling his hair a "corona." He was a good listener. Listening, he often covered parts of his face—his mouth, or his forehead. He smiled rarely, a beautiful, genuine, luminous smile. He handled all the divorce cases.

"He really listens to women," I said to Willie, who was getting ready to open some wine.

"Great," Willie said.

"And, for that reason, women really like him."

"Oh good," he said.

"Hey, it's not a trivial thing. It's a remarkably *unusual* thing."

"True. But I believe you meet with six enraged pals weekly to discuss this very subject. In fact, the entire white upper-middle-class segment of the population has already put in, by my count, about five solid years on the topic 'Listening to Women.' "

"Hey, five years hasn't quite done it! Why are you doing this? I just said he listens! I don't care if we spent nine hundred years! It's still *not that common*."

"I have no slightest quarrel with that," he said.

"You act like you do."

"Your point is unassailable." A pause, like clouds before rain. Then: "Dispositive it ain't."

"*What* doesn't dispose of *what?*"

"Simply put, lawyering demands, unfortunately,

substantially more than skillful listening, regardless of whether the lawyer is a man or a member of the besieged and neglected gender."

He smiled at me.

"Holy cow," I said. "You're a creepy guy."

Yanking on the corkscrew, he smiled harder. The cork pulled free.

I was faintly aware of my determination to remain innocent and press on. I said serenely, "Obviously I'm not talking about David as a lawyer, I'm talking about him as a person."

Willie said, "Few finer human beings exist. Boy, you don't quit."

He poured too much red wine, fast, into my glass.

We sniffed in our glasses.

After a pause I said: "David Grieves practically has an afro."

Willie cried, "We're also gonna talk about the hair! Will you *can* it?"

William and David had to part right away, because, Willie said, Grieves failed to take hold of the materials, to seize and shape them. This seizing and shaping was something William did so well. Learning a new skill, he talked about it continuously with steadily increasing sophistication and scope. When he was learning wine, I'd used to give him gifts in exchange for his not mentioning wine for a while—a T-shirt, a key chain, a fake Walt Frazier autograph. I pointed out that he had completely forgotten there was a time, back in drifting childhood, when he knew nothing of wine. William said, "Wonderfully fascinating, coming from somebody who doesn't think she knows it even when she knows it. Thank you, Joanne."

"You're calling me Joanne?"

"Joey," he said. "Okay? Everything perfect?"

I didn't, now, tell him my opinion that he parted with David Grieves because he struggles to get people near him and then kicks them till they back up again. He would say that's not him; it's me.

It was our tenth anniversary. I pointed out to Nora that she had a current events windfall, with the capture of Patty Hearst in distant San Francisco, and Nora looked confused—she had forgotten Patty. Then Willie and I had a brief, spirited quarrel, Willie maintaining Patty might've had free will. Then we spent the evening at back-to-school night—the kids full of pride and sweetness and astonished to be in their classrooms with darkness outside the windows. In the corridor, Nora took me aside. She whispered, "I wish you and Dad would get *haircuts*." I whispered, "Maybe Dad might not want any hair comments right now." She whispered, "I'm telling *you* this, in privacy."

Late at night Willie said he would like to go to bed for seventy-two hours and have "hard sex." It must mean deep massage, tenacity, orchestration: seizing and shaping. I thought maybe he wanted something more subtly voluptuous but didn't know how to say so. The week before we met, he had given up any remaining hope of ever becoming a movie director; now our potentially improved sexual life unfolded for him, frame by frame.

———

A man started calling me. "Joanne?" he said.

"Arden?"

"What do you mean?" he said.

"No, go ahead," I said, "I thought you were some-body else," and the phone fell dead.

The second time, he said, "I need you to listen."

"What is it?" I didn't hang up. I felt alarmed and interested—now I thought somehow it was my cousin calling, a man whose voice I hadn't heard since he was a boy.

"You can help me," he said.

"What is it?"

"You can listen when I call."

"Who is this?"

"Listen, I have things to tell you."

He had a soft, full, oddly beautiful voice. The sound of it seemed to cause me to slip very simply into a calm listening state, which lasted a long time. Finally, with a sense of suddenly waking up, I said, "You've got the wrong person!"

When he called again, I hung up; set the receiver on the desk; waited; hung it up again. He called, I let it ring for thirty rings, answered. "Help me." I hung up. The feeling he provoked was so familiar, the irri-tation, sudden closeness, then fear—that's how I real-ized it was the encyclopedia salesman.

When it rang again, I said, "Mr. Black, don't phone here anymore."

He said, "Randall-Black. Hyphenated. Oh I'm glad. You know me." He hung up and it stopped for a week.

2 1

William insulted me, I snubbed him, he touched me, I turned away; I kissed his face; he laughed, not nicely. We got very tired. On a Saturday morning, we were desperate to resolve our differences, and the kids stopped playing and came into the house and looked at us. Stop fighting, they said.

"Oh please," I said.

"Don't yell at Daddy!" Nora shouted. "I love Daddy!"

"I'm simply talking to him." In fact I had just pushed him, hard, but quietly.

"She's not yelling, she's talking," Zack said.

Nora embraced William's head and glared at me. He said, in a snuffling voice, from out of her embrace: "Norie, honey, we're having a discussion, Mommy's just telling me she—"

Nora: "Daddy, it's a big fight!"

William: *"Nora, we have to be able to have a private conversation."*

Zachary sat on the rug and started watching his hands twirl William's key ring—the one I'd given him two years before not to talk about Côtes du Rhône. "You're bizarre," Zack told the keys, and he almost began to cry.

I said, "Nora. I'm not hurting Dad. Dad can speak."

"That's it!" William shouted. "Sufficient! I already told her, she understands! Zachary, cut out the goddamn clinking!"

Zack stared at each of us in turn. Nora was far down in the couch, blotting her face on a throw pillow. I was at the table in my bathrobe above streaks of crumbs and breakfast litter. William was swaggering near the fireplace in his new tennis whites, looking aggrieved and helpless. His and my ensembles told, I thought, a usual story: he had a life, I didn't.

The phone rang and Willie answered in his most modulated voice, which was a joy to hear. "You were gracious," I said when he hung up. "Why don't you wear a powdered wig?" My heart wasn't in it, but I said it. I wanted him to say he would begin at once to talk syrup to me and indifference to everybody else.

Meanwhile he drew himself up and absently picked his nose. I watched him hard. I was readying myself to tell him that he obviously couldn't stand to relinquish the glow produced by the caller's chattiness and admiration, when he blinked and spoke. "Adjectival considerations aside—" he began.

"Inside is worse than out," Zachary said, and tossed his rubber ball, a SuperPinky, at Nora, and slammed out of the house. Fondling the ball, following Zack out, Nora gazed sadly at William and then at me, until we fell silent and began to feel, if possible, even more insistent regret.

Willie stood still and looked at me. "What do you want?" he said.

"I want you to talk as if they're your children too, as if it's your house too. I want you to talk as if—"

"Not how I talk. What the hell do you want?"

"Kinda Freudian," I said. He didn't smile. I got a sponge and came back and started swabbing the table, concentrating, sliding crumbs into my palm. I stood with my bathrobe caught in my rear, holding the sponge and crumbs. I said, "I want us to be together again."

He said glumly: "We're together."

Randall-Black called. "I'm not calling to hurt you in any way. Can I tell you one thing?"

I said, "What."

"I'm alone. It's not a sex thing I want to say, it's—"

As I set the phone down, I felt oddly sad. I thought, but I have to hang up, it's just a crazy pest on the phone. It's nothing to do with my real life.

He stopped calling. It occurred to me once that I knew his name and so I could reach him if I had to. I remembered him every day for months after he hung up—after "the last time we talked."

At the training school, surprisingly few boys tried to escape: only known runners, who always run. Arden was a reformed runner, still being watched. He had once run for five days, before they picked him up deep in Pennsylvania, among the Amish, in his pajamas with his feet bare. When he told me this, Arden started to remove his basketball sneakers to show me the scars on his soles; then he laughed and stopped.

I was interviewing Arden in order for us to write, in a booklet made of red construction paper, what he wanted to say about how he had lived so far: if nothing else, he could learn to read his own life story.

Arden's Chapter One: "This black guy named Cat,

when I seen him boxing I said He can't box! So for a year I was trying to train, to box him. But then I found out I'm not his weight—he's a featherweight and I'm a junior middleweight. So I could never fight him. On TV he looks like a normal size.

"I won in boxing though. When I got done, my eyes were bleeding and I went blind for awhile.

"When you get the plaque, you have to go up in front. I had my name in the paper: 'Arden James Sprague. Second place.' "

Do you still have the plaque?

"Nope."

Why not?

"Somebody broke in the apartment and stole every-thing. My mom knows who did it. It was the landlord who did it."

Why?

Arden shrugged. "They do it."

Dreams for Arden came to me. I wanted to save Arden so badly it would wake me in the night. I'd sit up suddenly in the dark, midrescue.

Arden's second chapter: "I was a third baseman until I got locked up. At a camp I got to go to. Two weeks. They got sand fleas. And we have to line up, we can't scratch, these millions of fleas hit our legs: 'Don't you dare scratch those fleas. You had your breakfast, so let them have theirs!'

"But that's okay. I've lived a dangerous life. I'm just living dangerously wherever I go."

What do you think you might do when you're older?

He held my forearm for a moment, the only time he had ever touched me. Grinned, looked away. He said, "Stay out of trouble."

At the beginning of November, when I went in one day Arden was gone. James, a short, wide black kid from Arden's wing, said he had last seen him the night before, watching the TV news. James was observant and shrewd. "What else?" I said. James laid his hand on his belly. He said, "Ate Doritos. Ate two stick of cheese."

"What did he talk about? Or what did he watch on television?"

James said, "We seen the lady, the president's wife. She say if somebody fucking her daughter she wants to know does he be *nice*."

I thought I'd tell a cleaned-up version of this to Nora: Susan Ford again. And when I came in the next morning, Arden would already be found.

The next day, when it was clear Arden had run and he wasn't at his mother's and they couldn't find him, I quit my job.

Willie asked what I had in mind, and I didn't know.

The school called to ask what he had told me and how he had said it, what light I could shed after two years of working side by side with Arden. I said I had nothing and I wouldn't go in to talk.

I told them that Arden had continuously apologized for not being able to read. "After every wrong word, he says, 'I mean!' " As if he'd misread the word by unprecedented oversight and were just on the verge of correcting it.

They said, we don't mean his language skills, we have to locate him, what about your notebook?

I said, "I don't keep my notes."

William and I fell into a good phase again. It was November, but I imagined it was warm, that nights in the neighborhood were still steamy when we dropped off to sleep. I dreamed it was summer—all night, the churning of the air conditioner, its condenser laboring through the cycles while we dreamed; Willie and I in bed, and near, floating on our sea.

In the night I would sometimes wake, read from my notebook and hear Arden's voice.

"I got one little sister, she's small but she's funny— she wants to box. I would have a brother but my mom had to give him up. My other sister went back down to Delaware with my dad—not my real father, he's dead, but my other dad. My sister wrote me a letter. I got it at Christmas."

How did your father die?

"Murdered, or accidentally killed, out in Partridge Street, that's a street near my mom's. Somebody said he was trying to run. But he got stabbed in his heart."

At this, I'd said that must've been hard for him and we sat in silence a while. He rubbed at his eye. At last he said, "You got a father?"

"Me? My father's dead."

"So he died of what?"

"A heart attack."

Arden's usual grin. He said, "Stabbed in his heart."

At the training school, nothing had been more important than incident containment. If a student wasn't yet frantic, you could sometimes settle him by threatening to reach for an Incident Report form, which listed the categories: *misconduct, runaway, property damage, injury, merit,* or *other.* It occurred to me that Willie and I and the kids could think about our family's life in terms like these. Misconduct and injury would appear with regularity; merit occasionally; runaway, never.

Thanksgiving was over. I had no job. My husband and the kids were standing in the living room loudly conversing, and their voices drifted up to me as I prepared to shower in the hamster bathroom. I opened the bathroom door and leaned near it, but why?—expecting, maybe, to hear some affirming comment about our elaborate life together.

The two hamsters shared a cage and spent their lives piling up mounds of sodden shavings and running in a circle all night in their exercise wheel. The bathroom smelled like a pet store. In the night if you walked around the house, you heard rattling, the hamsters side by side running and running. If I could've looked into the future, I would've seen that soon Ernie would die and Brownie would chew Ernie's head off at the neck and eat the brains out of Ernie's skull. I stuffed on my shower cap, sniffing plastic. Of course, looking ahead I would also have seen my husband falling in love with Jill Grieves, a woman as dog-tired as he of doing without any seizing and shaping. I would've seen Arden in Tampa; my own love affair; the kids in their beds at soccer camp; William and me divorcing. William going back to the Cape in August and learning more about tennis every day. William playing tennis on a clay court with a morose psychiatrist, while their new young girlfriends, silky hair swinging, look on. Red dust gathering on eight new white sneaks. The sun drops, the mist rolls in, Willie's backhand improves by the minute.

2. My Lover

I frequently had to make conversation with my lover. We had very little in common.

For years he and I had known each other slightly—gone to the same parties—but we'd never really spoken; it hadn't occurred to us to bother. Then there was a winter solstice housewarming party given by our friends Deenie and Michael Roseman in their big new glass-walled house. The Rosemans had a gift for befriending varied types, and by the time our family arrived the long snowy driveway was lined with everything—Volvos and BMWs and four-wheel-drives and battered Volkswagens and an old pink Chevy coupe. It was five o'clock and already black, the end of a day that had never turned bright. Nora leaned forward and whispered, "Mom, I don't want to go." But then she jumped out and followed Zack up the walk.

The front door was open. A square of green carpet had been laid over the icy step, so that you seemed to step into the house over a tiny frozen lawn. As I set my foot on the carpet scrap, Willie held my elbow in two fingers—an odd gesture, courtly but mean.

The kids had already disappeared. We were alone in the front hall in sudden heat. Pine branches lay along the banister, and from all the rooms we could hear the party roaring. I said, "Can we be nice to each other?" He was stripping off his coat and scarf, fast, in ferocious silence. We had been fighting, mainly silently, for two days.

I tugged at a piece of his hair.

"Look," he said. "Let's just do this party."

Deenie always greeted you as if you had been held hostage for months then debriefed in Germany and she was meeting you at Kennedy on the tarmac. Now she rushed in and beamed into our faces with vibrant sympathy. She was gorgeous, wearing a caftan and sending off clouds of jasmine perfume. On her chest lay a bib of silver disks, Tunisian, and, being hugged, I clanked against her; the embrace was so fragrant and vital and genuinely loving that I felt both comforted and demoralized in about equal measure.

"Was Roebuck hilarious today?" Willie cried happily. They had been in the same court, where the judge had skewered a young woman lawyer.

"He's a pig," Deenie said pleasantly.

She swept us before her into a swirl of people— elderly conventional-looking people, gloomy young hipsters, lawyers, potters, architects, psychologists, learning-disabilities specialists, political scientists in sport jackets; wild-eyed computer jocks; numberless serene leftists; poets, post-docs, and children. They all stood among naive paintings, Alaskan sculpture, Tibetan prayer cloths, arrangements of Japanese sugar flowers—it was a carnival atmosphere, full of color and movement, hectically festive.

I went up to David Grieves and said, "I'm always too nervous before a party."

3 1

He held his forehead and looked interested, then smiled the radiant smile.

A group immediately built up around us—Michael Roseman, our host, a small and comely developmental psychologist, wearing a silk aviator's scarf and protesting Saul Bellow's Nobel Prize; a demographer who wanted us to compete in listing the capitals of West African countries; Deenie's mother, a shrewd-looking woman; and an economist named Dan Marchand. The circle pulled in tighter, Deenie's mother stepped away, and Dan and I were facing each other, alone.

I said, "I'm always nervous before a party."

"About?"

"I guess, that I'll embarrass myself."

"Really?" He eyed me as if through a microscope.

"When I was young, at the beginning of a party, as I was about to be introduced, my father used to tear my eyeglasses off my face. I would stagger forward, blindly grinning."

He appeared to jump slightly. We were about equally surprised. I had been twelve when my father died; I had never told this to anyone; I'd forgotten it, until this moment.

After a while he said, "Where are your glasses now?"

"Contacts."

Dutifully, he moved to peer at me. We were exactly the same height. I held still. He took a short step, and, without seeing them, looked straight into my eyes.

We glanced around. We stared into our wineglasses.

"I worry too," he said finally.

"About what?"

"That I'll get bored and Kathy won't let me go home."

We gave up and fell completely silent in the din. People were laughing and festively shrieking and bumping us, and we had two empty glasses and we could escape each other.

I looked for the kids and found them in the kitchen with other children, trying to feed cookies to the parrot. All week Nora had been practicing courtly gestures, and she immediately lifted and kissed my hand.

My friend and host Michael Roseman came in and said to me, "Are you okay?"

"Do I look bad?"

He nodded. He stared at me, waiting.

"I'm sorry," I said.

Michael was one of my biggest supporters. He said, *"Do you know that I love you?"* We embraced like boxers and staggered around the room.

Several women were here in the kitchen, talking together in code, as if they were in the Resistance. I considered joining them. Instead, I went back out and talked with some teenagers, benignly smiling, taking the implicit position that, unlike their parents, I accepted human life in all its guises.

Nearby, a man told a woman something elaborate and she vivaciously listened. Near them, the same. Near them, the same. The women were more or less noticing what was happening. After a few more years of this, some would probably leave town in the night, stab the guy, or enroll in law school.

I could hear Willie somewhere in the crowd, and I looked around for him—his voice sounded happy, and I suddenly wanted to find him and say hello.

He turned up standing at the piano, listening to a quarrel between two beautiful women. They were Jill Grieves, the wife of his former partner, a new lawyer herself; and Deenie. The two were seated sideways on the piano bench, half-facing each other, like lovers, their knees touching. Jill wore remarkably high heels and a black silk suit. She raked her fingers through her cloud of red hair. As an adolescent she had been married for eight months to a black guy, and now she thought Deenie had said something racist. As I arrived, Deenie stood up and cried, "I must feed these people!" She whirled, smiled grimly, and rushed away.

Willie hadn't seen me yet. Jill said something quiet, and he leaned down. Her face was pale, with pink spots on the cheeks, and her eyes were unnaturally bright—she looked like a tall beautiful feverish child in a woman's clothes. I remembered somebody saying about David Grieves: he loves his wife so much he can't stand to watch her dance. She was talking to Willie, very low. He was close to her, listening hard.

Willie looked up and saw me. He said, "Hi!"

He excused himself and we walked outside. The terrace had been cleared and we stood on huge stones surrounded by drifts, and there were lights shining on a grove of birches and casting lavender light on the snow. We could hear the party behind us through the glass, but we stood together and looked ahead at trees and scraps of light and then darkness. We said we were sorry; we would try much harder; we cared.

Inside, somebody started to play the piano—an old man, a composer, about to retire from the university, playing Chopin. In waves, all the guests stopped talking—from outside we could see all the rooms, with everybody stopping their conversations, and we could hear the music clearly, fine distinct notes. In the kitchen window, a woman was doing dishes, but everybody else, even the children, stood still. They didn't look at each other. Snow gleaming, and silvery music rippling through the house. Willie kept his arm around my shoulder, at first efficiently, then sincerely.

Very late, outside, slipping around on the driveway trying to get to the car, I ran into Dan. He said, "That was an interesting moment. As if the music were trying to tell the party: Consider your life. Imagine your death."

I took this in stride, not realizing I'd never hear Dan Marchand say anything remotely like it again. "So you weren't too bored?"

"I enjoyed your being there," he said.

Nora was next to me. She suddenly reached for Dan's hand, picked it up, and kissed it. They both looked astonished, and we all rushed, thrilled, to our cars.

I was feeling wonderful—sad, strong, optimistic. Months later, falling asleep, I would realize: there was something wrong with the scene, a man like Willie never flagging as he listened to two women talk

Three weeks later, Dan and I found ourselves boarding the same train to New York. It was a Wednesday, the middle of January, temperature dropping fast. The glow of the party, of course, had worn off, but on the other hand we couldn't pretend not to

3 5

see and know each other. As we boarded, there was that strong smell of metallic smoke—it felt like a train scene in a black-and-white movie.

We declared that we felt an immediate bond because we had both decided against seeing Paul Taylor in favor of seeing Ballet Theatre, Baryshnikov and Fracci. Before the train pulled out, we stood in the aisle and quickly talked a lot about the shape of Carla Fracci's foot.

Then we sat companionably and opened our newspapers and saw what had happened the day before. Japan was ready to conclude a treaty with China, formally ending World War II. Egypt, Syria, and Jordan wanted the Security Council to ensure an Israeli withdrawal from the occupied territories; the Op-Ed Page of the *Times* had an article by Golda Meir. Fighting was spreading across Lebanon; the stock market was down slightly; Governor Byrne wanted some tax breaks for business and industry. And a thirty-year-old man had tried to walk across the Hudson from New Jersey to Manhattan, on two pontoons, using two paddles. Reporters had heckled him from a tugboat, and—this seemed poignant to me—he had said, "No problem."

Dan pronounced the Op-Ed Page inevitably more laughable than the guy on the pontoons. Then he explained all the rest of it—his airtight story made everything sound not just comprehensible but manageable; and by Elizabeth or Newark, our friendship, oddly, began.

We started to think of ourselves as being together, and time started to move.

Danny mainly phoned, from all parts of the world. He called from Indonesia: "Djakarta is changing and it's becoming visible. They'll have a middle class soon—they'll be ready for the fast-food and motorbike stage."

"Tell me about it," I said. This early in the conversation, I resisted trying to hustle him into an intimate declaration. There was a lag in the phone, and an echo; I could hear a voice like that of my younger self, tiny and far away, saying, Tell me.

He said, "It's a place that can't really be understood, I think, in American terms. In some sense, of course, the military is everywhere—but that doesn't mean what we think. You remember the Japanese had run the Dutch out? and when they declared themselves independent after World War II, the Dutch tried to take them back?" From across several wild seas, decades after the event, Danny sounded, in a restrained way, amused: "And if you can imagine it, the Dutch invaded!"

My husband was coming home from the office to pick something up, and I didn't have much time, but my new lover, who was incapable of saying anything romantic in the best of circumstances, continued in this vein. I thought I'd like to quickly get in a couple of endearments, in case we had to suddenly hang up. He didn't *have* endearments. He missed me. He wanted to talk to me. And this was how he talked.

Danny said: "The politicians gave up and the army didn't: the army ran the Dutch out! So in a sense the army established themselves as the preservers of the nation and superior to the politicians. So the influence of the military is social and political, rather than based in weapons. It's entirely non-Western: the army as members of society.

"Given that it's a country of some thirteen hundred islands, the military is oriented toward actual defense."

"Is, or isn't?" I asked.

"What's your question?"

"The army is or is not oriented toward defense?"

"Is," he said. "The military integrates itself into the life of the islands; they help build the roads and run the hospitals. And the theory is: If we're attacked, the people will rise. And the military will be like the Vietcong, the fish swimming in the sea of the people.

"To Western eyes, it looks threatening, as if you're caving in to a military regime. But it's much more benign than that."

I was starting to want him to recall who was on the phone with him, across oceans and continents. "Danny," I said, "I'm risking my marriage for you."

He laughed. "Oh, you were ready to risk it in any case," he said, and William's car pulled into the driveway.

He was right, I was. William always would be the love of my life—I could imagine the Dutch invading Indonesia infinitely more easily than I could imagine being parted from my husband. Being unfaithful to him had been a desperate move, and had made me feel at first like a sort of murderer, a crazy, lonely one, compelled to kill. After a while my feelings grew more ordinary, more correct. I started to feel just like what I was: faithless.

Dan was an international economist. What he liked to do, besides going to the ballet, was talk with his colleagues about economics or, in a pinch, with others in related professions about chaos or fractals or what OPEC might do. He could get pretty excited wondering whether Siegel's Paradox was maybe only an apparent paradox. In slow traffic, he'd refuse to change lanes because, he'd say, we'd already eaten up the disequilibrium.

For Danny, as it happened, this was a stirring moment in the century: the theory of rational expectations had just been argued by some Minnesota and Chicago guys (soon to be known as freshwater economists) to be broadly applicable. Their idea was so fundamentally destructive to interventionist economists' way of thinking that it was being widely ignored; Danny, nearly alone among the economists in the saltwater states, loved it inordinately. He appeared quite thrilled. At the market level, the theory said that future events now being anticipated are actually already having their effects; at the individual level, it said that on average your expectations turn out to be right. We talked about this halfway to New York, until I finally figured out what it meant: if you decide to do it, it's already done.

I told Danny, "I don't even see how we got started."

He thought. "We went to a ballet," he said. "We have a shared interest in it."

"So does everybody in the Metropolitan Opera House, and they aren't skulking around having an extramarital affair!" I felt pained, for the twentieth time that day.

He looked surprised. "I like the word 'skulking,' " he said. Finally he inquired, "Don't you think any of the four thousand members of the audience are having affairs?"

"I may not sound it, but I'm serious."

He said, "I don't find persuasive the idea that most of the people occupying those expensive seats, especially in the orchestra, are particularly interested in dance. They must be skulking."

We could go to these performances because we were married to these two people who didn't want to. Once a week, Danny and I took a train to New York, cordially chatting like the social acquaintances we had nominally been for years. We saw everything: Merce, small disorderly pieces in hot dangerous lofts, the Bolshoi, *Swan Lake*. We got to know the guys at the ticket windows, and we liked seeing them: the only friends we had who thought of us as a couple. In the ladies' room at the Met, I was often calm and happy, standing in line in the warm, comfy, urine-scented air, then tipping grandly.

Sitting in my seat, though, I always thought of Willie, who couldn't look at any painting or building or piece of sculpture, couldn't hear or see any performance, without rushing into the foreground with lavish remarks. I missed him. I thought, you're missing the old William from years ago, not the one back at the house. I rushed to think, William always has to jump in front of the work of art! I branched out and reviewed my husband's more serious failings, his anger at me, my anger at him, our shared confusion. If I didn't, it sometimes got hard to see why I was here with my lover.

Early on, the third time we went, I'd suddenly wanted to smash past people's knees and run out of the theater, to the train, and home. I would've been giving up a coveted seat, front mezzanine. It was a performance of *La Sylphide*. Little Baryshnikov, two short eventful years out of Russia, languished in the baronial hall in tasseled knee socks; the court promenaded; the sylphide appeared like a bit of mist, on a fieldstone window ledge, before a smoky midnight sky. Dan was cheerful. He was enjoying everything: the symmetry of Bournonville; the cognoscenti complaining about the tempo; the rows of sylphides in the forest glade, inclining their flowery heads. Who is this man, I thought, and I wanted to run. Gelsey Kirkland crossed the stage. I tried to look at her long foot, her stealthy jumps. When the sylphides regrouped, the popping sound of their point shoes, scurrying, scared me to death: I didn't know where I was, and my life seemed lost to me. In wisps of forest, Mischa licked the unseen beads of sweat from the tips of Gelsey's fingers. Then I looked over and Dan was watching hard, and he seemed to be trembling, because what he saw on the stage meant something real to him. I felt ashamed. As I often told him, virtually no encounters with my lover concluded with me feeling happy with myself.

Between us, we had six children, in grammar school together. He and Kathy had married, like me and Willie, when they were children themselves—sophomores in college—back in that old lost world; and immediately their paths had diverged. Their marriage, he once told me, was designed to have a shape very different from the one it took: not two lines traveling increasingly far from each other, but two parallel lines, wide apart but at a constant distance.

We were in a bar. He drew on a napkin:

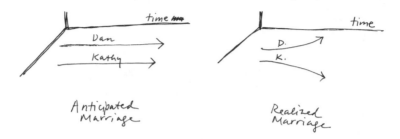

"They're both sad," I said. "But at least the first one looks permanent."

He said cheerfully, "No two people are together 'permanently,' just indefinitely. This is yours." He drew:

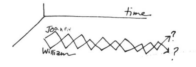

Then he said, "This is what you *think* your marriage is," and looked amused. He drew:

He said, "My marriage would be the same whether you're there or not. You think your marriage needs me to keep it in place."

Among the people we saw in common, it was known that Danny's marriage was terribly cool at best.

I said, "My marriage is the obverse of yours: terribly warm at best."

He stared. "I assume you're joking," he said.

People were starting to get answering machines; Willie spoke eloquently against this. But I bought one, and told everybody to stay away from it, it was mine. Talking to it, Danny was unusually expansive. He called from all over the world, while I was out. On the tape, he sounded real to me.

From Washington, he told the machine something I'd like: At lunchtime everybody walked over from the World Bank to the International Monetary Fund because at the IMF the subsidies were deeper; you got better value—more curry and sauerbraten and coq au vin for the money.

The IMF and the World Bank, in case I didn't know this, he went on to say, had been created simultaneously at Breton Woods in 1944; Keynes was at the meeting, and, for the U.S., Harry Dexter White, the only person McCarthy ever actually fingered, and— the tape ran out.

From a tour of the heartland: "As you know, Iowa is laid out on a grid. There's some kind of economic cost to not having towns be regularly spaced."

From Bali: "There's a reef a mile out and the water is flat and ankle deep. The beach is nice, if you want to watch Balinese babies play in an expanse of ankle-deep water." One in twenty of his messages was dreamy like this. During the lag before he spoke again, I imagined so fully the serene mothers, the little dimpled babies, the blue water glittering.

He would be consulting in Athens; he had rented a house on Crete for July, and he pretended I could join him: "You could have a commanding position over the Mediterranean, looking toward Africa." Affectionate chuckle about my pursuit of the best restaurant table, the best seat in the house: an awareness of me as myself! I could hardly believe my ears. This was one of the most romantic things he had ever said to the machine. He bounced it off a satellite.

"Possibly," Dan said, "you are made comfortable by the distance of the 'too-distant' lover?"

"Isn't that kind of Freudian for you?"

"I never recognize the stuff you call Freudian. But if you say it's there, I guess it is."

When pressed, he had a couple of ideas: "We're not necessarily on the wrong track," he'd tell me. "We won't see the path until we look back at it."

Once, sitting in an elegant dark bar, he explained that our relationship was structured in accordance with the principle of comparative advantage: I was better at "being intimate," so I should do that, and he was better at buying tickets and advising foreign governments, so he should continue to do those things.

"That's funny," I said, and I tried to laugh. The cocktail lounge glimmered around us. I suddenly laid my hands on the little table, palms up, in a standard gesture of despair. I cried, "All that intellectual power, trained on objects so far from . . . where we live!"

"It's trained on the stuff I know about," he said reasonably.

I said, "You mean, what's the point of devoting your mental life *to* your emotional life?"

He said, "I mean I can only think the way I do."

Then he took three salted peanuts out of the bowl and dropped them into my palm. I liked the gesture and I cheered up and told him so. He said pleasantly, "I never know."

From our hotel room, he made a call. This is what he said: "And on page two, you need to define the epsilon. . . . What is pi, in equation four? . . . Okay, on page twenty-two, there was something. Top of the page, there's, you seem to say something asymmetrical between imports and exports? . . . Right. . . . Oh sure! No, in the phase in which the dollar appreciated it would've *increased* imports and *reduced* exports, not the other way around. . . . Right. . . . Right. . . . Right. . . . Right. But then you should be saying there should be a smaller *decrease* in the volume of exports, not a permanent *increase*. . . . I don't think there's much more. I like the empirical results. . . . At one point you say some model is ad hoc. I don't know, for my taste there's no point in saying. . . . Okay. If you want. And page sixteen, you've got the 'permanently' again. You don't have too many 'permanently's, but they all have to go."

He was turned away, to create an office with his back, talking at the wall. I stood next to the bed, trying to retain what he said. It felt not just weird but improper, wanting to save his words, his ordinary voice.

Sometimes, unpredictably, Danny would tell his own story.

"My earliest memory is of my mother, gripping a pillow in her teeth while she put on a pillowcase.

"My second memory is of a woman rushing across a room to slap me. She was yelling, 'You've eaten too many of those carrots!' "

At the beginning, I had asked questions like, What's your earliest memory? Are your parents there? What are you wearing? and he continued, sometimes, to revert to that approach. "My earliest memory of being punished is when I was four. I think I was dressed in an itchy suit. I went into the hall and I called to my father, 'I'm like the Holy Ghost! You can't see me, but I'm here!' "

He couldn't recall much. He couldn't remember, for example, whether he had shared a bedroom with his brother—"but by the time he was born we were rich, so I doubt it." It was almost painful to imagine Dan as a boy. It ran the film backward, reversed everything he had done since, revealed him to be angry and frightened and small—what he'd truly never be again. An obedient, sneaky altar boy, stealing coins from his uncle the monsignor, catching fish in the cold early-summer mornings, riding alone on a train—he laughed at this stuff and even louder at my sentimentality about it.

But he continued occasionally to say things he thought I might find personal, irrational, or warm. When he got bogged down, he'd make love to me, kindly, with genuine competence.

"Where am I?" Danny said, through the sheet and blanket, and waited. We were in bed, in a Fifth Avenue hotel. He was at a conference, and I was spending a weekend with a friend on Perry Street. When I'd started this particular round of our continuing discussion, he had pulled the blankets over his face and lain perfectly still—an amazingly playful gesture for Danny, which made me feel almost proud of him: a man who couldn't play, making an effort to do so, purely out of unstated love for me.

One May evening, more than a year after Danny and I first went to the ballet together, when I got back from taking the kids to *Star Wars*, William was standing in the driveway under the garage light in the gathering darkness, trying to read a thick, expensive French magazine. Trees rustling. The kids ran off—their voices grew tiny as they moved away fast, down the street. The article was about Nureyev. As usual he was variously pictured as an odalisque, draped in a sable cloak, arching his famous back, making his famous *moue*. Danny had stopped over and dropped the magazine off.

"When did you talk to Dan Marchand?" Willie said.

"What do you mean? We run into them twice a month."

"But I didn't know you actually ever spoke to the guy."

"We had the same Ballet Theatre subscription."

"I know, but I didn't know you—" Uncharacteristically, Willie faltered; he stopped, confused. Then: "What does he talk about, marginal utility and its applicability to our poor little lives?"

"What's wrong?" I said.

"Also, why does he think you read French?"

"How do I know?" I said. "It's a university town. It's *your* university town. Everybody speaks French, he probably figures."

"But you don't," Willie said.

"But he doesn't know me well enough to know that."

Bugs were gathering, rushing the light bulb. The sky was turning navy blue, starting to glow. William looked irritated, and then, oddly, frightened. He said, "He knows you well enough to drop off a magazine with sexy pictures."

After the kids came in and went to bed, we sat out in the dark yard, listening to night sounds and feeling the trees nearby. We were silent, deep in our favorite canvas chairs, side by side. "Dan Marchand looked pretty sartorially amazing in complete blue seersucker," William said after a while.

"He's a college professor. That's what they wear."

"Terrific riposte."

"It's not a riposte," I said, "it's just a random *answer*. I don't know why you keep harping on Dan Marchand. I can't be responsible for every person who happens to stop over wearing an unstylish suit!"

I thought I had said enough, perhaps too enthusiastically. We sat quietly in the whistling of the crickets. Finally Willie muttered, "He looked like hell in it."

Without admitting I knew Dan at all, I wanted to tell Willie I hadn't intended to.

In fact this wasn't true. Around the time our affair began—but before we thought it would begin—some of our friends had been talking about some of our other friends, and one woman had said that Dan was so extremely self-possessed and so frequently out of the country that she couldn't quite see why Kathy had thought he was a good bet in the first place. Her husband, a usually silent econometrician, had said irritably: "He's a potent man with an elegant mind." And I'd astonished myself by immediately thinking, So *that's* why I want to be his lover!

3. The Earl and Bonnie Show

One morning at the end of May, Danny and I set out for a day at the beach—Atlantic City, perfect for adulterers, a resonant but forsaken place, disjoined from its promising youth. Keynes himself, coming to Atlantic City in the winter of 1944 to plan the Breton Woods Conference, had arrived by warship. We'd arrive by car, admire and ridicule the facades of the casinos, stroll the boardwalk alone. The kids would go from school to the Rosemans' and Willie from the office to court. By the time they got home at nine, I'd be in the kitchen making tomato sauce.

The sky was cloudless with the moon hanging in it. On the drive down, through farms and then a pine forest with a sand floor, I said I'd been hoping for weather like this. Danny laughed: In economics, there was no hope. There were expectations, there were probabilities—"but to hope is to imagine the mean is sort of better than it is."

I said, "You don't realize that sounds ridiculous."

"Similarly, dread, of course," he said.

"Dread doesn't exist."

"Yes," he said sweetly. "I suppose that cheers you up."

He wanted to make plans for a weekend in New York; of course, this would involve complicated lying and the concomitant guilt and dread and isolation and damaged self-esteem. It wasn't worth it, I thought, but our shared mood was so good that I considered it anyway. "Will you be under a lot of work pressure or would we be able to spend time together?"

He said, "Well, it's not clear. The probability distributions are bimodal."

I laughed and smacked him in the head.

My own car seemed unusually luxurious; the day seemed full of clarity, light, intensity, calm. Our love affair seemed real.

Willie caught me. He arrived in the kitchen crying, "What a gorgeous little sunburned face." This made me feel sorry for him, and deeply guilty.

"I sat outside." Now it was already too late to say I went to the beach.

"Car keys. I want ice cream."

"What's wrong with *your* car?"

"No gas," he said grumpily.

I was alarmed. Maybe I'd forgotten and left in my car some condoms from the fifties, used, or some sodden underpants, or the many pairs of ballet tickets, or the rumpled sheets from all the beds Danny and I had visited over the past year and a half. Or the divorce papers we'd implicitly contemplated filing but had never yet mentioned. Or the love letters we'd be starting to feel like writing each other any day. I wanted to return to my life with Willie—I suddenly missed him terribly, as if we'd been forcibly parted and I hadn't laid eyes on him in two years. I had become a lonely person: a liar. I was full of stage fright, suddenly very eager to be found out.

When he came back, for a moment he appeared to be dancing, maybe in a ballet by Agnes de Mille. He whirled in, into the light, hurled the ice cream into the freezer and waved his hands and signaled: stop cooking, put down the spoon, come here.

In the living room it was dark, and neither of us turned on a lamp. We sat. "What is wrong?" I said. This sounded natural. We were both always saying, What's wrong? We'd been at it a couple of years.

"There's sand in the car," he said.

"What?"

"Your car is full of sand."

"What?"

And that I'd gone to the beach with a man and Willie was going to leave me tonight.

I waited. I was wondering, slowly, why I hadn't said I'd gone to the beach. It seemed so careless as to be almost perverse. I was an irresponsible adulterer. I could hardly see him but I could hear his breathing. Then I noticed we were waiting for me to reverse direction and get this fixed.

"You're acting silly," I said. "I went to Atlantic City with Annie. I was starting to tell you. What's *wrong*?"

"You're involved with somebody," he said.

"Please. What is this, a soap?"

"You've got a guy."

My fingers started to tremble. Willie was counting on me. I said: "Call Annie. Do it. I want this silliness over."

He said, *"The woman's one of your closest friends."*

I said, "Oh, be sensible! *That's why I went to the beach with her.*"

We agreed that this sounded so realistic that it was true.

A month later, on a shimmering June day, Danny came over in the morning, in the suit William had hated—baglike, crumpled, baby blue. He was leaving for France, with his family, until September, and he stood out on the grass saying this was bad for us—

I said quickly, "Last week when we saw Martha Graham—"

—and he needed to try again with his wife.

"Now?" I said.

"I think so."

"Why now?"

I began to feel as if I were struggling to keep my balance, or straining to hear his voice. We could fix this, put it back the way it had been five minutes before. I said nicely, "Let's talk about it." We could do that simple thing. "We've always talked about ending it. It doesn't have to be right now, I don't think."

"For me it does," he said. "You can always go back. But I won't be able to, if I don't go now."

We were watching something precious falling off a shelf: it was about to land, and break. I sat down, in the luminous deep-green grass. "This is because I told you Willie was suspicious!" I cried. "I shouldn't have told you!"

"It's not that."

"What do you think this is for me? Some trivial thing?" My sadness started to pour out. It got out into the yard where I could see it—it looked to be a live solid thing, very healthy, like a rhododendron, or a tree.

He patted at my head. The theory of rational expectations seemed fully in play: If you've decided to do it, it's already done. Danny was already gone.

To be mean, I said, "I've betrayed somebody I love for somebody I like."

He looked shocked. He said, "Think about that."

I said it was all very decorous but in fact his chief concern was not for me and not even for Kathy, it was to protect his elevated opinion of himself—that I wanted to go back and tell my husband that I loved him, and that Dan Marchand had shown me how much. I stopped. I thought: I can't go back.

I said finally, "This has been the best year I've had."

"Not really," he said. "You've got a problem. And for a while I looked like a solution."

His face was pale. He walked toward the house, to go inside, to go out the front. I followed him. In the driveway, we stood in the brightness. He said, "You're somebody *I* love. I don't just like you," and he got into the car.

I leaned in his window. I said, "I just feel so alone."

"You'll never be that. They'll continue to beat down the door. I'll call you. I'll call from France."

"I can't stay married to Willie!" I said suddenly.

He turned on the motor.

"Do you need to go, this minute?"

"No," he said. "I'm not in a hurry. You're as compelling as ever."

"We've never assessed how compelling that is," I said. Then I laughed. Fuck him. I composed a vibrant, rueful smile, to portray myself as a resilient woman, aware she is being rescued by a sensible guy from spending more months or years on the wrong track. At the same moment, I realized that was exactly what was happening.

Brilliant sunlight. I peered into the dark car. I said, "Look. It's okay. I do want to be a normal person again."

Gracefully, surreptitiously, entirely appropriately, Danny shifted into reverse and backed out.

I composed a few letters I'd be writing to his wife — heartfelt, elegant, damning messages on heavy cream-colored paper. Or I saw myself at her front door like a woman in a movie, arrived to tell her what he'd done. I wanted to tell on him!

Then I thought: he's not gone. I called his secretary for his number in Paris and put it into my wallet. Most days I pretended I'd phone the next day. Falling asleep, I sometimes saw Danny's face, close to mine.

On the other hand, I walked through the house being quiet and precise, stepping carefully as if in someone else's footsteps. Willie said I was "inaccessible." I laughed, gratefully—he always said that.

For a month's stay in Wellfleet, we packed two cartons of books. I read them serially without a pause— finished one, dropped it, picked up the next.

Nobody seemed eager to talk to anybody else. On Wednesday nights we went square dancing in town: arrived early, formed squares with parents and tiny children, danced like maniacs, left late. Most other days, Nora and Zack stayed in the water all day, ate hamburgers, and fell asleep quickly with the sheets tossed back. William stood around on the burning sand as if expecting a bus—or possibly as if he were waiting for me to recuperate from an illness I'd been unaware I had. I started hugging him and the kids a lot. They'd stand patiently in my embrace. I felt shaky and strangely optimistic, strangely blessed, like somebody genuinely recovering: I was so happy to have, instead of a certainly hollow future, only a dishonest past.

Just before we'd left for the Cape, I had gotten a letter—a postcard, actually, inside an envelope, which had been lost in the mail for half a year. It showed a Kuwaiti tanker poised on a silvery sea. Danny had written: "Sad little about-to-be-rich country. Picture romantic enough?"

When we got back from the Cape, our house had been robbed. The robbers had stepped through the kitchen window and removed the stereo, the television sets, three silver bracelets, a fur hat, and the Toast-R-Oven. They had thrust their paws into hiding places and dumped our clothing on the rug.

Nora said, "Oh no! I knew this would happen!" Willie was already running through the house trying to put things back together. Zack got behind him and started following him everywhere.

How cheering. The results of the robbery—drawers standing open, our underwear strewn about—seemed so correct, so apt. I said loudly, "As Gertrude Stein said, Oh good, one of our favorite things broke!"

"Oh, stop," Willie said.

"Just a harmless burglary!" But then my mood dropped fast.

The children were afraid to sleep in their rooms. They dragged their sleeping bags into our room and lay down, and we rubbed their backs for a long time.

Willie and I walked downstairs on wobbly legs. We grew calm. We opened some wine, sat on the floor, ate scrambled eggs at three in the morning. We couldn't get sleepy, so relieved were we to be at home and thinking together about our disheveled house, and the situation no worse than it was. He brought me coffee and served Animal Crackers on a plate. He settled a pillow behind my back. I took off his shirt, kneaded his shoulders while we talked, licked cream off his fingers two at a time. I unzipped his jeans and bent and sucked a while, then came up wet-faced and gave him a friendly smile. Before he coaxed my head down again, I glimpsed a familiar face, from long ago—ardent; happy.

William and I declared that the burglary had put our problems in perspective. We stayed up all night in the wreckage and promised to try again.

We threw out the broken things and filed an insurance claim. Willie added two fictitious bicycles and twelve silver teaspoons that had been lost years before, and the company immediately gave us all the money.

We sent the kids for a week at soccer camp. As soon as they were gone, we missed them so much we pitched their red tent in the backyard. We slept in it for three nights. Arms touching, side by side in the rosy cave, we talked about the world outside. We stared up at our nylon roof, imagining the sky. Willie and I lay half the night watching the walls of the tent glowing, illuminated by the lights from our house.

In the fall, after considering it for two years, we tried Bonnie and Earl. Annie had recommended them. She said that she and Jules often found them useless, that that alone had drawn her and Jules together.

Bonnie was a shrewd grandmotherly-looking psychiatrist with expensive clothes. Earl was a tall young psychologist with an arresting Chicago accent. William and I began at once to invent a situation comedy about them and us. We said that either we were a particularly amusing couple or our therapists believed laughing was central to marital improvement. We said that often while Earl laughed—though in reality Earl had so far only chuckled, perhaps twice—he would wink at me and William. We said that when Bonnie laughed, she clapped her hands. We described her little feet in their elegant shoes twitching on the hassock.

Bonnie's house in the woods, we told everybody, had been designed by a young postmodernist with no sense of limits. Her husband, a cardiac surgeon, had been able to pay for the most insistent decorative refinements, so there were pink moldings and copper sheathing and oval windows and vast sections of glass brick. We met in a tiny separate building which had one wall of sheer glass. The clients sat with their backs to this window, while Bonnie and Earl gazed past them out into the trees. Driving to the appointment, Willie and I said nothing; driving away, we talked about nothing but the house. By nightfall we had new material for the Earl and Bonnie Show.

At the third meeting, Bonnie said, "Have you ever told each other what it is you actually want from each other?" Later Willie and I would tell each other that Earl had leaned forward and pantomimed tremendous exhortation, as if we were a little team and he our wonderful coach.

Bonnie to William: "What do you think you want?"

William said, "Fidelity," then jumped up and ran from the building, into the bright September air.

I turned to see him through the glass wall, the woods behind him, kicking with his highly polished loafers at Bonnie's imported stones. He looked lonely. I felt sorry for him, having such a wife. Anybody could see he was considering not coming back.

All September, I went to the ballet on Wednesdays and looked for Dan, who was out of the country. Twice, I saw him. Once, I sat next to a man in a tweed jacket like his, who positioned himself sideways with his back turned; when I bent to pick up my program, grazing his arm, he whispered, "I believe that's mine."

At Bonnie and Earl's, Willie said: all kinds of unhinged women's stuff, but then she quits her job! And now her job seems to be attending dance events!

I felt strange, thinking about what I was actually doing with my time: I was making collages—the words of Danny; and Nora and Zack; and Kissinger during the war, from my old clippings; and Janis Joplin and Billie Holiday; and remarks made by female tennis players; and things my mother told me when I was young; and the words of Arden from the training school, before he ran away, talking about his hopes for his life. Now I said, "I'm trying to write poetry."

Willie said, "Undeniably. Most lucrative."

Earl said sweetly, "Have you published some poetry?"

"Two."

"Thirty-five bucks," said Willie.

I cried, "Look, man! I contribute the money I got from my father and Gran, and I always have and you know it! And it's *a lot!*"

"Oh yes."

"Your law practice," I cried, "is about the least income-producing law practice in the county!"

Bonnie inquired, "Do you both contribute?"

Yes, we admitted.

"Oh heavens," she said.

In October, William told Bonnie it wasn't working and he didn't want to come anymore.

Bonnie to me: "Why don't you tell me everything you like about your husband."

I said William was dynamic, smart, spirited, in his own maniacal way I thought extremely devoted to me, sorry, I said, cut maniacal. Although his liveliness was immediately noticeable, I had always found him interesting in a deeper way, he was funny, dependably so, and that meant a lot to me, he was accomplished, he knew about lots of different things—

Earl: "Mmhm."

"Okay. Now, William, can you tell us what things you dislike about your wife?"

"Intelligent, pretty, sexy, diligent, uh, clever," he said grumpily.

Earl's head shifted slightly. Later, Willie would maintain that Earl had snapped his head as if shaking off water.

"*Dislike*," Bonnie said.

"Don't like?"

She nodded with her eyes closed. "Tell us what bothers you."

William said: unappreciative, perversely argumentative, competitive. Erratic, withholding, secretive, disdainful—

"*Disdainful?*" I said.

Bonnie: "Please"—showing me her palm. She nodded at him, and, growing steadily jollier, he went on with his list. Then he agreed to continue a few more months.

Earl asked what came to mind when we thought about our marriages. "Your two different marriages," he said.

"What comes to *mind?*" Willie said, evilly grinning. He said: Separate Quiet Time. The autocrat's dream.

It was a device of mine which I'd thought had been accepted and was well regarded around the house. From five to seven, and on weekends and vacations at other hours, the family had Separate Quiet Time: we might be together in the same room or the same car, or on the same beach; we could even work on the same project, side by side. But we could not speak. Nor could we try silently to get somebody's attention. Nora and Zack sometimes did a jigsaw puzzle, quickly, serenely, wordlessly, the pieces clicking into place. I loved Separate Quiet Time—it was one of the most wonderful things in my life.

"By royal fiat everybody in the family is rendered inaccessible," Willie said. His voice sounded unusually candid, tremulous but loud. He said, "It's like being married to the headmaster of a lunatic boarding school! Why does she live with people at all?"

Everybody looked at me. I suddenly couldn't think how I had visited Separate Quiet Time on the whole family—in a rush, it came to me that no other family did anything remotely like it. Families discussed issues together. They hung out together, sailed boats together, puzzled out the kids' homework, played Wiffle-Ball games, built new garages, all the while healthily chatting. Nobody but me had ever once suggested a period of Separate Quiet Time. After a while I said helplessly, "It's misnamed. We're not actually separate. We're just . . . quiet."

Earl looked at Willie.

"Aha," Willie said.

I told about a single incident, three years earlier. Willie had been working late. He'd asked me to bring him some dinner at his office on my way to yoga. I ran in, late, dropped the picnic basket on the desk, ran out. He followed me out into the dark, running along stroking my shoulders, nuzzling me as I tried to open the car door. I said, "I'm late." He said, "Looks voluptuous in the leotard," and kissed at the side of my head, hitting my ear. He was kissing me all over my hair, kisses falling everywhere as I struggled into the car—it was like trying to open a door in a high wind. I was laughing, saying, "You're *molesting* me!" While I rolled down the window, he held onto its edge. "Let go of the window." I was still grinning. He wasn't. He held on. I eased it into reverse and looked back over my shoulder.

The light inside the car went out. "Where did you go?" Willie cried.

"Let go now, Wil."

I started to back out, and he ran along holding on. I told Earl and Bonnie that we ended up fighting and I almost crushed his foot and I missed yoga and we never got talking to each other again for two days. Telling the story, I suddenly saw it was a remarkably modest complaint, and that it was also something precious— like Separate Quiet Time, something nobody else would think of doing. I felt at ease, talking, seeing on the rim of the window his crazy white hands gleaming, hanging on.

"These aren't such terrible grievances," Bonnie said.

"No," we said promptly.

Then we all looked puzzled, two of us for a fee. Willie and I were embarrassed—we continued to wrinkle our faces, like children hoping to imitate the adults successfully.

In December, we got into a quarrel about whether we wanted to take the kids to hear Bach in Carnegie

Hall at midnight on Christmas Eve—it took inventiveness and tenacity to quarrel about this: we actually both wanted to go.

Bonnie looked sleepily at Earl, who broke his complicated, active silence to propose to tell Willie and me what we were like. We each seemed to have a characteristic stance which could be summarized in a simple phrase, and these two stances regularly opposed each other, although in Earl's view they were only apparently, not really, incompatible. "Want to hear them?"

Bonnie: "I do. Otherwise we could watch these people play in the sandbox all night here."

William said, "All ears."

They looked at me. Unaccountably, I trembled. I said, "Sure."

Earl told us the few little words that summed us up.

Willie's was: *What you have to understand is*
Mine was: *Please! I've heard enough!*

In January, while I was talking, Earl chuckled and Bonnie grinned at him.

"What's so fucking funny?" William said. Then he and I enjoyed four days of honeymoon happiness.

Two months later, Bonnie broke her leg while hanging a mobile, and she had to be in a cast to her hip. Earl called to cancel two appointments, and Willie and I never went back.

It was spring. Things were often bad, but not always. We started to develop even more lavish impersonations of Bonnie and Earl. Willie would sit and jiggle his feet, I'd lean forward looking friendly and hectic. We only occasionally noticed that other people couldn't see the point. We went so far as to make a tape of ourselves impersonating the four of us, which featured admiring comments from the therapists about the view of the forest that the patients could not see. Once, late at night, we waited for the end of two simultaneous conversations—a discussion of drug use among sixth-grade children and an argument about the Israeli strike at the Palestinian sanctuaries in Lebanon—in order to play the tape for several friends, who understandably didn't know what to say. In the moments when we portrayed Bonnie and Earl, and in those moments only, Willie and I felt like two people in contact with a happy mystery—like a funny, loving, formerly desperate couple whose marriage had somehow been saved.

4. Commedia Dell' Arte

I got a call from Italy, from an old, not very intimate friend of mine. He was Paolo, another of Willie's and my mythic figures—marvelously tall, effortlessly potent, deeply intelligent, violently charming. Willie had met him once, and in his impersonation Paolo was always brushing back waves of hair with sensitive fingers, downing strong espressi, successfully selling short.

Paolo had a sixteen-year-old daughter now, who had been out of school this year—family matters—but wanted to take a look at the Ivy League: one month, perhaps two, and might she come to us?

Years ago, on our first joint trip to Europe, just before I got pregnant with Zack, in Piazza Minerva Willie and I had met the daughter—a tiny girl with hair curling to her waist, always at her father's side. She had eaten hazelnut gelato, silently stuck her spoon up for William to lick. We had driven into the country, and Alessandra had held out her baby hand and a butterfly had come to sit on her palm. Now we began to think of her as Alessandra the small and mighty.

———

It got warm—every day hazy gray and hotter. In the airport, Alessandra came toward us where we stood gaping on the industrial carpet—small and elegant, with black hair spilling down, white-blue eyes in a pale face. She wore a tiny leather outfit, Florentine boots on her little hooves. William hesitated, then glided toward her like a groom.

We were bewitched. While she went away to freshen her already alarming loveliness, we just stood there.

William: "Is that an adorable dumpling?"

"Incredible," I said.

Zack, with quiet feeling: "She looks like sort of a cat."

Nora stood watching the ladies' room door from which Alessandra would reemerge.

Alessandra did well in the heat; stepping out of the airport into gray, boiling air, she became, if possible, even more composed. She took her place in back with Nora and Zachary—three small people lined up, two sweating in T-shirts with wet hair clinging to their foreheads, one bisque doll in bronzed leather. She was planning to be an actress or a politician after college in the States. Yale, perhaps. Her scores would of course be low, but the interview would be a crazy success. She had left, back in Rome, a thirty-two-year-old boyfriend pining. He was a worthy man, sad and kind, who owned two Trastevere bakeries and some other, more profitable businesses. She had met him while swimming, in the Cinque Terre. She had lowered herself in waist-deep water, closed her eyes, and set out; she swam right into his arms.

Nora and Zack gazed at her. Into the front seat,

Alessandra talked on. "This situation is strahnge," she said. That she loved the man, of course, but she was young, quite obviously, with much to do. That even in the moment they were meeting—as she bumped him, stood up in the water, and saw his smile—she understood inevitably they would part. The splendid owner of bakeries could not yet see that she would become— what? to become older, to pass by?

"Outgrow him?" I said. She liked the locution, and she liked me: outgrow was precisely the word.

On the way into town, Alessandra said, "I like this bridge verry much. It's verry—" Helpless large gesture. "—good! Always I think when I come to cross over a bridge: my life will change!"

William, at the wheel, threw his head back and released a cathartic laugh, long and loud. He continued flushed and grinning, driving fast. Zack said, "Ground control to Major Dad. Come in, Dad."

Nora blissfully cried, "Come in, Daddy!" Alessandra looked puzzled, continued to smile. I continued to smile.

The first night, she wrapped my apron twice around her body and made linguine carbonara, using bacon instead of pancetta, breaking eggs tidily and fast, toddling in with the platter. She walked behind the children's chairs and took the spoons out of their hands, showed them how to twirl linguine on their forks: "You are Roman now."

The second night, she asked if she could sit in my place because the chair was higher. We all changed seats, twirled our pasta, smiled at her.

On Saturday William took her to the wine store to look at the Chiantis and Barolos. He had proposed a Dolcetto, but she had wanted something *not so young, not so fresh*. They ran into the Rosemans and she invited them, with their three children, to dinner. All afternoon she worked in the kitchen, making biscotti and involtini and porcini sauce. She told Michael and Deenie Roseman about her future acting career, her thirty-two-year-old boyfriend, and her plans for Yale; walked behind each of the kids and smoothed back their five heads of hair; poured Vinsanto into shot glasses, tossed hers back.

She told us about commedia dell'arte: that the actors married their roles, took them for life. For the rest of their lives, they improvised with increasing fluency, always elaborating and refining the parts they'd chosen when they were almost still children. She gestured boldly, whispered to Nora and Zack to clear the table—Alessandra, composed at the airport, had, it now seemed, been nervous and constrained. Michael Roseman had brought amaretto cookies in her honor, and she showed the kids how to curl the paper wrapper and set it on fire so that it lifted off the table and rose and became black ash drifting above us in the air. We all gazed up, unable to imagine life before Alessandra.

William came home early, carrying two barbecued chickens in bags made of paper outside, foil inside: tiny chickens like prisoners, their drumsticks tied together with string. He freed them, clipping the threads with a flourish, and declaimed the name of the chicken store: he wanted to show her some American food.

"Is this 'to go'?" she asked. "Food to carry?"

As usual now, he hurled back his head and laughed at the ceiling, then threw her a pink look. The cat suddenly woke up and ran out of the room. William glanced around as if to say, Look at this tyke, we raised it from a seed and now it pipes up and says these glittering things! Alessandra stopped applying Nora's lipstick. She looked worried. "Beel?" she said.

We all watched as Willie continued flushed and distended.

"Dad's choking on salivation," Nora said.

Alessandra looked confused, and irritated about it. With a yank she straightened Nora's chair, and Nora's neck snapped.

William's parents came up from Florida for the summer. They stayed with us for three days and joined the multitudes who were falling in love.

Lainie: "She's *very mature for sixteen*. She's *very bright*. She's *cute as a button:* Those big baby doll eyes—the whole bit."

Pep kept pulling people aside to say, "She's a darling"—just what he'd said almost thirteen years before, around the time of our wedding, about me. At every lunch, he arranged himself opposite Alessandra; he would sit down, immediately pile a plate with tuna salad or egg salad or slices of cheese, and, in perfect silence, shove it across the table in her direction.

Departing, Pep and Lainie waved excessively, until the car had disappeared from view.

———

Michael Roseman got his old Vespa out of the back of the garage and brought it over, and we all stood on the lawn and watched her swoop back and forth as if she were wearing a plumed headdress and riding a spirited steed, bareback. Dismounting, she rushed to Michael and told him, "I like always to be at the control!"

She interviewed at Columbia and came back reporting the school appeared "disorganized" and "without power." She sat on Zack and Nora's beds and told them about the Red Brigades and Aldo Moro. She laid them down on the lawn and rubbed their legs. Zack came inside and went out with his new Knicks T-shirt and handed it to her where she lay in the grass.

"That was your favorite shirt," I said later.

He whispered, "That's okay."

They started calling her Sandy. William started calling her "Sahndie."

Walking by the television room at night, I heard William say, "too easily faked out, by body fakes, shoulder fakes, and head fakes." It was summer—basketball wasn't on; but he was explaining basketball, *because of her T-shirt*, he'd said, grinning: *"You have to comprehend your own T-shirt."* Alessandra was sitting close to him on the rug in an artless, amazing posture, a half-crouch, sexual, and she was holding a pillow against her: she looked like a woman playing Spanish guitar. William tried to express the feeling of being inside Madison Square Garden: "This *thumping powerhouse event* where every spectator is *throbbing along*." Sahndie began to talk about Willis Reed, Walt Frazier, Lew Alcindor—she dropped these names with an air of embarrassment at the memory of her recent ignorance:

historical figures, American heroes, heretofore unknown. She dialed direct to Rome and talked for a long
time. We heard her say "Clyde" and "Earl the Pearl."

William bought opera tapes: Puccini and Verdi. In
the evening we'd hear his car approaching from blocks
away: Pavarotti and Freni exalted and belting it out,
declaring their love.

Before he left for work, he would come down smooth
and rosy from his shower and teach her to cook American breakfasts. In the mornings she looked even
smaller, with the apron folded all around her and the
tangled curls spilling down. He would lose track and
things would get overcooked. They would stand and
gaze into the pan, watching the eggs blister and their
edges turn crisp.

There was a Memorial Day parade downtown, jointly
sponsored by the borough and the university, to celebrate not only Memorial Day but long years of placid,
nourishing congress between town and gown. Leading
the marchers, the university president and the pro-
vost, two medium-sized, tentative-looking men, rushed
along at the side of the mayor, a tall, beautiful, blond
woman in a picture hat. They all marched proudly; they
knew themselves to be inextricably linked, their bond
to be, however uneasy, indissoluble. I didn't go. This
report came from William, who had decided to speak
to me again.

As soon as they got out of the car, Nora found my
wedding ring in the driveway, flattened but still
gleaming. "How could this *get* outside?" she said.

"Oh thank you! I lost this!" I trilled.

"You *lost* a ring for your marriage," she said. She put on her Wilma Flintstone look and tapped her foot. In fact I had thrown it out, the winter before, at an ordinary nadir. Willie had just hurled a cupcake at me, like a hardball, the fluted paper spinning, cake shattering and raining down, chocolate icing smearing the wall, and I had rushed to the door stripping off my ring and thrown it out into the night. "How was the parade?" I said.

"Verry American. Wanderfool."

Zack said, "Fogies and fogelettes. In their wheelchairs and whatnot."

Nora said, "How does a wedding ring get lost outside?"

"*I lost it, honey.*"

"That's a hot one," Zack said.

Nora gazed at him gratefully. She said, "I love that saying: 'It's a hot one.' " She took Alessandra's hand.

To get the kids to come into the house, I opened the screen door and shrieked. Alessandra looked at me with concern, as if I were running a dangerous fever. She said, "Would you prreffer to nap?"

"I can't 'nap' now, Alessandra. We've got a thousand things scheduled. But thank you."

She said, "Jo, Jo, Jo, Jo: You 'ave to try to be more trahnquil."

I told this to William. "Was this a bit much?"

He said, "Well, you said the family's powerful. She's probably used to jockeying for position. She's spent her life playing with the big boys." He looked proud.

Late at night I said, "She has a slight frown even when she's smiling."

William said drowsily, "Because of the flaw."

"What?"

"That little scar, above her right eye." He turned. "I'm dying here. I've got court, I've got depositions. I gotta sleep fast."

I found it—a mark like a bit of fine thread among the black hairs of her eyebrow. To see it, I had to pretend to accidentally bump her, and lean very close.

I went and found the kids where they were crouched gazing at anthills. I said, "Is Alessandra going to steal you away from me?" They looked, for a moment, curious; then, quickly, they lost interest.

I said to William, "Are you considering sleeping with Alessandra?"

"Are you nuts? She's a sixteen-year-old kid."

Then we had a couple of days of dazed, not entirely painful silence.

Deenie invited the kids to stay over, and when she came to pick them up they said they couldn't leave until Alessandra departed for Cambridge. She was going to spend four days deciding whether Harvard looked pleasant. She would be back before my birthday, and we would celebrate. Passionate, silent, Nora and Zack sat in her room and watched her pack. When the airport limo arrived, they stood in the driveway embracing her in farewell as if she were their entire family and about to defect.

We were alone in our house. All day William kept kissing and kissing me, saying, "*Almost a thirty-three-year-old lady!*" Finally I laughed and said, "Why don't you propose marriage to my birthday? I feel like a stand-in. You can't kiss my birthday so you kiss me."

"Unimaginable," he said, and started scrabbling through the tool drawer.

"It's a joke."

"Are you insane?"

"I was kidding!"

"I concede," he said. "You're jealous of your own birthday. I think it's really true. Fuck the fucking birthday and you celebrate it by your own unimpeachable lights."

It was still early, but he decided to go to bed. "I'm coming down with something," he said, and glared at me. In the night, he got up again and went down the hall and, I thought, talked a while to someone, in an uncharacteristically soft voice. I thought he was sitting with the kids on Alessandra's bed, his hand on her hair, Mediterranean daylight streaming in. When he came back I woke up, and for a long time he walked slowly around the room. Neither of us spoke. But I followed the face of William's watch, glowing, moving through the dark.

The morning of my birthday, William told me to go out for the day and he and Sahndie would prepare dinner. No, I said calmly, I will make veal cutlets. Okay, but after dinner I'd have to secrete myself while they prepared the birthday pageant. "Secrete?" I said, and grinned.

"Oops!" He clutched his mouth. "Too abstruse? Too fanciful?"

"I'll select fanciful." I smiled on, as if my continuing to look amused would make this moment be funny and make us be happy together.

"Splendid," he said, and violently drank some water.

I let my smile fade to something more winsome. But I wouldn't give up. We waited while he gulped and swallowed.

"Come on, Willie."

"You come on. You come on. My need for a vocabulary consultant has steadily waned."

The kids walked into the kitchen, cradling piles of magic markers in their arms. William said to them, "Watch it, the word police are out." They looked at him. They walked on through.

"Oh, Wil." Tears rushed into my eyes.

He didn't look at me, and he didn't leave.

They all went off on secret errands, crept around sneaking gifts into the house and whispering. The heat wave broke. It turned cool and the sun came out and everything looked sharp and bright and unrealistically clear. The toilet in the kids' bathroom got stopped up— two sad, symmetrical turds floating up near the lid.

In the evening they stood in the kitchen, while I dragged pieces of wet veal through crumbs and Alessandra sang the Sharks and Jets song vibrantly and sweetly like a well-loved child on amateur night. She moved through *West Side Story* until the veal slices were cooked and piled on the platter. "This has to be hot!" I cried. I rushed out, the kids jumped into their chairs, and she began to sing: "There's a Place for Us," but in Italian.

Imaginary strings soaring. I thumped the platter onto the table. Nora cried, "Sandy! Sandy! Beel! Beel!" Behind me, in the kitchen, she took his hands in hers, stood very near, looked deeply, all the way up, into his glowing face; sang on.

I went upstairs and with tiny scissors cut a pinhole in the front of Alessandra's leather jacket.

Then we ate.

Then I secreted myself.

The garden was warm and the scent of grass and flowers thick. Alessandra had dressed them. She and William wore Venetian masks—his the beak of the plague doctor, hers the blank face of Columbine, chalky white in the darkening green of the yard. Nora wore whiteface and a tulle ruff. Only Zachary's face was his own—his small tan face—but his hair was all gold and full of glitter.

Alessandra said, "It is our commedia dell'arte. And so we tell the story of our life."

"Improv is everything," William added in a fuzzy voice from behind his beak, and she gazed at him blindly. She said to me, "Mistakes occur. Persons are separate, but they find the other again."

The four groped in the shadows, pretended to look out windows, bumped into trees and mistook each other's identities. Zack stepped forward and stood in silence, his gold hair shining. Then he cartwheeled through the grass. It was going to end so soon. I sat in a canvas chair with an aluminum-foil crown on my head while night fell, and fireflies rose, and my family danced for me.

When they finished, there was still light in the sky but down in the yard it was shadowy. William set his beak on his head and carried out a tray of cakes. Nora stuck candles into the cakes, Alessandra lit the candles, and we all leaned forward.

Zachary's hair burst into flame.

The gold paint made the hair seem to be wildly flaring, when really it was only slowly burning. We turned slowly toward him, slowly I reached for him, Alessandra looked up, slowly William stripped off his shirt and wrapped it around the little gold head and smothered the fire before Zachary understood. Zack looked puzzled, peering out of William's embrace.

Then time started to move again and everything seemed to run together—the thick air and the dusk, the confusion, Alessandra's presence among us, the scent of burnt hair and chocolate icing. Alessandra suddenly sat down in the grass. Nora started to cry, and the tears streaked down her greased white face. William looked at me and I looked at him.

I went upstairs and sat on the edge of my bed. I thought: I can get rid of her.

At midnight as my birthday ended, while it was getting light in Rome, I called Alessandra's mother and I said the kid would be coming home early. Ginevra was concerned and intrigued: hair burning?

"She sprayed flammable paint into it," I said. "It wasn't a good idea."

"*Not* a good idea!" Ginevra vivaciously agreed, and then I told her how distracting and bewildering the visit was becoming for everyone. "Mmm. Mmm," Ginevra was saying mournfully. Especially for Zachary, I said (completely untrue). I said he was just terribly taken with Alessandra and almost disoriented by it.

Ginevra, after a pause: "*Cute. How he wands to be a mahn.*"

Late morning, I knocked. "In a moment," she said, but I went in. She was in bed not sleeping, black makeup smudges under her eyes, the shades drawn. "A moment, Jo," she said.

"It's my house, Alessandra."

She scrambled up, leaned against the pillows. She said, "I will go, Jo."

"I think that makes sense."

She looked extremely self-contained. She lay her hand on her beautiful chest, where Willis Reed was rushing the net. She said with dignity, "I am sorry if you don't like my visit." Then her hands flew up, her face dissolved, and she began to cry.

"Zack is fine," I said. "There's no real damage. I just think the visit has been long enough."

She grabbed the sheet and scrubbed at her face. "May I speak?"

"Of course. Speak."

"I know little Zachary is well. It is something else. You 'ave been a friend to me, and I 'ave to tell you some information."

I suddenly wanted her not to say anything. I said, "Alessandra, you're wanting to discuss things because you're far from home, and you think I'm mad at you, and you've gotten out of your depth. It's really not necessary."

"It is my guilt," she said. "It is about Beel."

"William?"

"That we 'ave been lovers."

"That you and William have been lovers," I said.

"Oh, Jo, I must offer my apology to you!" She began to gasp and sob.

I turned my back. I looked out the window, down into bright-green lawn. Nora was crossing the grass toward Zachary, carrying plastic glasses on a tray. Distinguish yourself, I thought.

She was poignantly sitting with her small hands folded, letting her tears drip onto the sheet. I said, "You know, dear, William and I don't really, strictly speaking, have secrets. We *tell* each other what we do."

She gazed at me.

I said, "This is a *marriage,* dear. Now that's a complicated thing. An event like this doesn't really have the kind of impact you might've expected. Do you understand what I'm telling you?"

"I don't know," she said.

I talked on. I said that whatever impression she'd gotten, I didn't think she ought to trouble herself further. Really, to not keep crying now. This sort of thing was of remarkably little significance either to William or to me, and there was no necessity for her to continue being so upset. I cast her a full look of simple high-minded clarity. I went to the bathroom, squeezed out a washcloth, noticed in the mirror a grim, stubborn, saintly nurse. I said, "Wipe your face now."

She looked at me miserably, dabbed at the corners of her pale wet eyes. She said, "I permitted my Tampax to go down the toilet."

"I know," I said. "Now why don't you pack."

William was at work when the limousine came for Alessandra. We walked her out. As she bent to kiss him, Zack whispered, and she set her bag down, unzipped it, and pulled out his T-shirt. He closed his eyes and held up his arms, and she slipped the shirt over his head and smoothed it down.

She said quickly, "Thank you, Jo," and kissed my cheeks, and turned. She glittered at the limo driver, who looked excited, held the door tenderly, said, "I think you're Italian."

As the car pulled out, Nora bitterly cried, "Beel! Beel!" and grasped Zack by the neck and tried to kiss him while he silently struggled. The limo pulled away. We watched its brake lights flare, and then slowly it turned the corner. The weather had changed again, and the day was hazy, with heat steadily building up in the haze. The kids immediately went inside and came out again wearing bathing suits. They coasted down the driveway, suddenly began to pedal, rounded the corner.

I went in and dialed William's office. She had left the white Venetian masks behind, and they sat on the counter side by side, their eyeholes watching me as I hit the buttons.

Tracy said, "We're not calling him William Green anymore. We're going to call him Your Greatness."

"I can't laugh right now," I said.

She said, "I know the feeling."

Then I stood, on hold for a while, listening to distant elevator music, waiting for my husband to come on the line, to see if he felt like talking about whether I still wanted to be his wife.

"Be less cryptic," he said. "We're swamped here."

"You can't sleep with people and not be found out. I cannot see how you'd imagine you could."

"I'm gonna close my door."

"Swell," I said.

No footsteps—his step was muffled by thick Berber carpeting. Door clicking shut. No footsteps.

"What are we talking about?" he said.

"I talked to her, William, and she told me."

There was a silence. Then, "Let's hear this again."

"On top of doing it, you're going to lie? How could that possibly be worth it, when I already *talked* to her, and she *told* me?"

"It's not possible."

"She volunteered the information!"

"Jill wouldn't do that."

"Jill?" I said.

He said: "*Oh man.*"

5. Matrimonial

We talked and wept. By morning we were hoarse, as if we'd spent the night smoking and dancing, living festively, back in some earlier or half-imagined life. Willie showered and stumbled off to work; I fell asleep again, and slept until the room heated up in the afternoon and the heat woke me. The kids came home from the pool with their hair in strings and their fingers wrinkled. They stood in the kitchen, gulped down hot dogs without chewing, and rushed back into the neighborhood. Willie came home, we waited for dark and went back to bed and lay close and turned our backs. I touched his calf with the sole of my foot and we slept.

False dawn had ended, birds were peeping, traces of blue would soon sift into the sky. Willie continued to sleep in cold soup with the air conditioner stirring it. I woke up and came down and leaned out the front door. It was still dark, with fog, and the cat was purring and walking back and forth on the porch. The air smelled like rubber. Squirrels fizzed on the wires.

I turned on the television and started writing William a note. The static died, the sermon swam by, and some podiatrists sprang into view, seated on loveseats before a wallpaper depicting ferns and wicker trellises. At issue were implant procedures, callous formation, severe degenerative process, hammertoes. The interviewer was preoccupied with deformity, the doctors with evaluation, biomechanical and radiographic. "We can't divorce the foot from the rest of the body," the most mournful podiatrist said, while I waited for the gas stations to open and Nora and Zack to wake so we could get in my car, roll down the windows, hang our arms out, and drive away.

Because I didn't know what else to do, I was going home—to my mother's summer home on the Cape. In the pale light, I woke the kids. They stood up, walked like sleepwalkers, put on bathing suits with their eyes closed. Nora pulled on red rain boots and descended carrying her budgie, Amy Carter, in its cage, with the cover on to keep it serene. I imagined Amy C.'s pale feathers, her small glittery febrile eyes, her stillness on her perch. "Okay," I said, and they put the cage in and climbed in without asking anything. Nora said, "I still can't believe the real Amy Carter almost got crushed by that elephant. I hate the hamsters, who cares, Dad will feed them." "Red Scott night, sailor's delight," Zack told me from the back seat, and we all remembered the evening before, an uncommon dusk full of rosy vividness.

I put it in neutral and coasted down the driveway. Nora turned to watch. "I just remembered I miss Sandy," she said.

"I miss Sandy too," Zack said.

"So do I," I said, surprised.

"Also I forgot—Sandy wrote you a letter," Nora said, and handed it up to me. In Alessandra's large, round hand, on my own stationery, it said she was sorry to have lied about William, that she had been just so unhappy at being sent away. That I was a friend to her. That she felt obliged to admit her guilt and make it right. Her written English was surprisingly compelling and represented her well. I turned on the motor, and we left home.

Morning. My mother's house in Wellfleet had been built up over forty years, around the much smaller house where Rhody and I had spent our childhood summers. It was inside the National Seashore, and at times over the years the authorities had spoken firmly with Mom about staying within their modest renovation guidelines. Mom wouldn't listen. She just built. Now the house was huge, set back in the pines behind the high dune, and sea breezes blew through it like a house in a dream. Somewhere inside this place, I often thought, the small original house remained.

On the screened porch, facing the Atlantic, Mom and her brand-new husband reclined on chaise longues. They were reading the newspapers. My mother wore a little red bathing suit and a leopard-pattern visor, while Stu was entirely dressed, in resort slacks and leather slippers. He was a Philadelphian, retired from menswear; Mom had met him at the coat-check area in a restaurant, where he had taken a sincere interest in her coat. Stu was as natty as Willie, but color-blind; in order to dress himself in his many color-coordinated outfits, he'd had little numbers sewn into his clothes. He sat with one hand on Florence, my mother's labrador pup. Absently, continuing to read, my mother lifted Stu's hand off the dog's back, folded it around her own tiny hand.

Zack and Nora were jumping on a trampoline set out in the trees; they flew up, dropped, hit, did it again, hundreds of times, their voices small and far away. In a chair next to the house, very near the house like a baby lifeboat clinging to the *Queen Mary,* I lay with the sun getting hotter behind my eyelids, watching blackness shot with white points. Dozing, I saw Danny's face. Alessandra had orange hair like cotton candy and her black silk suit. She and Danny seemed to be twins, which was odd—the one so expressive and beautiful, the other not.

The house was small again, I was small. Although I had spent my summers here, as a child I didn't know much about the beach. I knew nothing about crabs or the seasons for fish. At some point I did know how clams were dug but not whether quahogs were found in the ocean or bay. I did not know the location of beds of oysters, how to shoot ducks, get gas for the motorboat, or read the channel markers, or whether the lobsters in the restaurants were local or Maine. Everybody seemed preoccupied with these issues. I had no idea how to look into the subjects. I spent my time climbing down the dune and running on the beach in a daze, memorizing the colors of the ocean. I would discuss with myself all the stuff I didn't know. Of course I knew about the public lives of movie stars, and of course I knew I wanted to be immediately given in marriage to a man who would tell me: Darling . . .

I was asleep.

Mom came out and sat on the end of my chair. The sun had moved and it was cooler. Nora and Zack's trampoline was empty, the radio was still.

Mom said William had called to say he was driving up.

Mom wanted to talk, but I didn't have the heart. She wanted to talk about Stu, and marriage. I said I'd talk about anything, after I woke up, and I let my eyes close.

When William arrived, we walked onto the dune and sat on the deck of Stu's new gazebo. It was the end of the day, and far below us tiny surfers were sitting like birds on the water. He said that Jill felt as badly about this as we did, that she was a wonderful woman. He said she had grown up in Orlando. She was an accomplished diver and water-skier. She had once been Miss Florida.

"What?"

"Miss Florida," he said. "Miss Florida. Miss Florida." He looked confused.

We needed to talk, but if we said things it might get worse. It occurred to me that I loved William and I wanted to stay with him. Or perhaps I wanted to stand up and slam this tall, doleful man against the side of the gazebo. His head would bounce, he would look amazed.

I said, "She comes from Florida? But wasn't she married to somebody black?"

He said, "Sticking it to her parents."

"Are Jill and David staying together?"

"Yes," he said. The surfers caught a wave, and plunged toward us, a scatter of black dots. "Are we?"

It was becoming hard to speak. "What sort of lawyer is she?" I said finally.

"Pardon me?"

"What does she specialize in?"

"Oh, matrimonial," Willie said, and looked rueful, and we grinned bitterly together.

Much later, when it was getting dark and starting to seem that nothing could be done, as we stood up to go I said, "I hate you for what you've done."

"Oh I know," he said promptly.

The next morning was hazy, gray and damp. Willie and I got in my car and started driving up the Cape, to try again to talk. My hands were icy. My heart jumped in my chest.

We slipped into the line of cars already creeping at a walking pace toward Provincetown. We were polite, talking about the rainy-day traffic, and I kept forgetting what we were doing—it was possible to imagine we were friends, chatting, out for a time-killing drive.

In Truro, I turned off and pulled over. Why were we parking here? I turned and told Willie about my second-grade class trip to a lighthouse. I didn't know anymore where that lighthouse was. But I remembered a long ride out of Boston in the bus, the moment of arrival at the edge of some broad, undulating dunes, the blind ascent inside the tower, and then the brilliant opening-up, bay and inlet and sea, water everywhere and we were in the sky. I had stood holding hands with a precious friend—I couldn't remember her face now, only the intense joyful love I had for her—and we had held hands behind the rail and looked over the blue glitter to see Portugal. I turned the car around and pulled back onto Route 6, heading back down. The tight line of cars eased toward us, stuffed with families anticipating their upcoming strolls through Provincetown, ingestion of linguiça and fudge and cotton candy, surreptitious observation of homosexual couples, buying of weird hats. Willie and I started to ride in silence back down the Cape, fast now, alone against the traffic.

He said finally, "One thing I'm particularly unimpressed by: the posture of unimpeachable blamelessness."

Which meant what?

He said he meant Marchand, the self-important professor with the diversified portfolio.

Thick pines lined the road here, a lovely wall of blackish green. I accelerated, shifted, drove on.

"Do you think I'm a fool?" He pushed my thigh. The car swerved.

"What are you doing! Stop it!"

Willie pushed me again. The car paused, jumped ahead. "You've been fucking Marchand for two years! I talked to his wife, and you know the woman's got it right."

He reached out and hit at the side of my head, fast, once. His fingers flipped my hair up and scraped past my ear. I kept driving. He took out his wallet. He screamed that Dan Marchand was a wealthy man, *rich, rich, rich, rich*—

Please stop, I said.

William pulled out a pile of dollar bills. One by one he crumpled them and he started trying to stick them into the air conditioner and the little vents at the top of the door, grunting and trying to force the crushed dollars into every orifice. The holes were too small and the bills stuck only a moment before falling to the floor. I accelerated. I drove on. The wind, carrying mist from the ocean, poured in the windows. He scooped up the crumpled bills and threw them at me in handfuls, and they bounced off the side of my head and fell lightly around my hair and onto my shoulders like rain.

When I was a child, staying here above the ocean, I couldn't usually hear the water. Other people would talk about the sound of breakers rolling in, and I'd strain to hear. The sound seemed to have been with me, then, all my life, and it was like pure silence.

Willie and I lay all night on our bed behind the dune, and thought about how we had screwed everything up.

Halfway through the night he said, "You don't like me much. You haven't liked me for a long time."

He was weeping. We both were. I said, "I like you, Wil."

Much later, as light was starting, he turned toward me and I rolled into his arms. Now, lying with my husband, I could hear waves breaking.

Back in New Jersey. Willie did the next thing, a surprising thing, in his characteristic sudden way—he rushed out and rented a new home.

The day William and I drove over to look at his apartment, the temperature was still around ninety, and stepping into the rental office was mildly thrilling—it felt like stepping into a refrigerator. Two young women were sitting at desks, wearing gleaming lipstick and silk dinner dresses, in the chill. They looked like anchor-women. "Twenty-one inches, standing," one said into the phone. Any pet would be allowed to live here if it came in under these dimensions.

I looked at Willie, who was reading his lease, just as he lifted his eyes and grinned. His face was very shiny and remarkably familiar. He walked over and pulled open my shirt pocket and stuck his nose into it. He said, "Down, boy."

Bulletin board. Poster about happy hour. They have it every Friday in summer, on an expanse of concrete patio between the diving and lap pools. An image rose: William prominent among the revelers—golden people dropping their heads back to laugh; twin bodies of water turquoise and glimmering; the sun still high.

In the apartment, he pointed out the amenities— trash compactor, paint on the walls, newness—and the view through the sliding glass door, a vista of fields, former truck farms awaiting development, with tiny resting bulldozers and a blue line of trees at their distant edge. I chirped about the velour furniture, the dining area rheostat. "It's perfect, it's great," I chirped. He stood behind me, folded himself around me, rested his face on my hair.

Unlocking the car, I thought, She's an adult; she locks up. On the way home I was driving slowly, not thinking, blinking in the glare—trying to avoid displays of regret or fear. Halfway home, with cars pulling out around us, Willie jerked in his seat and shoved

the dashboard so that the glove compartment fell open.
He let his head dip. He tenderly felt the front of his
shirt with his fingertips, as if his chest hurt—a gesture
both comic and sad. When I got home, I wrote it down.

In the middle of the night when I woke, I made
notes. After a few nights of this I wondered when the
poems themselves would get written, and I thought:
much later, far from here.

Some notes:

—Willie, sad, palpating his chest.

—the Versailles bomb—destroyed irreplaceable art
and blasted through the ceiling.

—Zack's Mem. Day traffic deaths—508, way up
from last year.

—N. in the bath, singing about sea voyages, floating to rinse out her hair. William called her a mermaid.

—The cardinals' nest. The adult cardinals calling to
the half-feathered babies: fly higher, fly higher.

We couldn't tell them.

He would move on September first. We agreed we
couldn't tell them now because it would ruin Fourth of
July for the rest of their lives. We thought maybe they
knew—they had become so silent, although it had been
months since I'd had the nerve to request Separate Quiet
Time. On the fourth, we all dressed in tricolor clothes
and rode downtown and sat on the soccer field to watch
fireworks flaring above the trees. We sat quietly, lined
up in the haze of smoke, sniffing the sulfur—Willie

and I very still, as the showers of sparks crackled and rained down.

He and I drove to New York City to shop for his apartment—Saturday afternoon, into the hot, quiet streets. We bought two TV sets—I thought I could bear Willie's buying a new television if I got one too. We went to buy him a coffee table, and I bought one too. In the driveway, late at night, the television sets were gone from the trunk. Willie called the precinct house and shrieked like a maniac. The officer on duty said, "Wha'd you expect, man, this's the Apple." William screamed, "*Are you beyond help?*" As this was happening, we recognized it was going to become one of our divorce stories. We told it to each other, making it nuttier and funnier every time.

We couldn't tell them and July went by.

On an early August evening, at the movies—16mm, minuscule budget, a heartbreaking story, about street boys in Morocco—behind me, a woman talked to her husband. I turned around and looked hard in her face; she stared back, hard.

I looked at the screen. She talked.

"Please be quiet," I implored her.

"Uh oh," she said to her husband.

I turned back. The smallest boy picked a pocket and ran alone through the swirling streets of Marrakech.

She talked.

I whirled. "Look," I said. "We come to this little theater to avoid people like you. It really would be better if you went to a mall, or stayed home in front of your own television!"

She clicked her tongue.

"You better shut up, lady!" I cried. William looked at me, amazed.

"I'll talk if I want to, darling," she said amiably.

I stood up and leaned over and shoved her shoulder, and she slapped at my hand. William tried to grasp the tail of my shirt. People were yelling at me to sit down. *Shut the fuck up,* I said, *or I'm gonna push your face in.* Then I smashed out of the row and ran out of the theater. Out in the cool night, I felt surprisingly well. I had never done anything remotely like this in my life. I looked around in the black rustling summery air for new challenges.

September came and we couldn't bring ourselves to tell them. They went back to school, to third and fourth grade. Our first floor was scheduled to be refinished, and one day the men showed up. They laid a plank on which we could walk from the front door to the stairs. We started living upstairs, sitting on beds eating sandwiches for dinner. William paid his first month's rent but he didn't move out. Each day we didn't tell them was a lovely day.

We grew exhausted. We were becoming too tense to say much to each other. Willie and I were confused, sort of breathless, plummeting ahead; as our marriage had, our divorce seemed to be making itself, picking us up and carrying us on. If I turned on the light at night, he didn't move. Very late, while he slept, I'd sit making notes for poems, waiting for something. I'd remember things we'd done together and things that had gone wrong, and I'd listen, as if for his car to arrive. Once I said, aloud, in a low voice: Come back.

I left a big heap of clothes on William's chair. He rolled each piece up, and hurled them one by one across the room: keep your stuff on your side.

That night, in lieu of hitting him, hugging him, begging him to reconsider, stabbing him with a knife, while he slept I uncapped a pen and drew on his back: a black dot.

Finally, after dinner on Friday, we threw away the paper wrappers from our sandwiches and asked them to come in and sit on our bed. We had, we said, some thing serious to say.

"Oh no, somebody died," Nora said.

"Who died?" Zack said.

Nora said, "Mom, this is what I told you I worry about. When I hear that somebody died, I smile. I can't help it."

No one died, we said. Everybody's okay. Let's sit on the bed.

Nora said, "Why are so many people dying! How come these days! Sometimes I think it's planned."

"Elvis died on the toilet," Zack said. "There was that picture in the paper."

Nora: "*No.* I didn't see that!"

Zack: "Last year! You forgot?"

Guys, we said. Sit on the bed.

I said that Daddy and I have not been getting along well enough—they must've noticed—and now we had decided to separate for a while, temporarily, in the hope of getting some perspective and eventually being able to resolve some of our differences.

"I didn't notice anything," Zack said. He twisted the edge of his shirt. "I didn't notice any fighting," he said.

"Well, you certainly know we don't get along as well as we should," William said.

Zack looked blank. "I don't know that."

Nora was sitting with her head down and her face turned away. She lifted the edge of the quilt and put both hands under it.

"David Beecham's mom and dad *really* fight," Zack said, to nobody. "That's what I call fighting."

"I don't call anything fighting!" Nora said, and she started to cry.

Zack said to her, "It's not really real."

For a long time, Willie and I sat there and incompletely described ourselves: our efforts, our slow recognitions, our hopes, but not our doubts. We portrayed ourselves as having finally arrived at confidence in the rightness of our plan for Willie to spend some time across town. We sounded like wonderful human beings and we felt like murderers. When we finished, Zack looked hopeful. He said, "Dad. I'm not sure you're doing the right thing."

Dizzy with uncertainty, we said we were sure. It was long past their bedtime. They put on their bathrobes and we all walked down the stairs, across the plank, past the empty rooms and through the smell of wood stain and polyurethane, and got into the car to go see where their father would live.

It was the first cool night, black and starry, and as we rode our spirits lifted. They wore pajamas, it was late, it was exciting to be riding through the night; we let the ride comfort us. Nora sat on my lap and looked around urgently, as if being given a tour of a foreign city, about which she would later have to take an exam.

We drove past dark low woods and fields, heading toward where the road would cross a highway. Ahead, above the trees, was a pale haze.

"Two glows!" Zack said from the back seat. "It looks like something's burning! It looks like two clouds side by side! Mom! I know what it is: the malls!"

"It's both of the malls," Nora told Willie.

Zack said, "Dad is staying temporarily near the malls. We can see him when we go shopping."

"You can see him whenever you want," I said.

"You'll come and stay with me all the time, honey," William said.

Zack didn't answer. He didn't seem to be listening to us anymore.

In the apartment, the electricity was off. They walked around and around in the dark, tried to turn on the lights, used the toilet, sat at the dining table, lay on the bed and shut their eyes. From the couch, you could look through the glass door at fields and black sky and high stars. Finally we sat there together looking out for a long time, as we would've if we had all just moved in.

Zack couldn't sleep. He couldn't lie in his bed. He walked around his room in the dark.

He called into the hall, "Mom? Will you make me a sandwich for school in the morning?"—as if, when the morning came, perhaps I'd have moved out of town.

Late at night, he was standing by the side of the bed. William was in the bathroom. Zack stood carefully. He touched my arm. He said, "Is Dad gone?"

Because of the floors being redone, all our downstairs furniture was piled in the garage. On Saturday William got up early and came home with a truck and started to load it. In my sleep I heard the garage door open, a rumble under my head—I thought it was a train, carrying away somebody I'd known all my life.

Much later I woke to a cold bright day, and William's rented truck in the driveway half full. His new coffee table had gone in first, and then all the furniture from his study, and then a big object which stood like a wall inside the truck—the armoire we had bought in Maine the first year we were married, when we were young. I saw it and I was frightened. "Who said you could take that?"

"Who *said?*" He grinned. He went back into the garage.

"You were supposed to leave everything except your own stuff. We agreed the furniture would stay with the house."

He was in the garage in darkness, pulling at the corner of a desk, trying to extricate it from the pile. In the sun, the truck stood waiting.

"This is the reason we rented you a furnished apartment! So the furniture could stay with the house!"

"Not with the house. With you," he said. He kept pulling at the desk.

I went in and stood behind him. "What are you doing?"

He kept pulling.

"What are you doing?" I cried. "My mother gave me that desk! You can't take my desk!"

"I'm taking it."

"You can't!" I cried, and tugged at his sleeve—it was surprisingly soft, cashmere. I was alarmed: *he can't take the furniture away.* "You said you were leaving it here! We agreed!"

"I changed my mind."

"You can't! You can't!"

I kept pulling at him, he kept pulling at the desk. I was crying and he was almost crying and we were screaming. "I need this furniture!" I cried. "You can get more furniture! This is mine!" Willie turned and hit my head. My head snapped around, and the bright day came into my eyes, and Nora and Zack out on the driveway pretending not to hear us, standing just outside the doorway of the place where Willie and I were trapped alone.

An hour later he came into the bedroom with a glass of iced coffee for me. I sat up to talk with him. But he bowed like a stage waiter, and set the glass down hard and it splashed on the table. He said, "Just because you despise me is no reason for the flow of services to stop."

He ran out. In the driveway, the truck started.

Cold sweat came out on my face. I went into the bathroom and vomited. I sat on the bathroom rug with my head leaning against the cold tiles. All of us in this dream, and unable to wake up.

I slept. I dreamed about struggling with Willie in the garage—I was pushing at his cashmere sleeve, feeling the softness powerfully, shoving, stroking his soft arm.

When I came out of my room, they were sitting together in the hall. I said, "I'm so sorry." "Okay," they said.

Nora went into the back of her closet and got out her baby books. She started reading aloud. She declaimed in a high steady voice. Nora read all afternoon to Zack as they lay on the carpet, and he listened as if the books were all about what he needed to know. Princesses walked in forest glades, raccoons got tucked into their tiny leafy beds.

After William left, I thought he was still in the house. I had heard him downstairs kissing the kids good-bye, and I'd heard him run down the driveway with a light quick step, and the truck starting. But for a day I thought he was still there. In the morning I walked back and forth upstairs, convinced he was downstairs. When I came down and he was gone, I walked from room to room, looking for him as if he were something I'd mislaid—I knew he was with me and I'd see his face soon. At night, after he'd been gone a day, I went out to the car and looked in, to see if he were lying in the back seat. It was dark. I pressed my face against the window. His suitcases would be hidden in the trunk or squashed down behind the steering wheel. He would be lying flat, breathing quietly, watching the perforations on the ceiling; patiently, pliantly waiting for me.

Monday night, William phoned, to speak to the kids.

After they hung up, I went upstairs and called him back. I told him he could have the desk.

"Impressive largesse," he said. "It's my own furniture."

"The desk isn't." My mother had bought it for me the week I came down with pneumonia when I was twenty. In the attic we still had a Polaroid photograph, now starting to fade out as it had faded in: Willie and me wearing new bell-bottoms, flanking the desk, blinking in sunlight like kids getting their school pictures taken, trying to keep our eyes open and smile at Mom. "I don't want it," Willie said.

"Let's stop this."

"Oh, let's. As long as you get to keep everything and I absent myself quietly and sit out in a potato field."

I laughed. It sounded so much like him—"absent myself." While I was laughing, encouraging him to join in, he hung up.

My day was busy and long and empty. I drove all over town doing errands, then finally sat on the porch watching for the kids. When Nora arrived, she said, "I can't go to school tomorrow, Mommy."

Zack stepped through the screen door after her. "You're not kidding," he told her. "It's a bitch."

She said, "I feel like Daddy isn't my father anymore,

he's just somebody to be nice to. Mom, I haven't been very nice to Dad this year either. I've been fighting with him a lot."

"He didn't leave because of you," I said. "It has nothing to do with you."

"I'm sort of embarrassed at school," she said miserably. "I don't like to look at my friends anymore." My children had never talked about any one thing so much in their lives. Zack mumbled, but we could hear him. He said, "I feel like a stupid fool."

Nora went inside. Zack stood near me, looking out the screen.

I said, "I think maybe it's good that we're talking about it."

He looked at me. "It's good to you. Lots of things are good to you. Because it's your fault."

"Oh, honey, I'm sorry." I reached and tried to hold his hand. He set my hand onto the table and pressed it down.

"Your sorryness is for you to know," he said. "You wreck everything."

He said that I made people stand in driveways while I hit people, that I was the ugliest woman he had ever seen or known, that this was not his house anymore, and he was sobbing, and I was too. He cried, "I wanted that moving day to be fun! But I couldn't make it be fun!" Because you won't let us. Our lives were ruined and I had ruined them. I agreed with Zack.

6. At the Rosemans'

All fall, I slept.

Twenty minutes before the kids got home, I would toss back the blankets and stagger to the shower. I'd rush out to the supermarket, as if I'd been hurrying all day, one of the people who is too busy to think. As the day ended my spirits lifted. For one so shaky, I was remarkably strong. I'd lug the groceries home, hurl them onto the porch, then drag them in like a stevedore. At dinner, nightly, I improvised a persona and told the children at length about her plans—projects that sounded likely for a woman as indefatigable as she: to write long poems for impressive magazines, immediately learn Spanish, lift remarkably heavy weights. I drank wine and smiled erratically and grew flushed. The kids gazed at me cautiously, with saddening respect.

My friend Annie invited me for lunch. I knew she had twice entertained William at Saturday dinners, along with several of our friends. I said, "I don't want to come. I won't acquiesce in being socially demoted, Anne, just because I'm alone." She was upset that I'd called her Anne and said I had misunderstood. I told her I hadn't misunderstood *anything at all* and I was *affronted and hurt.* While she was patiently, sympathetically replying, I hung up. I went back to sleep.

Willie called, ready to fight like an animal to take the kids for Thanksgiving weekend, and I said, Take them. Deenie Roseman invited me for Thanksgiving and I pretended I was already going to Annie's. Before ringing off, Deenie tried to encourage me to converse normally. "Have you been reading about Jonestown?" she said. I said, "Of course I know all about it! Stop taking my pulse."

Thanksgiving was a dark day, with sleet falling. At four, I drove over to William's and rode slowly by; then I rode by again, trying to catch sight of my children, as though they'd been gone for years. There were two extra cars out front, unfamiliar ones—for a moment I was afraid one of my own closest friends had bought a new car.

On Sunday I took the train to New York, where the museum was swarming with couples old and young, physically or spiritually entwined. In the Egyptian galleries were a fat man and his little wife, gazing at the Egyptian couples, Fifth Dynasty, made of stone. He said, "See, that's his wife? See how much smaller she is?"

His bulky, sheltering arm all around her shoulders. She smiling up from inside his armpit. I watched with my mouth watering.

In December Annie invited me to a dinner party to meet a man.

He was newly separated from a woman he had

known since grammar school, and we sat miserably together in the candlelight through the long meal, side by side in perfect sympathy. Happiness seemed to be lifting off the other guests like light; they were all married to each other. The mantel in the dining room was strewn with Christmas ornaments, and tiny white lights glittered behind the man's large, shapely head as he told me about his wife. When the sachertorte was served, the others applauded. The man whispered to me, "Do you make dessert for yourself?"

I received my first Christmas card alone, and ripped it open. It showed a sleigh rushing over frozen fields—purple shadows, spirited horse, two revelers under a lap robe. Inside, it said: "Never a Christmas morning, Never the old year ends, But someone thinks of someone, Old Days, Old Times, Old Friends. Harold's Sunoco."

4:30. December afternoon—red streaks in the blackening sky. In the shopping center parking lot, the lights were already on. Crossing the parking lot, I noticed the feeling I'd had for months now—it was as though I'd been living in some watery element, breathing a sort of fluid, never air. I walked into a cloud of exhaust from a bus. Emerging, I was almost run down by a Cadillac—I slapped its fender, ran after it to keep slapping until it pulled out of reach. Then I jumped into my car, banging my knee, and sat trembling for just a minute. Then I turned the radio up and drove home 100 miles an hour.

At home, the phone was ringing. It was William, of course, swimming back into my life.

We met at a bar and talked until it closed. We wanted to light Chanukah candles together with the children! We laughed: we were so assimilated, we had heretofore celebrated Chanukah only once, and trimmed five Christmas trees. Under pressure, apparently, our true religious affiliation asserted itself and the tree fell away.

We didn't know if we could ever be together again, but we didn't want to foreclose the possibility. We wanted to see each other in some limited way and possibly it would not be impossible to think we might someday be able to talk. We said the word "possible" so many times it started to sound bizarre. We said this was too hard this way! We had grown up together, we agreed—begun to grow up. We wanted to be civilized. We wanted to be friends.

The bar was quiet. In the gloom, Willie and I made identical faces—rueful, sanguine, almost wise. Our hands lay on the varnished table, and Willie held two of my fingers. Over and over, his hold tightened; I wiggled my fingers; he loosened his grip.

The East Coast was having a cold spell, and there were days of brilliant sunshine, light pouring down all over the snow. Right after Christmas, William took the kids to Florida to visit his parents. I had been too demoralized to shovel the driveway. Nora and Zack ran out to William's car through a narrow corridor between walls of snow up to their shoulders, like Japanese in the north in the middle of the long black winter, calling to each other about how happy they were to be going. For days after they left, my heart kept jolting, as if I were constantly on the verge of receiving terrible news.

New Year's Eve 1978 found me at home. I had made no plans. I was celebrating the imminence of 1979 by walking around my house. Sitting on the edge of my bed, I ate popcorn and drank most of a bottle of champagne. Then I went down and found two joints in the flashlight and hammer drawer, rolled during pre-Watergate days—Julie and Tricia days—and I stood in the kitchen and smoked them. I bent and sniffed the cat's head—scent of wild animal and flea bath. I said, "I believe I have to cry." Crying was something I'd only recently begun to do with regularity; now my noisy, rasping, faraway sobs echoed in the empty house.

A long time went by. The light got unprecedentedly brilliant. I became remarkably aware of the shiny white appliances, and stood there swaying half the night.

Much later I sat at Nora's piano, which I didn't know how to play, and turned on the metronome and listened to it snap in the silence. I ate fudge, drank cognac, stayed up until dawn, then hung up my clothes on the rug.

Two days after New Year's Eve, I still had a hangover. My car was dead. I took a cab to the Rosemans'.

Deenie answered the door wearing a napkin on her head. Deenie was the most capable person I knew— she could do anything. At the moment she was training the green parrot, Beautiful Girl, not to sit on her head anymore, and the bird was going crazy, setting out and flying toward Deenie's hair, starting to land, catching sight of the dangerous slope of the napkin, screeching to a halt in the air.

Outside, where I was standing, it was still and bright—snow with sunlight blazing off it. I stood looking into the dimness. Summery air poured out.

"It's perfectly safe to enter," she said.

I reached in and pulled a corner of her napkin. I started to speak and my voice caught—I was trying to make my first remark in three days. Finally I said, "That was smart, to think of the napkin."

"I'm smarter than a parrot," she said. "Step over the threshold. It won't be so bad."

For a long time I walked around the big glassy house full of objects from other moments in the century and other parts of the world, looking at every familiar thing, as though this were my own home and I'd just gotten back from far away. The Tibetan hangings lay against creamy walls, the Japanese sugars glistered on the coffee table. All over the tables were scattered ACLU newsletters, pornographic comic books, essays about the Tasadai, biographies of Mary Wollstonecraft and Freud. There were framed photographs of Deenie and Michael on the Amazon; their sons Andrew and Jacob before a Mayan ruin; and their eldest child, Daria, fourteen, in Kyoto. Daria looked dramatic—the picture emphasized her long, beautiful limbs and fingers and her extravagant gold hair; she was towering over three generations of Japanese, at the Great Hermit Temple of the Daitoku-ji.

I felt light and shaky. Everything here was so lively, and everything was shared. The whole house was filled with emblems of Deenie and Michael's love and its elaborate ramifications. Every object seemed to exist for the purpose of remarking that the Rosemans were together for life.

On the shelf next to the photographs, under a sliver of light, was a tiny stone head with a wrinkled brow. I picked it up, and from my palm it looked up at me, pre-Columbian, worried. I decided to take it. They wouldn't miss it for a long time, and it could live with me. I'd steal a little person, centuries old, far from home, belonging to my best friends!

In the kitchen, Deenie was rolling pork cubes in a dust made of crushed coriander seeds. Her son Andrew was menacing Beautiful Girl with a wooden spoon, forcing the bird to back up through the cage door. Andrew bumped the refrigerator, and tiny watermelon wedges clattered to the floor, releasing a frayed picture of Rosa Parks. He was thirteen, a musician, tall. He glanced at me and left the room.

I said, "The pre-Columbian head is in my pocket. I was considering stealing it." I looked at Deenie—normally, I thought.

"*Oh sweetie,*" she said.

To converse, I told her about my high school boyfriend and wondered for the first time in about sixteen years where he could possibly be—I recalled all that lovemaking on the beach, the sand and dunegrass and mosquitoes, the friendly amiable adventurous sex laboratory we had together, and what his hands looked and felt like, his long muscular arms, delicate ears, wonderful slippery tongue . . .

When I wound down, she said, "Are you going back to work?"

"I'm writing poetry, still."

109

"Could you maybe write poetry at night?"

"Great. Good idea," I said. "I've heard it from everybody." I gave her a stubborn look and she paused a moment.

"Have you heard from Dan?"

"Every three months."

"Do you feel disoriented?"

"No."

She looked at me until I laughed and said, "Yes. I'm disoriented."

"Maybe you're not."

In a determined way, I chuckled on. I sounded like two people: a raucous one and a helpless one.

She said that just because people constantly got divorces didn't mean it was easy.

"We're not necessarily getting a divorce," I said, fast.

She rushed over, took my face in her hands, and stared at me, miming intense love. There was a strong, pleasant smell of coriander seed. Pretending it was an entirely normal invitation, she invited me to stay overnight.

As we sat down to dinner, Michael came in with the dog. "You're here? Where's your car?" He looked as usual—small, golden, alarmed.

Andrew jumped up and rushed to the dog as if back from the war. The dog ran to meet him, reared up, thrashed in the air.

"Out at once!" Deenie yelled. "Put him out! Put him out!"

"Ooooh doggums boy," Andrew sang. Gritting his

teeth, he hugged the dog and tried to get it balanced on its hind legs for ballroom dancing.

"Take the dog out!" Deenie cried. She started running across the kitchen.

Michael kissed his little son Jacob's head. "So?" he said to me.

I struggled to look amused. I said, "I'm here to tell you that you just won a big important grant."

Deenie, rushing past, gave me an encouraging smile.

Everybody sat down and we began. Michael rehashed the Shah of Iran's history and told us the many reasons the Shah was finished. Daria told Jacob about karate—what the belts meant. Deenie told about her favorite client—breaking and entering, repeated assaults with a deadly weapon—a white guy who would act normal for long periods and then break up his dinner plate and eat it. Andrew, humming, buttered three bread slabs, stuffed them down.

Michael started to fantasize about an upcoming trip to the People's Republic of China with some other psychologists. He would immediately manage to find the currency black market, eat in a people's noodle shop and drop his scraps on the floor like one of the people, get a bike and ride through the hair-raising streets of Beijing: he was planning to fit right in. We had already heard all this; we chewed, he talked on. He told us that the Chinese have innumerable wonderful sayings, that the Taoists know everything, that the Taoists say: If you have two cowlicks, you are either magical or very smart. Deenie fixed him in a madonna's gaze.

He said, "I have the impression I'm being tolerated."

1 1 1

"Finish what you were saying," she said.

"Before you started tolerating? I pick up the thread where, 1961?" he said, looking happy.

"*Go on.*"

So Michael announced that the Chinese were a minority: "There are probably even more Chinese than women!" Everybody laughed steadily for a while without comprehension. It was hot in the kitchen. The dog lay down, and the windows steamed up. We ate like a family, attending to our plates.

At last Michael asked, "What do you hear from William?"

Deenie forked snow peas onto Jacob's plate. She said, "Not right now."

"No?" Michael said. " 'Not right now'?"

She shook her head slightly.

Michael said, "No?"

"After dinner," she said.

Michael said, "After dinner, not during dinner? Again in life I said the thing at the wrong time? Is this now a new idea we developed in psychology to save feelings? Deenie, *what?* I'm coming in the house with big muddy boots? People move out but we pretend they died?"

"He's fine," Deenie said. "He took the kids to Florida."

"She's trying to keep me from feeling sad," I told him.

"You're sad?" Michael cried. "Of course you're sad! It's a big, momentous, very significant, very monumental, once-in-a-lifetime situation. What do we do in our lives? We get born, we get sick, we get laid, we get married, we work, we die, we get divorces! What is this, Deenie, our new method is we don't mention it so the divorce doesn't exist anymore, if we don't mention names her husband didn't move out, he's actually back at the house? *Of course* you're sad! *Be sad,* honey! You *should* be sad!"

"We're separated," I said. "Not divorced."

"Fine!" he said. "Separated. Whatever."

Grinning in the candlelight, Daria started violently playing an imaginary violin. Her head was bent, her hair flying. She said to me, "I don't mean this against you."

"No, wonderful," Michael said. "What is going on here? Any action to avoid a simple straightforward experience of a real thing! *I can't believe this family.*"

Daria bowed harder. Andrew said to the dog, "Isn't this fun for doggums boy?"

Michael cried, "Listen, people, guess what, we all agree: *Nobody should get hurt in the world.* It's a bad world where it happens! Nobody should insult anybody's tender feelings, nobody should feel devastated, nobody should feel *badddd,* nobody should go away from anybody . . . it shouldn't happen! *It should never happen.* So, as a defense, let's all play games and let's all keep our collective mouth shut about significant events, and"—he glared around in triumph—"that's the method of choice!"

I sat and chewed my salad and imagined Michael lifting me onto his lap and promising to care for me alone among women through the long years ahead. In real life, even given other constraints, he was far too small and I too large for us to pull it off. But real life had slipped out of view.

After dinner, Deenie and Andrew had to go out to look at dogs. Across town were some baby Chesapeake retrievers, and Deenie said it was necessary to look at retrievers if only to rule them out.

"My wife is a known saint. First a parrot. Now two dogs."

"Come with us," she said.

"Don't expect me to help bring home an animal," he said.

"A couple of people need a little silence for a while." She looked at him until he saluted, put on his leather jacket, and walked straight out.

Jacob went to the computer, Daria to her room. Things fell still. The place was full of quiet, and again I started to walk around. I circled the first floor, aimlessly for a while, then opening all the doors. In Deenie's study I looked into the closet at legal pads and manila file folders, extra boxes of paper clips and pens. There was a walk-in closet, and I walked in. I tried on her coats, then Michael's parka, then a shawl. Folded on the shelf I found a kimono, and I tried it on. Finally I put on Andrew's satin Dodgers jacket, went upstairs and lay down on Deenie and Michael's bed, and dialed Willie at his parents' in Florida.

The kids were at the movies. I told him where I was.

"Oh, the virtuoso family," he said, after a pause.

"So you'll be marching on Washington, of course, while dilating upon the novels of Kawabata."

"Don't do this now," I said.

He said, "Michael Roseman really telling it like it is?"

"I don't feel like hearing this now."

"I imagine not," he said.

"Anyway, I'll probably stay here tonight."

He said, "While everything continues brilliant and fey for long, unendurable hours."

Tears flashed into my eyes. I said I was so *fucking tired* of his competition with Michael, my voice rising, the tempo picking up, that he had been jealous for years and it was babyish and it was pathetic, he was obviously still consumed with resentment because Michael and Deenie were my true friends instead of his, "and you continue to abuse me and make a complete fool of yourself about it!"

"You're remarkably unhinged," he said.

"You are horrible!"

"You can stuff it," William replied pleasantly, and the phone fell dead.

I went into the closet. It was huge and lined with Japanese paper—giant peonies, magenta on ivory—and filled with jeans, bathrobes, Michael's jackets, Deenie's caftans and her six business suits. On a hook was her silk nightgown, flesh-colored with lace, an anniversary gift from her husband. I took off the Dodgers jacket and put on the nightgown, which was designed to almost bare the nipples—in it, I had a dejected, soft-core look. I stood looking in the mirror until the phone rang. It was William, apologizing.

I thanked him, three times. He told me that Zack had seen a barracuda and flown out of the water, straight up. I lay on the bed and laughed. Then we told old family stories—Zachary trying to comb baby Nora's hair with the hammer; Nora refusing to go out because she was afraid of the fighting on the sidewalk, a battle between red and black ants; Zack getting interested in a record by a guy named Moe Zart. I turned off the lamp. Except for a sliver of light from the closet, the room was dark. In the silky nightgown, I got into the bed. From downstairs, Jake's video game faintly, steadily beeped. I looked up at where the ceiling must be, and Willie's voice buzzed in my ear. For the first time in months, I felt okay. I felt fine.

On January 4th, home from the Rosemans', I rose full of resolve and got the car battery charged, then drove to the garage. Courtly mechanics, streaked with grease, in green coveralls: "This is the problem." It calmed me right down, having professional help.

My mother had given the kids a kitten, Bonky Boy—now an adolescent cat. That night I took Bonky to the vet's evening hours. I was weak and cheerful, like somebody whose fever has just broken, playing the tape deck loud, driving through snowy fields in the dark—on the way, I saw a raccoon standing in the road, leaning over a bit of food, fluffy stripes dragging, and named it Stripe.

The vet's office was afire with fluorescent lighting and smelled terrifying, that antiseptic doggy smell. Here seven veterinarians had come together in tedious, lucrative practice. They were walking about in white coats

and running shoes, carrying charts and morosely calling out the names of the owners of the ailing. While
Bonky stayed in the car crouched and craning his neck
and screaming, the vet's assistant wrote: Bonkyboy
Green. Castrate.

After the anesthesia, Bonky's head wouldn't drop
down. The vet, a young man in a down vest, said,
"You just stand here and pet him and when he's unconscious we'll do the deed." The vet said Bonky's head
would drop in a minute, but it didn't, and two more
vets stopped in to check him out.

"You can give him a little more. I read that somewhere." This was a breezy ancient woman who'd managed to stop in the operating room, a Doberman owner
in cowboy boots.

One of the younger vets came in and offered to give
him a bit of pentothal to put him under. He shaved
the shin of Bonky's front paw and gave him the pentothal i.v. while his aide, a teenaged girl, stood under
the blazing operating room lights and held Bonky's paw
still and told the vet every twist and turn in the plot of
Raiders of the Lost Ark, which she had seen on video for
the third time on New Year's Eve.

Bonky disappeared, his eyes wide, his tongue sticking out. Sprigs of black fur lay next to him on the table,
which was actually a metal grid over a sink, where blood
could run off. While the vet did the job I walked away.
He whistled "Moon River," and had only got to Twooo
drifters, off to see the world, when Bonky Boy's balls
were gone.

For a moment, I had the fantasy I'd brought the
wrong cat, that in my distraction I'd grabbed up our old
gray cat, Kibbie, and dragged him off to be neutered

all over again. I'd picked up the wrong cat and brought him two towns over in the dark, driving fast, listening to Bach concertos while the wrong cat walked around my shoulders, and thinking about nothing except all the implausible ways I might possibly get my own derailed life onto some track.

Actually, of course, it was Bonky. At the front desk I bought a cat carrier, cardboard, with a picture of a tabby and a cartoon balloon saying I'm fine, thanks. Inside it I laid, with his neck weirdly bent, boneless Bonky, who looked dead at best.

"What should I do for him?"

"Don't leave him where he can fall down stairs or get his head in a water bowl," the vet said. Absently, he fingered the ventilation holes in the side of the carrier.

"That's all?"

"That's the aftercare," he said, smiling oddly.

On the road on the way home, Stripe, the raccoon, was dead, curled on his side, his red mouth ajar, his eyes red beads in the headlights. I was busy, talking to unconscious Bonky, telling him I was sorry he was having such a demoralizing time.

They got back from Florida three days later in the middle of the night. The kids' faces were vacant and brown and gleaming. They stumbled to their beds.

Since his surgery, I'd been allowing Bonky Boy to sleep in my room—in the night, Bonky kicked the hair dryer and it turned itself on and started roaring.

I held the clock up to my eyes—four: in an hour, William would have to wake up and sneak out. I couldn't see him, but I thought he was asleep. I was already used to sleeping alone—with two people in the bed, it was too hot.

Willie suddenly said, "It's a sauna!" and sat up fast and peeled off blankets. Then he stamped across the room and turned off the hair dryer and threw it on the rug.

All night I'd been waking up—turning over, clutching the sheet, sighing. I'd kept saying, "I'm sorry. I don't know what I want."

Rhoda, my sister, called from Vermont and handed the phone to her husband, Tom. As a young man, Tom had married the same woman twice. He had known they were reconciling when "furniture started drifting back to my house"—he had seen that she would finally come home, by increments, following her tables and chairs. He thought something like this could happen to me.

I said, "But I don't get the point of the story. Besides the fact that Willie didn't take the furniture, you're married to Rhody now. So it actually didn't work out."

"Oh Christ, I'm a bozo!" he cried. After we laughed a while, Tom yowled at Rhoda to take the phone, that he was full of self-doubt and had to go out in the air.

Willie started coming over. Two or three nights a week, after the kids went to bed I'd listen and wait, sitting on the couch like somebody in a waiting room, with Bonky in my lap. When they slept, I'd phone him. I'd walk out onto the front lawn and watch for his headlights. Standing on the frozen grass in the dark, I was an addict about to binge—queasy and eager and compelled, alone with my secret craving. By day we continued to complain about each other, exhaustively and sincerely, to our friends. We didn't tell any of them about our nighttime life: they couldn't take it. Our illicit congress was making us very lonely.

The car would wheel in and brake as if hitting a wall. He would drop his arm around my shoulders, then walk like a man in a hurry into his former home.

We didn't talk. We lay there and made love for long hours, elaborately and hopelessly. We woke at five and he tiptoed out. In four months I never saw his face in daylight.

When summer came, we were still married.

7. Deaths of 1980

In the night I thought my life was over, and woke refreshed.

As soon as Willie tiptoed out, in the early dark I got up. Outside, it was steamy and warm—almost morning. I drove away carefully, as though I were leaving him behind.

Twenty miles away, I parked in gold and pink rising light. This was Partridge Street, where Arden's mother had once lived, half the dead afternoon in her bed, in the street half the long, tangled night. I was going to sit in my car and ask myself questions and think about how to proceed.

The city seemed quiet, as if before a storm. The street was empty. Three stories up, an air conditioner dripped; otherwise, Arden's building looked uninhabited. On a wall, a billboard still showed one corner of its story about the communal gaiety induced by cigarette smoking, but most of it was torn in strings, as if somebody had stabbed it. Tiny blue scraps of paper, the remains of the stabbing, blew on the sidewalk like butterflies. Arden almost could've been walking here, kicking along, causing the blue scraps to fly.

I got my old job back.

Almost four years had passed since Arden had run and I had walked out of the boys' training school. I asked about him—he was twenty now, and in real prison, brought back from Florida where he'd been found in Tampa in the third Mercedes convertible he stole. The story came from an officer who knew his mother: When the police pulled up, he had been parked at the curb, about to eat three burritos off a Styrofoam plate—the smell of the food filling the car, Arden's big delicate hands peeling open his paper napkin, Arden thinking about his future, where he might go and how he might begin to live when he arrived. He had turned, looked at the policemen crossing the street, and started stuffing himself like a man in a pie-eating contest. He got all the burritos down.

Most of the boys were smaller than I'd remembered. On my first morning back, Billy, a little black kid, who had stolen cars obsessively, unbelievably often, said he wanted to work with me again and he would try this time. He had turned over a new leaf: he was eating broccoli and salad; he didn't watch only kung fu but tried to watch and comprehend the news; he was lifting—he showed me his small powerful forearm, made the muscle twitch. When Billy had first arrived here, he'd been given an unusually bad blanket party—folded in a blanket so he couldn't see out, and kicked by everyone in his wing until he fainted. Talking to me now, he rubbed the hem of my jacket with his thumb. I pushed his hand away. He grinned and licked his fingers. Billy was a boy who couldn't read at all, and, I thought, never would. Later that week, he stood next to Roy and farted, and Roy broke his nose.

The electricity went out, taking the air conditioning with it, and the house filled up with tropical air, thick and cloudy. "This is sort of fun!" I said, and started portraying an indomitable, madcap mom. We went out for Chinese food and read books by flashlights. We took the frozen stuff to the neighbors' and poured out the souring milk. While I was planning my call to the electrician, three days went by.

Nora said she couldn't stand the heat upstairs and began to sleep in the living room, lying on top of her sleeping bag. If Zack or I walked through the room at night, any hour, she said: "It's okay. I'm awake."

The fourth night, while I was reading by candles, saving the flashlight battery for bigger things, Zack came down. He had on his football uniform, which slightly shifted as he walked, and which made him look enormous and fragile. He smiled a wry smile, but then he suddenly got tears in his eyes. "I'm up there feeling around for my pajamas, blindly sweltering," he said. "Please, Mom! I need my room!"

What am I doing?

"Mom, y'see—"

"Oh, honey, I'm sorry about the delay."

Delicately, Zack palpated his own big false shoulders. He said gently, "Mom, we can't just keep our house this way."

"Without lights?" I said. "Of course not! I'm getting the electrician!"

"Also without the refrigerator and the air-conditioning."

"Of course!"

"It's bad this way," he said.

Then I suddenly finally noticed the badness of it—the electricity becoming a thing I was avoiding, and actual darkness descending.

"You probably called him today, right, Mom?"

I blushed. But of course it was dark, and, anyway, not to embarrass me, Zack had already turned away. As he tiptoed past her, Nora said to him, "I'm awake. Hi. I wish that we could have the lights also."

In the morning I woke thinking that things would be better if we had much more money—I meant enormous amounts of new money, the sums made in an evening by rock-and-rollers and movie stars, to hire housekeepers and gardeners and secretaries and drivers, or, more precisely, numerous companions—people to care about the kids and me. I told this to Deenie. "In fact we *do* care," she said grimly, and she planted some bleeding hearts in my yard and dialed the electrician.

He told me there was nothing wrong with the electricity; it had been turned off! I had paid the other bills, but this one envelope had looked off-putting. Now, galvanized by the electrician's sensible presence, I finally ripped open the envelopes and read the notices in which the electric company had issued its increasingly frank warnings. Willie had always opened the bills and written the checks—any day now, I'd been planning to start to do the job as thoroughly as he.

In the night I half-woke, dreaming about somebody

familiar: it was the electrician himself, in a business suit, checking out my wiring, then standing very near.

The next week, while the Rosemans and I were out eating pizza with the five kids, Michael Roseman said that a friend of his had "gone gay" after twenty years of marriage. "Drove him to it," he said genially.

From the booth behind us, Nora looked shocked, then screamed, "Ha! Ha!"

Deenie turned and said, "Ignore your Uncle Michael. He's an idiot. We take him on these outings."

The waitresses were rushing around in sky-blue nylon skirts with tiny aprons, and nurses' shoes, attending to our needs like real nurses. The air conditioner was blasting cold wind into the hot restaurant, high above our heads. The air was thick with pizza scent. Deenie was laughing and looking disgusted and arguing with Michael.

He said to her, "*Yes* I had diverse sexual experience. And ultimately I didn't choose homosexuality—that's *one* difference."

"Stop now," she said. She sucked in smoke, set down her cigarette, half-turned to the booth behind her, and started arranging her daughter Daria's hair. Daria shook her head. Andrew dropped a pizza slice and started crawling under the table. Zack and Jacob were intently chewing. Nora looked up and said, "There's Daddy!"

He was holding the door for Jill Grieves, and she was turned back toward him. We all looked. We could see her pale red hair, and Willie's grin, his shining eyes, his whole face bright with happiness. Behind them, the night sky.

Nora and Zack slid out and started running. Deenie got up and rushed toward William with her arms already opening. He looked at them all in a dazed way, the last I saw before Michael Roseman started feeding me with his hands.

He was ripping off bits of pizza and setting them into my mouth, letting the hot strings of cheese drip back onto his fingers. "Look at me," he said, "and just taste." I looked. He was smiling ardently, as if long into a relationship so complicated and gratifying and deeply sexual that only by hand-feeding me for another lifetime could he begin to express his commingled gratitude and lust. The pizza tasted surprisingly good in these tiny bits, sweet and salty. A scrap of crust dropped onto the table. "Oh look," Michael whispered, "it's jumping around. It's excited about entering you!"

Deenie and the kids were sliding back into the booths. Willie and Jill were passing the table, and there was a little scatter of hellos like flashbulbs going off. Michael greasily brushed at my cheek with one hand and waved with the other—a flutter of the fingers of a man so distracted by love that he can't get it together to properly wave. After they passed, he said to me, "Now aren't you happy I didn't go gay?"

What my friends said: Marriage is insurance. Marriage is a matter of being with the one who knows your history. Or: with the one you can trust, at the end, to pull the plug (Michael, grinning and drooling at Deenie, who ignored him).

Everybody had an opinion. When you're single, the highs are too high and the lows too low. On the other hand, when you're single, you can go straight out and find young men, men like beautiful boys with strong smooth arms, who haven't yet earned their faces, and with these fellows you can rediscover tenderness (Annie) or fuck your brains out (Michael). How the hell did my friends know this stuff? According to magazines, half the country was divorced. All my friends were married.

But I leaned toward them day and night, snapping up their advice. I'd been fooling myself: Willie was gone. At the same moment I realized this, I also started to see what everybody had been avoiding mentioning: married life is the only life there is.

I said to people, I'm sliding. They said no no. For the first time in my adult life, I couldn't tell my husband, the only person who would understand.

Willie and I didn't speak anymore. We had lawyers. The first week of every month, he'd be mailing me a check. I was planning to open the envelope.

All summer, whenever the kids spent the weekend at their father's—eating in restaurants, sleeping on futons—I drove, seven manic hours, to my mother's house at the Cape.

In the mornings, Stu and I took long walks on the

beach, me near the water, Stu near the dune, in opposite directions. Mom stood high above the beach, at her easel, in her bathing suit, on a little rubber bathmat set on the sand, painting large luminous pictures of water and sky.

In the afternoons, I'd sit with Mom and Stu on the screened porch, where we all read the paper. They offered me the front page, but I graciously declined, numbly studied the business section. Late in the day there'd be a pale version of Willie's and my old newspaper reports, lacking our emphasis on sensational private violence, charisma, celebs. Over dinner nightly, we conversed, while I waited until I could drive back down to New Jersey, to the sidewalk in front of William's apartment, and pick up Nora and Zack and go home. Mom and Stu told me about the Soviet invasion of Afghanistan; I told them about the price of gold rising.

One weekend at Mom's, during the night, a cold August night, I walked downstairs in a blanket and stood in the living room with the windows black, the scrub pines swinging outside, pine needles scratching at the house. The lamp casting its pool of light; darkness beyond.

My husband was out.

I kept phoning half the night. Every twenty minutes I came down and dialed again. It began to seem appropriate to enlist the aid of the operators—I started asking them to place the calls. Small faraway voices under the steady ringing, static on the line, the operators chatting, bustling in their chairs and sharing sandwiches at the noon hour of the night shift. When they spoke to me, it was in unusual, though not surprising, tones of intimacy, even complicity, induced by the late hour—just us here together murmuring in the dark. At three in the morning, an operator let it ring thirty times, knowing without my admitting it that I was trying to wake a man.

The next day Willie phoned, from my house. He and the kids had gone over to use the barbecue and the Ping-Pong table and ended up using the beds. "You go back to your own house!" I cried. But why? So he'd be where he ought to be, when I called.

I ran into my mother in the hall in the middle of the night. "What's going on out here all the time?" she said.

"Nothing," I said, and went into the bathroom. When I came out, she was waiting. The Chinese lamp was on, and, standing in its light, wrapped in Stu's big elegant dressing gown, Mom looked tiny but unavoidable. She followed me back into my childhood bedroom. Of course the room had long since been entirely refurnished, and next to the bed was a slipper chair which seemed to've been purchased years ago for just such a moment as this: me in the bed; Mom on the chair.

With sudden vehement little jerks of her feet, she kicked off her satin slippers, as if they'd been biting her. She said, "Maybe you and William never should've gotten married in the first place. Maybe that's true. Maybe I should've been a better mother and said something at the time. Some people thought you were both too young. Well, you *were* too young then! Let's face it: you're too young *now*."

"Ma," I said.

"What? Tell me."

"This is not really too helpful."

Outside, over the ocean, the sky was getting ready to lighten. Mom leaned and peeked through the blinds, looking for the beginnings of sunrise. "Well, what *is* helpful?" she said irritably. "You tell me and then I'll just do it and try to *help*."

"I'm not sure," I said.

"Which means what?"

"I think," I said, "I probably have to get through this myself. I think I have to try to start figuring things out for myself. I really appreciate your—"

She held up her hand. "Oh please!" she cried.

I was sitting with the quilt up to my neck. From her perch, she studied me a while, concentrating, as if trying to pick me out of a lineup. Finally Mom said, "Oh, you chick. I feel so *responsible*. You obviously just do not have the *slightest idea*."

Nora said this had been the worst year of her life— "and I'm only ten." She was standing on the front step, wearing new ponytail holders and holding a new Miss Piggy lunchbox. She'd had to keep going outside, she said, even in winter, to get away from our marriage. She was glad this was September, the first day of school—the beginning of the new year. "No! Don't answer me, Mom!" she said. "Don't tell me anything."

Zack said, "She couldn't anyway." Nevertheless, we stood there together for a long time, while I tried.

———

Nora said it seemed that William in the past weeks had been constantly giving them things, buying them things, being nice, in order to get them to like him. It reminded her of a boy at school, running for class president, who had passed out hard candies wrapped in little red papers saying Vote for Bob.

Nora: Daddy bought us notebooks. Daddy took a shower this morning at his new girlfriend's, Mary Leigh—

"You mean Jill," I said. She looked confused, dreamy, shook her head.

—Daddy might be going to Barbados with Mary Leigh, his new girlfriend, although it might be too expensive. Daddy and Mary Leigh took Mary Leigh's baby in bed with them! A long peroration about Mary Leigh's children, their names and ages, and William's attempt to get Zack to babysit for Mary Leigh's little boys, and Zack declined and "Daddy took him in the bathroom and yelled at him."

While Nora told me this, Zack stood in the doorway, as if eavesdropping, trying to pick up some information about his own life.

His junk mail still came to my house—I wanted to keep it.

I wanted to keep his leather gloves, hidden in my desk drawer. We conferred with our lawyers. Mine was Linda, a nervous, clever, prettily dressed woman with a noisy briefcase. "If you want it right away, we can just get it on mental cruelty," Linda said.

"There wasn't any," I said.

"Be serious," she said, snapping the briefcase hinges. "I had three counts at my house this morning, and I'm married twenty years."

I wanted to keep talking with Linda about Willie, whom I thought about a lot—nobody else, sensibly enough, could tolerate hearing about Willie anymore; Linda was fascinated. I wanted to have extra meetings, to hang on the phone making divorce plans in increasingly fine detail. I imagined his apartment, then the grand new house he'd eventually buy, filled with people, filled with light. I didn't want to take back my own name.

March came: William and I had lived apart a year and a half.

"It's not really an official eighteen-month separation," I confessed. "We were sleeping together for a while."

"So what?" Linda said.

"So we weren't really apart."

She was sick of me. "I hope this one's a joke," she said.

"You mean we'll have to wait longer?"

"Does he want to contest?"

"No."

"He still wants to end the marriage?"

"Yes."

"*You* want to end the marriage?"

I hesitated. Intently smiling, she pumped her head up and down. "Yes," I said.

"Well then, you got it." She smashed her briefcase shut. "If sleeping together was a hindrance to divorce," she said, "everybody in America would still be married."

More months slid by. Finally Linda smiled her complicated smile and said that William Green and I ought to "bite the bullet" and actually get a divorce. She pronounced it "boo-lay," as if it were French. It occurred to me to bop Linda, my most important ally, in her little beautifully powdered nose.

My heart jumped. Trying to write a poem late at night, I thought someone was touching my back.

It was December. At the training school, hopelessly, we'd been decorating; two of my boys—Billy, car theft and joyriding, and Malcolm, armed robbery of a convenience store—had painted smoky white corners across the windows. An anonymous donor had distributed red and green jelly beans, but they hadn't worked out: some people had forcibly used them on some smaller people as suppositories.

Willie's and my lives had rolled on. Suddenly, implausibly, we were getting divorced today.

"How old was your father when he died?" This was Nora, dressed for school, standing in my doorway, embellishing her family tree.

"Forty-three," I said. Coincidentally I had just finished dressing as for a funeral, in decorous black. I was late. I pulled some suede pumps out from under the bed and stepped into them fast.

"Very young man," Nora said.

"Yes, he was."

"We learned about cholesterol. Heart attack?" Nora said.

"Yes."

"How old were you?"

"Honey, why are you asking this right now?"

"Mom. Can't I ask?"

"Twelve," I said. I ran into the bathroom. There was an unfamiliar woman in the mirror—in lieu of dwelling on this, I started drawing makeup on the unknown woman's face, trying to improve matters for her.

Nora called, "In twenty-two days *Zack* will be twelve. Then next year I will. Do you remember that, Mama?"

Mama? Instead of having coffee I'd sit down on the bed, put my arm around Nora, and answer her questions, tell her the stuff she'd forgotten or never been told. For a moment I thought to tell her about an earlier life of mine—my young father's sudden death, my young mother's sudden frightening quietness and her immediate flight to Rome, our apartment all that summer and through the fall, my mother at her easel on the terrace from early morning until the light dropped and on the Janiculum the umbrella pines stood out against darkening blue sky. Of course I wouldn't tell her about Rhody's and my pain and confusion in Italy, and worse pain and more elaborate confusion when we suddenly returned to our unfamiliar home. I wouldn't mention all the lies Rhody and I practiced telling, and told for months, in an attempt to keep our spirits up. The small change we stole, the creepy smiles we affected. I wouldn't mention our discussions in the night, nor the sheets of thin blue airmail paper on which we wrote our plans to grow up and find families and *live normally* and *be good*.

When I came out of the bathroom Nora was gone.

In the courthouse, the first person I saw was William—I was thrilled to see somebody I knew so well! He was standing alone, holding one end of his expensive silk tie, fruitlessly studying it for flaws. His lawyer, a pal of his, sidled out of the men's room like a criminal. Linda was at my elbow tugging me down the hall. As we passed Willie, he stuck his hand out behind him and squeezed my hand.

Then we went into the courtroom and affirmed that our differences were irreconcilable and that we had lived apart a long time and that we had been unremittingly careful in reflecting individually and jointly upon the irremediable nature of our lamentable shared situation and that everything had been tried. We affected low soft modulated voices, impeccable posture—we were like two longtime students from the same fictitious finishing school. Willie and I clearly shared the idea that if we didn't appear to be a remarkably sensible couple, and of one mind, they wouldn't let us leave each other.

Linda looked exalted and kissed my cheeks, as though this were my wedding day. It was a very cold day, getting dark fast. I turned the heat up and drove straight on to school, and spent the last period playing four-letter Scrabble with Billy, who kept muttering, as usual correctly, "Can't make shit with four letters." Then I drove to the supermarket and filled up a cart like somebody buying for a family of ten, and dropped the bags of groceries into the trunk, already forgetting them.

At eleven, I took off all the black clothes, quite roughly, preparatory to giving them away. For a long time I sat on the edge of the bed, looking toward the television picture, listening to the quiet house. John and Yoko slid across the screen. The sound was off. I didn't bother to turn it up and hear what the rhapsodic two were planning now.

In the morning when I came down, the house already smelled like toast, and "Rocky Raccoon" was playing—the Apple label spinning on the turntable; Zack circling too, on the rug, sighing with anxiety. The kitchen television was on, showing the Dakota, and people behind barricades, weeping. Nora said, "Mama, John Lennon got killed! And we were just talking about your father! What a coincidence! I can't believe this!"

" 'Mama'?" Zack said. His eyes were pink in his pale face. "Who's 'Mama'?"

Yoko asked us to plan to participate in a ten-minute vigil on Sunday at two from wherever in the world we were. That night, on every news show, we saw John and the boys when young, John coiled around Yoko with his nakedness partially obscured, John and Yoko older, the sidewalk in front of the apartment building, people holding each other and sobbing in Central Park; late at night, rock-and-roll writers with large heads of graying hair were asked to reminisce. In bed, Nora and Zack tuned their clock radios to the same station—the house humming with "Lucy in the Sky with Diamonds" and "A Day in the Life" and "Imagine."

Michael Roseman called, to talk about how much the clamor was irritating him. "This man is not a president!" he cried. At the training school, it was like living in the television; we stopped classes to look at

Beatles documentaries, ran discussion groups, tried to decipher the captions under the photographs in the newspaper. Billy said unhappily, over and over, "This be a black dude, *none* of this shit in the paper."

Three days later Zack still couldn't sleep. Very late, he came into my bedroom and sat on the edge of my bed and told me, while I woke up, about his research. He had a partial list of recent deaths: Steve McQueen, the Shah of Iran, Alfred Hitchcock, and the "Born Free" lady.

"These were all this year," he said. "And Peter Sellers died, remember that? That was the bad one, Mom—that was even worse than John."

"People dying is impossible to understand, isn't it?" I said sleepily—not the sort of thing I usually said. "We spend our lives trying to figure it out."

He didn't answer—I thought perhaps he hadn't heard me, or perhaps I hadn't actually spoken. Then he said, "It seems like you just get to know the person right before they leave."

It was very quiet, and I couldn't tell how late it was. Then heat came on and for a while we listened to the hot air swirling up into the house.

Zack said, "You believe in God, right?"

"Yes," I said. "Do you?"

"I'm pretty sure," he said. "Could you make me some of that milk?"

In the middle of the night, walking down the stairs with my son, into the darkness, to turn lights on and heat up a pan of milk, I let myself notice, as if in passing, that I had landed in the middle of my life. And that Nora and Zack were with me temporarily. And that Willie was gone.

Part II

8. Mousetrap

When I visited, Mom asked me questions. "What is love?" she wanted to know. "Do you believe that hearts can truly break?" In the year since Stu's death, she'd never stopped asking.

Mom was sixty-three now, tiny, deeply stylish. She had new MTV hair, so short it was fuzzy, dark with a whitish glaze on it. This time I was visiting for her neck lift, a surgery to fine-tune her already startlingly youthful appearance and complement the wonderful-looking baby wolf's hair. As I traveled toward Boston, the train always seemed to rise; I'd ascend into the North, finally stepping out into sheets of wintry air. Mom lived these days on a square like one in London, in the interesting, changing South End. As usual, Mom was on some kind of cutting edge. All around her, the neighborhood was shifting economically —some areas drastically gentrifying, others falling into neglect.

Back in New Jersey, I was trying to grow up. On Union Square, in the foyer, pleasure would drop over me; being a child again, in my mother's house, just gathered me up and carried me away. Faint music was always playing in the background, at Mom's. Before I got my jacket off, she'd be asking, "Could you put a baby up for adoption?"

My mother's old friend Hilary from Newton took me aside. Hilary was a large imposing woman, a former actress, disorientingly flashy, a wearer of cloaks and scarves. On her right index finger, she had a tiny jewel screwed into the point of her polished nail. She followed me into the pantry, pressed me against the cabinet, and told me about Mom: "I'd say *aren't you cute* to visit, but it's so much more. How crucial you and Rhoda are to Mother! Stuart was irreplaceable! Who does Mother have?"

Hilary and Mom, one big, one little, were, in some way, about as glamorous as you get. Hilary was Mom's surgery mentor; she'd had her entire face tightened and polished twice, back in her glittering other life. Several times a week, Hilary drove in from Newton and sat on the velvet couch until Mom was ready to go out. Today, after the pantry, she took her place on the middle cushion, while I worried about her question.

Well, my mother had Florence, her labrador, and Baby Blue, her Burmese. She also had Raymond, a sort of boyfriend, eighty years old, whom she claimed to hate, in the brownstone across the square. Their windows lined up precisely. Several times a day, Mom looked carefully out the living room windows, from her house into his, to be sure he hadn't fallen unconscious.

Hilary said, "Ray and Mother are like Beauvoir and Sartre."

"Snooze on," Mom said. She left the room and immediately returned—this was an old habit of hers, departing the conversation for a moment; if you waited a couple of beats, she'd come back. Today she was wearing a Chanel suit, carrying a crystal atomizer, spraying about her throat. She said, "Raymond — it takes a lot of applause to keep *that* Tinkerbell in the air."

Hilary shrieked and fell on her side into the pillows. "She is so adorable! She is a cute adorable little minx, your mother! What a troublemaker!"

Mom's face got pink. She said, "If you think this codger is a boyfriend of mine, Hilary, you are losing it. You are *lost in the wild.*"

Mom and Hilary tried to decide where to eat. "Hilary wants it cheap," Mom told me privately. And to Hilary: "I won't go to the Italian place. Last week the lettuce tasted like a rubber raft."

In the Palestinian restaurant, a fly was on its back in the Arabian salad, kicking its little legs. "Oh stop the fuss, Hil," my mother said, and flicked it onto the floor.

When I got back from the bathroom, they were talking about medical matters, and Mom was curled over the table, impersonating a friend with a back problem. Under her miniature suit, she had got her spine bent like a twig.

The friend needed surgery on a disk and had consulted two doctors, one empathic, the other brusque.

"It sounds like a good cop/bad cop routine," Hilary said.

"It's not that he's such a good cop!" my mother

cried, sitting up and shoving at the pita basket. "But he's *sentient*. Unlike this Thanksgiving turkey she's employed to be her surgeon!"

Inevitably, over the honeyed pastry, we talked about Raymond—talking about him, Mom pointed out, was an index of our exaggerated collective longing for men: "Are we *so desperate* that the discussion has to be continuous?" I told her she was right—it does, because we are. Actually, for some months I had been seeing Steven, a handsome, consistently pleasant lawyer, who mainly acted as if, out of deep reserves of goodwill toward humankind, he were *letting* me date him. The kids didn't like Steven and they couldn't say why. They disliked him the way a dog might.

"I envy you, Lolly," said Hilary. "You know I am no groupie for Ray. You're right he's a sob sister. But face it, dear, at times he can be a nice surprise: perceptive and acute."

Mom said sweetly, "Doddering, and arch, and blind."

"Blind?"

"Literally, no. Figuratively, almost completely," she told us. She waved wildly at the restaurateurs, who were clustered in the back on the phone to the West Bank, and one of them rushed forward, looking at her with what appeared to be love. When Raymond died, as he certainly would before Mom, she would say that he was the sharpest, warmest, most intelligent old man she had ever known. She would lay his silk hankie in her underwear drawer, folded like a little flag.

———

Earlier today, before we had come out to lunch, Ray had said, "I would just wonder what your mother— all you girls—think about this fellow Jackson."

Mom looked suspicious. "Why do you use the term 'fellow'?" She flushed and her eyes grew bright with unshed tears of rage about racism.

"Oh Lolly," Hilary said. "Go right on, Ray. And please continue to call *me* a girl whenever you see fit."

Raymond said genially, "Lolly, you're full of soup." My mother spun around and looked at me and crossed her eyes as if being garroted.

My sister, Rhoda, and her husband were also in Boston, for the year, trying it out—Rhody was teaching drawing and printmaking. Hilary was sitting in the club chair looking interested, wearing a silk jumpsuit and silk dancing pumps. Tom was telling Mother Stories. His mother had once taken him to a rodeo, claimed her dress faded, and dragged him home by the leg, screaming *I'll never take you to an outdoor event again!*

We moaned and laughed. Mom went to the kitchen and came right back.

Tom said, "My mother equated inconvenience with death."

Rhody grinned at Mom, who cut her dead.

Tom said, "While I was at school, she gave my dog away. This was during Korea. She said, 'Our president came on the radio and asked us to contribute to the war effort, so I gave Captain to the Defense Department.' I remember thinking, 'Well, maybe he'll be an asset. After all, he's a biter.' "

Hilary and I got hysterical. Mom said, "Oh poo. It's always the mother."

"Not always," Tom said, smiling. "Frequently."

Mom stood up, looked at us, and walked out. When I found her in the bathroom, she said, "Please make an excuse to your sister. But get that lightweight out of my house."

Tom was Rhoda's second husband. After they left, Hilary said, "Tommy is charming. Not constantly spaced out, like number one."

Mom regarded her with elaborate interest, then walked out again. When I found her in the bathroom, she said, "Get Hilary rolling."

Sleeping in the television room, in the middle of the night I rolled over on the clicker and the TV turned on. A younger Telly Savalas came into view, tough and disgusted, reflectively sucking his lollipop. I had to sleep again, fast: late-night loneliness was starting to crash over me like a wave breaking. From three rooms away, I could hear my mother's music playing, in the walls.

In the morning, when I came out, everything was cool and quiet and the Burmese had thrown up furry puddles. On the polished floor, the wet spots sat like tiny islands crossing a luminous calm dark sea. Baby Blue lay staring in the cat opium den, upon a square of Bokhara where he habitually did his catnip.

Mom came out, looked at the puddles, and peered at Florence, her labrador, then identified the culprit. She cried, "*Don't* you try that!" as if the cat were still in the act of vomiting. She crept along in her satin pajamas and scrubbed at the floor. She glared at Baby Blue under the armoire: "Doesn't he see what a burden he is?"

In the dining room, surrounded by hammered silver bowls and crystal goblets behind glass doors, we ate cinnamon toast together. We said what we'd been saying all year:

"How's it going?"

Mom: "Sucks."

"Oh, Ma."

"Well, please correct me and then I'll be quiet: does it suck to have nobody, to have no friends— "

"You do have friends. You know a hundred people—the phone rings constantly." This was true, but a wrong tack.

"What would you say if I said that to you?" she cried. " 'Not helpful'! And you'd be right!"

"Maybe it doesn't help very much. I know it's hard without Stu. I'm just saying you do have a lot of nice friends."

"Acquaintances. Not always such nice ones either."

"What about Eliot, who we ran into on Appleton Street? He was wonderful."

She snorted. "A lonely man with Scotty dogs."

"Mom, you *do not have no friends.*"

"I have a limited circle. You don't realize. Yes, Hilary I have. A Nobel laureate she's not. I'm not criticizing her, but one friend coming over to wait for me to ferry her out to a restaurant hardly constitutes a broad social network. Raymond, as you know, is hopeless. His idea of a hot time is sitting in the Barcalounger nodding off while in the act of dialing the weather."

I laughed. Mom looked pleased.

"So, see?" I said. I was as stubborn as Mom. "You have some friends."

My point, though not precisely relevant, was supported by evidence. In fact Mom had given a New Year's Day party only a month before, where eighty people had embraced her until her hair was mashed and her face was smudged. Two young men had grabbed her by the head and, together, pressed her to their shirtfronts, crying, "Prom-night noogie!" A beautiful young Swedish woman in a velvet hat had said Mom was her best friend. The caterer, passing a tray, had said Mom was *his* best friend. Nobody was smoking, everybody looked serene and healthy, the room smelled like a garden. There were three hairdressers (the youngest, who appeared to be a boy of twelve, had created Mom's new look), several painters and print-makers, two psychiatrists, two gallery owners, a woman filmmaker named Sluggo, a genial and sneaky-looking Harvard Medical School student, Mom's yoga teacher, Mom's accountant, Mom's lawyer, Mom's dentist, Mom's dog-walker and cat-sitter, Mom's women's group, and a superior court judge. The mean age of the guests, even factoring in Raymond and Hilary, was about thirty-six.

When reminded of her huge social world, Mom liked to say, "My life is *colorful*. That's all it is." Now, she said instead that she'd forgotten how to feel like getting up in the morning—it was like a skill she'd just lost.

"Oh Ma. Do you feel that bad?"

"What can I do?" she asked, quite seriously.

Talking too loud, I recited a list of things she could do—take or teach a painting class, study at Harvard extension, volunteer at the Gardiner, help feed the homeless, read to the blind: a boilerplate version of the sincere advice I'd labored over as a child. When I was young, in the year after my father died, while we tried together to figure out the shape our life might assume, the moment she would become happy was always just ahead. I was trying just as hard now—the time ahead was short.

I said that Stu hadn't been gone very long, that this was probably still the hardest part.

She pinched at her sprigs of hair. "Did I tell about the mousetrap?"

They had had a mouse. Ida, who comes to clean, had gone to buy a trap, and they sold her a little glueboard: the mouse gets stuck by its feet. When Mom came into the kitchen late at night, the mouse was attached and struggling.

"I thought, 'I can't face it.' I went to bed. In the morning he had dragged it all the way to the sink and ripped his front feet off, but his back foot was still stuck. He was getting exhausted. He could still move, but he was permanently bogged down. I'll never set a trap like that again. It was horrible for him. I thought: 'Little rat, you're acting out the story of my life.' "

"Oh Ma."

Mom, grimly chewing: "Yes. 'Oh Ma.' "

I touched my mother's hand.

She looked at my hand on hers. My mother said, "I never say this. But I am dead-ended here. I am sixty-three years old. I am behind a wall. And I cannot break through."

———

1 4 9

Two days before the surgery, on a morning of sudden spring weather popping into February, we visited with Rhoda in Cambridge. In Harvard Square, where everybody on the street had a crazed look of penetrating intelligence, we walked around, Rhody and Mom and I, passing Rhoda's baby back and forth. We sat at a tiny table and drank coffee, and Mom dabbed a bit of cappuccino foam on the baby's lip. "Oh, I recall you both as babies," she said. "Can you imagine, you're this big and you were *this* big?"

Rhoda, gazing at Nicholas in his little seat: "It sounds like we just now attained our full growth."

"You were *this big*. Are you saying it isn't amazing?"

Of course it was. I remembered her leaving for the hospital when Rhoda was to be born—not what Mom looked like herself, but the hem of her skirt as she climbed into the car. Now I thought, like a child: I don't want her to go to a hospital again. That morning Mom had stood looking into the bathroom mirror with her palms flat against her temples, tightening the skin of her small, already beautiful face.

In the ladies' room, Rhody said, "Is this whole thing fucking nuts?"

In the mirror I pulled at my neck from the sides and stared myself down. I said, "I'm thirty-six. Soon I'll look older than Ma."

She laughed. "You already do."

"I might do it myself," I said.

"Pardon?"

"I think I'll have some kind of lift myself when I'm fifty or sixty."

She looked at me until I felt shy, then closed the stall door.

"Are you sorry she's doing it?" I called to her.

"Oh no," she said. "Not at all. This is a fragile old lady getting shot up with anesthesia in order to smooth out three lines in her neck area. It's not fucked up in the least. It's valorous and adorable." A minute later, coming out of the stall: "Have you been getting letters from Ma?"

"This year? Sure," I said, surprised. Did she think she was Mom's only daughter? I actually had been in that position, and could almost remember it: strolling on green lawn, a cloud of scented air, my mother's hand in its kid glove.

On the way back to the table, Rhoda told me she sometimes waited to read Mom's letter, because she felt anxiety shimmering off the envelope. Also because it was a chore to get it open. "There's so much Scotch Tape sealing them up, you have to practically break in with a crowbar," she said, sliding into her chair, snatching the baby out of Mom's cradling arms.

Mom looked at us. "What's so funny?"

Nothing, we said. I was laughing, Rhoda was chewing the baby's arm. Our mother was already on her feet. "I am exiting, you people," she said.

Ma, sit down! Sit down! we cried. We pushed her back into the chair—I was amazed that it was so easy to sit her down genuinely against her will. She struggled and grabbed for her coat, but she was lighter than ever: each contributing one hand, Rhody and I could easily keep her seated. "Stop it!" she cried. "I am not going to be ganged up on!" She ripped twenties out of her bag, threw them on the table. Her eyes were bright. But as we kept our hands on her shoulders, she stopped being frantic and became merely restive, then subdued, then calm. She sipped coffee. She waved at the baby, into the baby's eyes.

My sister's hand on Mom's cashmere shoulder had been slightly blue. Rhoda's hands were always faintly stained with pastels, the nails edged in fading color. My mother was still painting too, but erratically now— her dreamy landscapes had recently given way to huge canvases thickly covered with oil paint. All year as she'd become noticeably sadder, the paintings had grown more lavish—the most recent were giant abstractions painted in flamboyant, despairing strokes.

Mom talked about colors as if they were people, or animals—their special natures, the way each typically behaved, what it was like to enter a room where one of them was dominating the scene. This year she'd stopped getting excited about finding new ones. "Do other people get starved for colors the way I do?" she occasionally asked, staring out the window like a child forbidden to go out into the bright street.

That night, two nights before the hospital, Mom and Hilary had a fight. Hilary wept, took me into the pantry. "Mother doesn't realize how she treats me. I am sensitive about being talked to roughly, and Mother doesn't see how she hurts my feelings. Just because I don't say what she *wants*."

Fierce and pale, my mother held her palm an inch

from her face and stared into it: "This is how Hilary sees."

She wouldn't call Hilary and she wouldn't talk about it. We stayed up and intently watched Henry Kissinger converse with Ted Koppel. Mom and Koppel looked alike: somber, quietly angry. Mom, through clamped teeth: "Mr. Koppel, siss iss a comblete lie. . . . But I know this lie egg-sists. It follows me everywhere, ass I dravel siss verld."

The next morning, her face was puffed up and she went back and stayed in her room. Her eyes swelled. She came out and walked back and forth in the dining room, the glasses in the breakfront tinkling. She walked, talked for hours, grew hoarse.

I think she's depressed, I told her—she's bereaved; maybe we could talk about it, maybe she could consult a shrink, somebody who could actually help, give her some perspective. I talked on like that for quite a while.

She looked away.

She said, "I am not going to tolerate being condescended to. I am still a piece of the person I was."

The next night, when the kids called, Nora wanted to know how to help Zack press his shirt for his eighth-grade dance. "He's freaked," she told Mom, and Mom sang, "He won't be all freaked when we get him pressed!" She stood in the kitchen on the phone for a long time, running an imaginary steam iron over the sleeves, then the back, then the front, then the placket, of Zack's imaginary dance shirt, talking Nora through it. "Now hold it up!" she cried, and she mimed holding it up, and stood back. "Doesn't it look flash?"

For the calm hopeful minutes Mom was on the phone, she looked familiar: as I remembered her from some earlier time.

Finally the surgery was over. Mom and I were staying together while she recuperated for two nights, in a hotel attached to the hospital, where, painstakingly patting at their lips, the guests sipped meals brought on trays. The neck-lift surgeon was an old friend of my mother's, "Uncle" Daniel, a man I found I resented, as if he were the culprit, the person who had—done what? Taken Stu away. Dealt my mother the gratuitous blow from which she must now hope to recover. He stood in the doorway, hale and effervescent, teasing Mom while I subtly snubbed him. I now recalled that as I rode up on the train, I'd imagined the surgery might change her horribly. But she looked like a cartoon character—a cunning little rabbit with a toothache.

Later, she took a Valium, shredded her napkin. "Should I have not done this? Was this crazy? Did I make another mistake?"

"Not at all, Ma," I said. "You haven't really been making mistakes, have you? Isn't it just a bad year?" Together we were casting our doubts in the appropriate interrogative form: How best to live?

Mom asked: "Do you believe that people can ever truly heal?"

"In most cases, absolutely. Don't you?"

"And in other cases?"

"I want to think they can."

"But do you?"

1 5 4

I said, "I'm sorry. I'm not sure."
Mom said, "I knew it!"

After dinner, I finally made us laugh. I was telling about a bat mitzvah, how the Resnik boys—now two melancholy grown men wearing crumpled suits—kept coming up and asking about our family, crying, "*What ever happened to Rhody?*" Finally I'd said to one of them, "Bruce. Please. Nothing happened to Rhody. You just haven't seen her. Just because you haven't personally seen somebody doesn't mean they died." My mother started shrieking, "My stomach hurts! I'm wetting my pants!" and jumped up and crossed her legs. As she staggered toward the bathroom, her pajama cuffs dropped over her pretty little feet.

While she was in the bathroom, there was a knock on the door, and while I was letting Rhoda in we heard a thud. Then silence.

Ma, Ma!

Mom had fainted deftly—not cracked her head against any porcelain, just folded onto the bathmat and the floor. She was lying on her back with her eyes open. She was looking at the ceiling, which had a gilded wallpaper describing outer space as a sort of supper club—festive planets and opalescent moons, comets trailing silver dust.

"Don't pick me up yet," she said. She batted our hands away, as if we were trying to knock her down. Then while we made some further assisting gestures, she sort of gently smacked at us, until finally we gave up and stood still. Mom had a point: Rhody and I were young and robust and Mom was old and lying on the floor—there was nothing she'd let us do to obscure those facts.

The planets twirled above us. Mom kept looking up, blinking fiercely, as if the stars could rain down and fall into her eyes.

After a while Rhody said, "Wow, you fell beautifully."

"You didn't hit your head," I said. "Your fall was actually perfect."

Rhody and I were out of moves. Mom was out of questions. "Oh poo," Mom said. "What a picture. The gang of two. There you are just standing there, upside down in space, saying the things I knew you would say before you were even born."

9. Down in Florida

A few days before New Year's, William called and asked if there was any chance I'd consider accompanying him to Florida to visit his parents. Lainie was in the hospital with a stomach pain that had started to go away—maybe nothing serious, but Pep was terribly worried—and did I feel like flying south?

"Why do you need me? It doesn't really sound necessary," I said.

"Uh-oh, this is unmanageably devastating!" he cried. "You're not considering not going?"

"Well." I probably didn't have a reason not to. I knew who would stay with the kids. "I mean, would you buy my ticket?" I said.

After a brief silence, William said, "Of course!" as if he had said it immediately.

"Okay. If I can."

"Why is it in doubt? What does it hinge on?"

"I have to see if I can cancel plans with my putative boyfriend," I said. (This was my one repeated effort at wit during that strained period, an allusion to my old wisecracking self—two words: "putative boyfriend.") Long silence. Then William recovered, which it was in his interest to do.

I called Steven to cancel New Year's Eve; he tried to be gracious about it, but he couldn't entirely conceal the fact that he didn't really care. I called William back. "It's all set," I said.

"You won't regret this act of charity. Well, undoubtedly you will, but by then you'll already be down there," he said. He sounded genuinely grateful.

Pep picked us up at the West Palm Beach airport, with his friend Herman riding shotgun. Pep was minuscule, Herman slightly larger. Pep, a natty dresser, was wearing some kind of fancy miniature windbreaker with lots of grommets, and Herman was wearing an ordinary nylon windbreaker and a golf cap. Immediately, they seized our suitcases and demanded we get into the car—they were so insistent and shoved us in with such ferocity it was like being kidnapped. Then for a while we heard them out behind us in the dark, wrestling our bags into the trunk.

William and I settled into the back seat and started asking questions. Pep sat on a flattened pillow, peeked over the wheel, and drove us slowly down a boulevard where it was foggy and neon lights were flipping past in the haze: "Galaxy Skateway," "Cinema Ten." Herman said, "This is the era of discounts for senior citizens at any given time. You don't have to break your neck for the twilight show. That's one of the beauties of down here."

We asked about the beach. Was it relevant? Was it rocky? Was it nice? Pep didn't answer. He put on his turn signal long in advance, and, while we all watched, finally made a left. Herman said, "We don't go. Nahh, it's a big sandy beach. We don't go."

Several times while we were married, William and I had thought of traveling to the Keys, but we'd never got around to doing it. Often during the winter we had imagined ourselves driving a car along a spine of land with glassy water all around, riding to Key West. We asked Pep and Herman about the Keys. Isn't it spoiled, we said.

Herman said, "Nahh, when I went it wasn't worthwhile going. This is a period going back thirty-five years ago."

Herman's subjects were four: Florida. What used to happen. What happened this week vis-à-vis his health. And the locations of the apartments of his and Pep's friends along our route. Herman said, "I doubt you know: the population of Florida is increasing at the rate of seven thousand new people per week."

Herman said, "We were talking today about my thing: calisthenics. Once upon a time I used to do handstands. Weight lifting. High bar. I was excellent, may I say."

Herman said, "Yesterday I thought I had a miracle and I took a Vibramycin. On your right, you're approaching Leo."

William tried an old reliable attitude of his—urgent joviality. As we passed a small shopping center, he leaned near the back of his father's head and announced, "That store wasn't here last time! That's right, Peppy, I've been keeping track of every establishment. And so I am able to tell you that two years ago when I came down, Happy Traveler and Golden Dragon did not flank World of Hair."

Pep said nothing. Under us, the plush seat shifted, and we rode along in the murky Florida night.

At their apartment complex, Herman left us near the swimming pool and took off for his own place with a jaunty step. To get to Pep and Lainie's, you crossed a shallow artificial ravine on a wooden walkway held up by ropes—a walkway suggesting adventure, but remarkably easy to navigate. Pep looked down and watched his foot in its two-tone loafer step onto the first plank, then shook his head all the way to the front door. "That guy," he said.

"I thought he was a pal of yours," William said, and looked at me.

Pep had switched on a little flashlight attached to his key ring, and was getting the door open. "He's a jerk," he said.

Inside, it was colder. We set down our suitcases and immediately started aimlessly walking around. The furniture was rattan, and there was a pattern of palm fronds and giant tropical leaves all over the cushions. There was a bamboo pattern on the bathroom wallpaper and a trellis pattern sweeping across the kitchen. At the rear of the apartment was a tiny atrium with a terra-cotta floor, and a mesh roof through which we could see clouds and light night sky.

A little cream-colored cat walked out of the bedroom and into the kitchen and looked at Pep. Pep said, "Okay. Okay. It's coming. It's coming."

William joined his father in the kitchen. "Who's this? Butter?" he said, and bent and absently patted at the cat. Pep held up a cat-food can and stared at the label.

William slipped off his shoes, opened his suitcase, and started strolling from room to room, brushing his teeth. He went back to the dining area and called, through toothpaste, "So, Pep, Herman's not really a close friend?" He was still trying to get his father to look at him, to talk.

Now Pep was working on serving three gigantic rolls and a paper tub of cream cheese. He said into the refrigerator, "That's right, he's a friend. Y'know, Willie, he's a talker. He can get on your nerves. There are times too much of a friend can be too much."

After the rolls, we got back in the car and went to the hospital, to show Lainie that William and I were there and to say good night. It was a low, modern hospital with lots of windows, sitting all alone out in a flat, new area. It looked like a regional school. Inside, it was decorous and quiet—there seemed to be very few patients.

In Lainie's room all the lights were on, and she was lying on her back wearing a Walkman and gazing at the ceiling. She pressed a button to sit herself up. She lifted off the headset, and for a moment a tinny version of Vivaldi's *Four Seasons* fell out into the room.

"Hi, dear," she said to William warmly, and then the same thing to me, as we kissed her in turn. Her blond hair was arranged in its pageboy almost as smoothly as usual; she was wearing giant gold hoop earrings. Amazingly, she also had on a pink satin quilted bed jacket, like a woman in a forties movie, and in recognition of our arrival she smoothed it out and retied the bow at the neck. Pep went right into the closet and started rummaging around.

Immediately Lainie asked questions about our trip

and related topics, moving rapidly from the specific to the general—had we encountered *traffic* on the way to Newark airport, was traffic on the turnpike as *horrendous* as she recalled, wasn't the East Coast becoming an untenable *megalopolis,* and so on. She flung her arm out in an arc, then a wider arc, to indicate a megalopolis growing.

At once, William was driven wild. In an effort to contain the topic, he applied his usual verbal tourniquet: he adopted a tone of mingled irritation and nonchalance and barked out a rapid series of yeses and nos. Before Lainie could even approach the indignation stage (lively sympathy for her remarkable child, who was spending his valuable time sitting in imaginary traffic), William succeeded in getting her completely discouraged.

William, Lainie, and I settled in and readied ourselves to converse. "Dad always has to poke around," Lainie said. She called, "Sweetie, what are you doing? Come out of there!"

Pep came out of the closet, carrying big knitting needles holding the beginnings of a blue sweater, and tried to put the knitting into Lainie's hands. Lainie said, "Sweetie, why are you giving me this? I don't want to knit now, I want to talk to everybody!"

"Yes, talk to us," I said. "First of all, Lainie, I have to say you look wonderful. You look fine."

"Remarkably well!" William said.

"Who's staying with the children?" Lainie said.

"The gym teachers," I said, and William and Lainie looked at me.

"We are nonplussed," William said. Sexy grin. "Tell us more."

I explained that the boys' gym teacher and his wife, the girls' gym teacher, sometimes slept at the homes of students while their parents were out of town, and that Nora loved the gym teachers both as a couple and individually, and in anticipation of their arrival had baked some brownies and dusted their room. Lainie gazed at me, smiling, shaking her head.

Pep walked over and felt the air-conditioner vent. "I had that Herman with me," he said morosely.

"We thought he was Pep's best friend," I said.

"Dad's being silly," Lainie announced. "Herman Simon *is* his best friend. Dad's just feuding with him because of some little nonexistent thing."

"The guy's a *bocher*," Pep said. He looked at me. "Know what's a *bocher*?"

"Pep, once again you don't think I'm Jewish?" I said, and I cast him a flirtatious look, thinking to cheer him up.

Lainie said, "It means an unmarried man. Which is *absolutely ridiculous* about Herman."

A discussion ensued about whether Herman was really in any meaningful sense a *bocher*. It turned out that Herman had the habit of playing pinochle at night, and that Pep didn't approve.

"Sit down, sweetheart. Why are you walking in circles?" Lainie said, and Pep sat down.

He said, "You ever saw Herman's wife out at night?"

Lainie said, "Dad thinks Herman's wife should get out more. But Esther really isn't that well. Maybe she doesn't *want* to go out constantly. She makes an appearance when it's called for."

William laughed. He said, "Mother, on how many occasions could the appearance of Herman's wife possibly be 'called for'?" He reached over and tweaked the bow of her bed jacket.

"Excuse me!" Pep said loudly. "Where did you see Herman's wife? Name one place! Name one place! At night this is!" He said to William, "She's never seen Herman's wife out anywhere this whole winter, and still she defends Herman. Your mother is a very generous woman, but at times a little too generous for her own good!"

In a small way, William started helplessly laughing, slightly falling apart.

Pep stood up. He leaned and grasped the back of a chair, looking excited and earnest, rather as if about to accept an Oscar. He said, "*I* wouldn't want to leave *my* wife home for the evening!"

"I don't know why Dad has such a grudge against Herman," Lainie said.

Pep flushed. He said to her, "Herman's wife never goes anywhere. You haven't seen her out because she hasn't *been* out."

That night William and I slept in the living room, on two twin-bed couches set at right angles to each other along the walls. The air-conditioning was blowing up near the top of the room, and we lay under blankets made out of some fine synthetic thread, which fell lightly over us like velvety sheets of blue spun sugar.

"Feel your blanket," I said.

William said, "Oh, this blanket? Why, this blanket is made of pure Heroicon, or Modernelle." I thought this was very funny. I was feeling really comfortable.

Except for a few lapses early on, it had been three years since we'd shared a bedroom.

For a while after we got in bed we outlined our tactics—how we would talk to the doctor the next day, how we would try to persuade Lainie to go to a more high-powered hospital if it seemed necessary, how we might confer with specialists when we got back home. Then for a while we rolled around and laughed about the discussion of Herman, taking turns playing the parts and telling each other what our faces had looked like and what Pep had said. Finally, when it was really late, we drifted into just talking, with many long pauses, up at the ceiling. In the dark, we could still see we were surrounded by Caribbean leaves and fronds. We didn't face each other: our beds met in the corner at a table holding a ceramic lamp, and the top of my head wasn't far from the top of William's.

About three in the morning I said, "Have you noticed we've made no effort to turn and look at each other?"

Dreamily, Willie said, "Because you're divorced and down in Florida, you already forgot my face?"

I woke up first. I stepped outside in my nightgown and looked along the catwalk and across the court toward the swimming pool. It was seven o'clock and already bright, and far down the way a small woman was walking a small reddish dog. Pink sky—it was cool and blowy out, not sultry at all, nothing like what I'd expected of Florida in the morning.

I went in and got back into bed. William was sleeping. As I lay down, I heard him say, "You're waking me up because I know you're awake." He opened his eyes and tipped his head back to look at me upside down. "I can't see you," he said resentfully, while he reached behind him for his glasses. He put them on, but then he didn't look at me. When I woke up again, the curtains were open and sunlight was streaming in, the shower was running, Pep was pouring boiling water into decaf powder, and it was time to get up and go back to the hospital.

As we walked into Lainie's room, a round young nurse said, "Here we go! Here's your family!"

Lainie started brushing at her face to dry her tears. Pep walked over and handed her his handkerchief, then sat down on her bed.

William said, "Lainie, dear, what's going on?" and Lainie ignored him. She talked to Pep: absolutely nothing was being accomplished here; if they were doing tests, she would probably be feeling like a guinea pig, but as it was she was just sitting here cooling her heels all week like a bump on a log; when was she getting out and what was the prognosis; that Dr. Astrakhan was so helpful at first and now he hadn't even been in in two days; she felt perfectly fine now and she had felt perfectly fine the whole weekend; if it was really true that she was here only for observation, how long should observation drag on and on and on?

"Lainie, today's the day we're hoping to talk with your doctor," William said. "I'm sure he won't be in the least reluctant to give us some answers."

Pep and Lainie ignored William. Lainie didn't unfold Pep's handkerchief but used the folded square to blot at her eyes. "I'm on an emotional roller coaster," she said to Pep.

"That's right," Pep said.

"I see *no reason whatsoever* why I should continue to be confined here. I want to see Butter! I miss my little *cat!*"

William and I stood there for a while wearing sympathetic expressions, with Lainie and Pep ignoring us.

"There's nothing trivial, Mother, about wanting to see a beloved pet," William said.

"Is there something we can do?" I said.

"Pep," William said. "This is a not unexpectable situation. How about if we all sit down and try to thrash out what's going on here?"

"You don't mean 'thrash out,' " I said.

"Mother, it seems to me crucial in this situation for you to try very hard to maintain some consistent sense of perspective and proportion," William said. "The fact of the matter is that—" Pep waved at him. William stopped talking, turned his back to Pep, threw open his mouth, and frantically bit the air like a maddened dog.

Lainie leaned against her pillow and shut her eyes. Pep held her hand. He didn't bother to turn and look at us, but spoke over his shoulder. We listened to musical clicking as he felt in his pocket for his keys. He said, "You can go out and give yourselves a tour of the area, and we'll see you back in a couple hours."

William and I went out into the bright hot day, got into Pep's car, and drove two towns over. On the way, I said, "Wouldn't it be great to not talk for a while?"

He looked wildly insulted. "Entirely fine," he said. "Mandate what you gotta mandate."

1 6 7

So he treated me to a silent trip around Palm Beach, driving slowly past many pastel buildings and the fire company, with its chartreuse fire engine, and down the avenues of high palms, sharing the road with glittering cars with sunlight flashing off their fenders—Cadillacs, Jaguars, and Silver Clouds.

We went into a restaurant for lunch, ordered a bottle of Chardonnay, and in silence drank it fast. We ate chicken-salad sandwiches, licked our fingers, ordered slabs of cake.

When we came out, it was almost four o'clock and still hot, and inside the cash-register hut the parking-lot attendant was singing a Buffalo Springfield song: "There goes another day. And I wonder *whyyy*. You and I. Keep tellin' lies." How could a guy young enough to be parking cars remember the Buffalo Springfield, or had there been a revival of interest? I waited for him to come out so I could look at him. Of course he was grizzled and wore a ponytail—the one he started growing around 1965. I was somewhat drunk.

In the car I said, "It's always so strange and sad that so many of the guys who went to Vietnam look like hippies now. All the people who were home looking like that and protesting the war have inevitably moved on—you know, they're academics or they're lawyers, or M.B.A. people, or whatever they are, and these vets seem to be the only people who are stuck back in that time. And they remain isolated, and ultimately they're still on the outside—except now they're the ones wearing long hair, wearing headbands, smoking dope. I don't know if I told you about my friend Barney, who—"

"Oh, good. Good. This is what you decide to break

the sacred silence with?" William said. "Something really very central to the problem at hand." He looked mad, but also as if he might be about to cry. "Jesus Christ. Let me off the hook," he said, and peeled out of the lot.

When we turned in at the hospital, we saw Pep out in front. He was standing on the step, carefully watching for us in the other direction. When we got near him, he suddenly turned and started leaning over the hood and waving at us through the windshield.

"Pull up! Pull up!" he called. He pointed to a spot in the driveway right in front of his foot, where the car should land.

Lainie had gone to sleep. She felt much better. Astrakhan had called to say he wouldn't be able to get in until late tomorrow—New Year's Day, but he'd be there. William started saying, "Did you tell him we want to—"

"You don't just tell him like that on the phone!" Pep cried. Pep stood in the driveway leaning into William's window, and now he was talking. Angrily, he gave us his thoughts: that the doctor is a busy man and you don't just jump in and pressure him on the phone, that he and Lainie are perfectly satisfied with the care here, that they have no intention, in case William was thinking this, of going up north to another hospital, that they have been completely comfortable living in Florida these past six years, they haven't wanted for anything, the environment is excellent, they have about forty-five friends here. Pep looked furious and ready to stand his ground if we moved to try to rip him away from his friends and the home he had come to love.

"Pep," William said, "we're really ranging far afield here. We completely understand your and Lainie's situation. Believe me, everybody here wants the same thing. Nobody's trying to pull any wool over anybody's eyes. Nobody's trying to arrange anything that doesn't comport precisely with what you and Lainie would wish for yourselves. So how about getting in the car?"

Pep wanted to drive. He had his hand on the handle of William's door, but he didn't open it. He just kept standing out in the hospital driveway in the late-afternoon sunlight, waiting for his big dominating son to relinquish the driver's seat, to voluntarily hand it over.

At night, after some bagels, we called Lainie, and we each got on to say Happy New Year. She told us, listening on three phones, "That nice Astrakhan called *again*, and he said he wanted to reassure me *again* that he does *not think* this is going to turn out to be anything serious at all, which I thought was so thoughtful. So I feel fine now, and I want to knit and go to sleep."

"Wonderful, darling," Pep said.

We called our children in New Jersey, but the gym teachers said they were out. William went out and bought a bottle of champagne, and we prepared to spend New Year's Eve in the atrium. Around eleven we rolled out the television and plugged it into the outdoor plug, and while we were getting it set up the doorbell rang and it was Herman.

"Herm, everything's all right?" Pep said at the door.

"Nahh, sure. New Year," Herman said. He yelled into the house, "Hi, kids!"

"Hi, Herman!" William and I called in unison, as if we really were kids.

"Keep your jacket on," Pep said. "We're outside. We're out in the, uh, tile-porch area here . . ."

"Essie conked out," Herman said to Pep. He came back to the atrium and sat down and looked around. He said, "So. Where's the cat?"

"He's around. We just saw him," I said. "Oh, here he comes back!"

"Hey. Margarine," Herman said.

"A little bubbly, Herman?" William said, and brought him a glass. Herman took it while he stretched and poked with his foot, trying to touch the cat.

"She's standoffish," Herman said.

Pep came out and sat down, and Butter immediately fell over and lay on his foot. "Turn off the volume," he said to William, and the roaring of Times Square stopped. A few big drops of rain were falling in through the mesh roof, and we could suddenly hear drops snapping on the leaves of the philodendron, but nobody suggested going inside.

William came up behind me and put his arms around me and starting singing "Do Nothing Till You Hear from Me," the Otis Redding version.

"Is this your idea of New Year sentiment?" I said.

He made his voice dense and oily; he sang like a man deeply sick with pneumonia and love. He nipped at my hair.

"Would this be some warped notion of a rapprochement?" I said. We were really starting to feel better. On the television the revelers were packed into the screen, silently pushing each other and bellowing.

"Pep, you used to go to Times Square every New Year's Eve, right?" William said, from close behind me.

"Nahh, we both went together!" Herman said. "In days of yore we did *all* these things!"

"In my early days—" Pep began, and he shifted to settle himself in his chair, so we could see it was going to be a long story. Pep grinned. He lifted his glass at his son. He said, "And I can tell you, Willie, take my word for it: I was much, much younger at the time. That's how long ago we're talking about. When even my friend Herman here was still expecting to stay young."

10 Snapshots of our Trip

After William's and my Florida visit, Lainie got better, and a year went by when neither of us saw Lainie and Pep. Finally, I decided that while Zack stayed with Willie over Easter vacation, I'd take Nora to visit her grandparents. We'd do things together. Everybody would benefit. I had something riding on this—what the hell was it?

"Is it possible to bring Tibby, or no?"

Tibby at thirteen was extremely tall and white and silent, with studs stuck through the cartilage of one ear, describing its edge, and pale-green hair. She was deeply, wonderfully shy. She was constantly inviting Nora to go to Atlantic City to the track. "Grandma and Grandpa might have a little trouble," I said.

Nora phoned Lainie: "Do you and Grandpa have cable? . . . Well, did you ever see this thing called vid eos? It's like playing songs, but you have a little movie with it? . . . Yes, Grandma, it's on the television. . . . Well, if you haven't seen it, it doesn't matter. I was trying to tell you about what my friend Elizabeth looks like. Wait! Did you ever hear of a pib? . . . A person in black . . . Oh, well, never mind. Oh, Grandpa, you're on here also? Hi! . . . Tibby. *Tibby.*

T-I-B-B-Y . . . That's right. Well, thank you for letting her come. She's a little not too talkative. But she's a *very* nice girl." Nora hung up. She had worked it out: she and Tibby would live in the closet.

I was feeling good. When Willie and I parted, he had kept the camera and its zoom lens and flash. I'd intended to buy a replacement immediately, and this week, four years later, I'd bought it. I had already taken about fifty portraits at the boys' training school, most of the subjects striking fabulous poses, pretending to be rich, famous, beloved, white, or free. Now I picked up the new camera and, blinding her, snapped a close-up of Nora dialing Tibby, as if at this moment we were setting off on the first leg of our journey.

On the way down, Nora and I squeezed into the bathroom where we depressed the water handles for each other and pocketed some little soaps. With the airplane roaring around us, my former baby daughter and I stood nose to nose. She told me that she and Tibby had high expectations of Florida: palm trees, flamingos, creamy Kahlua drinks in pineapple boats, fuchsia and turquoise, *hot*. I said, "Are you saying 'Kahlua'? The liqueur?"

They were right: it was hot. The east coast of Florida was in extremis—layers of heat and high winds, for two stunning weeks so far—and Pep and Lainie were staying indoors.

"*You* prefer the outside air," Lainie told me. She led us through the cool apartment and straight out into the hot little shaded atrium, pointed at some straw chairs, and went away.

Nora and Tibby sat very still, where they'd been put—Nora like a polite bird on its perch, Tibby like a member of the rock-and-roll royal family.

Nora looked at me. "Uh-oh, I don't know," she said.

"In a minute you can excuse yourselves."

Pep came out, slowly peeling off his golf sweater while we watched; underneath, he wore a sport shirt showing diagonal rows of miniature golfers teeing off, on a ground of French blue. He stood, resting a hand on his blue chest, while I took his picture, then eased into his chair. "It's a scorcher, darling," he said to Nora.

"It feels *nice*, hot like this," she said. We were surrounded by potted plants. Nora reached out and held onto a giant philodendron leaf and looked at it. Tibby leaned and snapped her fingers at the cat.

Lainie returned with a tray—huge glasses of iced tea with mint leaves floating in them.

"Here's our girl," Pep said.

I pointed the camera. She paused with the tray, adjusted her gaze, and flashed me a professional smile.

"Don't we get *orange juice?*" Nora said cheerily.

Pep pushed himself out of his chair.

"Where are you going?" Lainie said.

"They want juice."

"Oh Grandpa, I was making a joke, because it's Florida!"

Pep kept walking. I said, "Pep, they don't need orange juice." He was at the door. Tibby looked as if she were witnessing a car accident. Nora said, "Grandpa, ice tea is great! We love ice tea!"

Finally Lainie cried, "*Sweetheart, they were joking. They want the tea!*" and Pep came back and sat down.

Lainie passed a plate of her homemade pecan

cookies, defrosted for our visit, and Nora and Tibby ate steadily while answering questions about school. Nora said that Tibby sang in the chorus, and Tibby suddenly turned a delightful true pink.

"Singing is such a marvelous, challenging discipline," Lainie said.

"I can't sing," Nora said to Pep, but he didn't hear her.

"It's my secret desire," Lainie said. "If I could've done anything, I secretly would've become an opera singer."

Nora said, "Dad says that you should've been a senator, if—if I'm not sure what."

"It has always fascinated me. *Thrilling* voices. To be able to musically project such a range of emotion—the whole bit!" Lainie threw open her arms, to encompass opera's breadth, and I took her picture.

"That was a great shot," I said to Pep, who coughed. "How's our favorite grandson?" he said to Nora.

Nora looked addled. She held up the last cookie and gave Tibby an intimate, searching look, and Tibby shook her head. Biting, Nora said, "Oh, just wonderful. Just my favoritely wonderful brother."

While I worked my way through the first roll of film, Nora asked Lainie about her jewelry-making, and Lainie walked around dipping her head for us to finger her earrings—large, fragile silver feathers.

When Nora asked if it were possible to use the pool at night, Tibby looked extremely alert and Pep and Lainie said in unison, *absolutely not*, night swimming was absolutely never even considered. In their seven years here, nobody within earshot had considered night swimming.

More questions, and they eloquently described the heat, unremittingly like an oven, the winds blowing dust and paper and lawn furniture past the window, all this unforgiving weather preventing Pep from tending his plants and Lainie from visiting sights of interest. I felt very cheerful—it was so boring to listen, but at the same time so familial and safe.

"However, Mother's a go-getter," Pep said. Lainie had recently phoned some high official of their municipality and, persuasively chatting, had managed to end up with the city sending a bus to take her and fifty of her acquaintances on a tour of nearby Palm Beach.

"Grandma, that's amazing." I snapped the last shot: Nora—young, beautiful, admiring, stunned.

Lainie frowned. "Many people our age are not in a position to be constantly driving cars all over the landscape," she said. "Why shouldn't people tour the area comfortably!"

But how did she accomplish it, Nora and I effusively demanded.

Pep said, "Mother loves to take on the establishment!"

Pleasantly, Tibby and Nora turned their shiny heads his way.

She had just dialed, she said, and reached a Mr. Spanier and told him that Palm Beach was a historic place; many people had no trouble driving in, but for others it was a burden, and why couldn't he make available some alternative?

"She's on a first-name basis," Pep said. "She calls

up: 'Hello, Dick? This is Lainie Green.' *'Lainie, how are you?'* " Pep looked animated, gazing at his wife with consuming pride.

"That's not the point," Lainie said. She started to say what was the point.

"It was all completely on the up and up! And she got a big new bus, all new upholstery, *excellent* air-conditioning! A young fellow to give the tour. It's unbelievable to me, what Mother does when she puts her mind to it!"

Lainie stopped trying to speak and stood up with the pitcher and frowned at Pep.

"Watch out when Mother takes on the powers that be!" he said gaily.

The ice cubes clacked as she violently poured a wave of tea into Pep's glass. She said, "Sweetie, I don't know why you keep *saying* that."

Nora and Tibby did turn out to be sleeping in the closet—arms touching, on foam slabs in a tiny storage room near the front door. I was sleeping in the living room.

I wanted to take the kids to something like Sea World, but Nora said *Please*, they had already *seen it* on TV, a porpoise getting his teeth brushed, was it a crime to get a little rest and a little tan? So a routine developed: Nora and Tibby would wake early and whisper in the closet, then sneak past me. The shower would run a long time. They'd sneak into the kitchen and eat Danish pastries and drink many mugs of coffee. They'd put on bikinis and sunglasses. They'd stand in the hall oiling their bodies, and the living room would fill with the smell of coconut. They'd tiptoe to the front door with their radios and towels; they'd release the chain, reach for the doorknob. And Pep would come out of the bedroom and try to go with them.

The first morning he said, "I'm showing you the ropes."

Nora whispered, "What do we need to know?"

"I'll familiarize you."

"Grandpa, it's not necessary," she whispered.

I opened my eyes. Nora had got the front door open and sharp light was pouring in. I could see Tibby already out on the step, wearing a bikini of glittery green stuff, in which she looked like a big preoccupied mermaid. Lainie came rushing down the hall, tying her bathrobe, also whispering at Pep. I said, "It's okay. I'm awake," and they all looked at me.

"Sorry, Mom. We tried to be quiet."

"Good morning, dear," Lainie said to me. To Pep she said, "Let the girls go."

Pep looked confused.

Nora came back in. She took his hand. She looked at him as if he were a puppy trying to scale a high step. She said, "Okay, Grandpa, you come this time and show me and Tib how everything works."

The second morning when he tried it again, Nora again gazed into his face. We were as before: Tibby outside, Lainie in the hall, me in bed on the couch. Nora said warmly: *"Grandpa. It's okay."*

She yanked the cord and the blinds flapped open. She said, "Grandpa. See that swimming pool?"

We all looked. No people were out. The wind was

up again, and the surface of the aquamarine water was ruffled. Triangular flags were strung up nearby, flipping in the breeze. Nora said, "Today we can walk over by ourselves."

She lifted the cat off a chair and, holding him curled in sleeping position, set him on the carpet. She said, "Grandpa, you can stay here in the cool. I'll bring this chair over and you can sit and watch us the whole time through the window." She started dragging the chair through the shag.

I said, "Tomorrow I take you to Sea World."

"*Fine*," she said grimly.

We woke to thick rain—blackish sky, sheets of water blowing past the window. "We're burnt anyway," Nora said, and she and Tibby switched the lamps on and prepared to spend the morning eating doughnuts and reading magazines. I started to take their picture, and Nora held *Life* in front of her face. From behind it, she said, "Could we please stop the camera? It's starting to get horrible."

I went into the kitchen and asked Lainie if there were at least some movies. Through the pass-through window, Nora heard me. She came over to the window, and we heard a little voice say: "Don't bother. We're fine."

I said desperately, "You're *not fine* sitting in a house eating sugar and looking at pictures of models and rock stars! I want you to be able to *do* something!"

"Believe me, Mom," she said, "Tib and me have seen more movies in our life than you."

"Well, you can see a couple more," I muttered.

Through the little window she whispered, *"Mommy. Please stop it."*

After lunch, Pep announced that now he'd give the girls a Cook's tour of the mall.

They stared at each other. Tibby said, "Sure."

They let Lainie dress them in her two raincoats, Nora in a trench coat and Tibby in a yellow plastic slicker which couldn't be buttoned. Tibby looked at her own forearms protruding from the sleeves. She pressed her arm and watched the skin turn white and the florid pink rebound. "God, I'm purple," she said. Lainie tied them into transparent rain bonnets, and Pep suited up and brought his big sedan around.

Half an hour later there was a pounding on the door and I opened it and it was Nora, streaming water. Behind her were Tibby, water blowing around, and Pep's car pulling away like a slow boat toward the garage.

They rushed in, soaking the rug, and repaired to the closet. Pep arrived, looking downcast, and went to the bedroom for his almanac; but then he didn't come out. Nora emerged and called me into the bathroom.

As I stepped in, she reached behind me and swatted the door shut. We were in a wonderful little Florida environment—tiny soaps formed like periwinkles and venus clams, satin seahorses floating on the hand towels, wallpaper depicting bamboo stalks enmeshed and rising to some exotic sky. She eased the toilet seat shut and sat on it. She said, "Mom, we have to do something."

"Was there a problem on the ride?"

"Everything is the same. *Grandma* isn't bad at all, but *Grandpa!* I always used to get along with him, but now—"

Had they gone to the mall?

"We went," she said. "But Grandpa wouldn't let us do anything!"

"You couldn't go into the stores?"

It turned out Pep had driven to the entrance of the biggest department store and said he'd wait there at the curb. Nora had asked if he wouldn't park and join them and he'd said no, he'd wait. Even Tibby had tried to persuade him, but he'd said no, he'd be waiting.

"So *of course* we couldn't look around! I mean, how can we walk around the mall if we know Grandpa is out there *sitting in the goddamn car with the motor running!*"

I laughed.

Nora glared at me. She looked very young, with her wet hair combed back and her face shiny. Her face got even brighter—she was about to cry, but instead she laughed. She said, "Mom, I love Grandpa. He's a wonderful person. But you've *got* to get the damn guy off our back!"

During supper William and Zack called, and Nora went in on the bedroom phone and talked to Zack. She cried, "Zachary, you would *not* believe it!" and "No you would *not!*" and "Ha! Ha!" and rolled on the bed and shrieked.

William and I were the last pair to talk. He said, "We hear you guys are experiencing dramatic weather."

"In more ways than one."

"Oh, is that right? We got some vibes. What's the situation?"

"How shall I say," I said.

"Should I intuit? I assume this kid Tibby is creating some kind of problem?"

"Not at all, but somebody else is."

"Really?"

"Absolutely. It's very unusual."

"Pep?"

"Yes. And I mean day and night."

"Is it extreme?"

"*Quite*," I said.

"Extensive grousing?" he guessed.

"No."

"Provoking 'Mother' by exaggerated pep-talking and ear-splitting compliments?"

"A little of that. But no, that's not really it."

"Let's see—overprotectiveness? Getting on Lainie's ass?"

"Not Lainie's," I said.

"Not yours," he said.

"No."

"So, Nora's," he said.

"Right."

"And Lainie and this kid Tibby are also fully aware of this?"

"You could say that."

"And so I take it some kind of possibly subterranean struggle has ensued, some feelings have been hurt, things have become contorted and strained, every player is involved, and there is no resolution in sight," he said.

I said, "You got it."

But by the time Lainie and I were scraping the dishes, the rain had stopped, a rosy sky was blooming, Pep had invited the girls to walk with him on the wet sidewalks of the apartment complex, and the three had gaily set out.

Lainie said that Tibby was certainly a long drink of water, but her heart didn't seem to be in it. After a while she said fervently, "I don't know what gets into Dad! He is so worried about those girls. Since I had that stomach thing, he has become overprotective! He overdoes it! Frankly, it's getting on my nerves."

The three blasted into the house and walked past us and out to the atrium, and soon we began to hear Pep loudly describing some great moments in Florida history. By 8000 B.C., according to his almanac, the first human inhabitants had migrated to the peninsula. By A.D. 1500, aboriginal Indian tribes were joined by Cubans and Mexicans. European seamen began to explore the coastal waters. Later, Sir Francis Drake razed St. Augustine. Then Pensacola was founded by a Spaniard; in 1719, it was captured by the French, recaptured by the Spanish, recaptured by the French. Tibby and Nora, on the edge of their seats, agreed that in high school, should high school ever come, they would *take Spanish, not French*. By 1795: Spanish-American border disputes. 1803: Louisiana Purchase. U.S. claims West Florida. "Good-bye, Spain! Hello, America!" Nora cried. 1821: U.S. acquires Florida! "DadadaDAAA!" Nora sang, and pounded her cushion. 1836: Florida's first railroad! Nora: "Da-dup duh-DAAA!" Tibby started acting as the chorus, stamping and singing, "Dump dump dump dump. Dump dump dump dump." Her voice was strong—silky and resonant. By the time the state had finished with its yellow fever epidemic and was furnishing salt, beef, and bacon to the Confederate Army, Tibby and Nora were on their feet and marching on the terra-cotta tiles. Lainie and I rushed in to see them: invisible muskets at the ready, singing and saluting, on they marched, circling Pep's chair as he happily cried out the facts of the whole long complicated history of the great fuchsia-and-turquoise Kahlua-drinking state of Florida.

The next day, it was cool enough to breathe. Nora and I had a barely audible fight. In the bathroom, I fiercely whispered (sounding like Willie), "And I resent your sniping at me because I have the effrontery to suggest we go out of this apartment for ten minutes and *do something!*"

"Mommy, you are kinda pestering us," she whispered.

I whispered, "Well, what are we *doing* here then?"

She whispered, "You brought us here, Mommy."

I whispered, "Well, *what the hell are we supposed to be doing if you girls won't even go out?*"

Nora looked into my eyes. Sweetly, she patted my face. She whispered: "We're supposed to be visiting our relatives."

Lainie and I decided to take everything out of her kitchen cabinets and put down sticky shelf paper. We were galvanized. The job was enormous, meaningless; it made sense to us. We drove to the hardware store and rejected shelf paper featuring hibiscus and semaphore flags and agreed at length, like child-brides making a crucial selection for our long fruitful upcoming life, on blue and white stripes. Back at the apartment, I went straight into the kitchen and got on a stepladder and started handing stuff down—Neapolitan platters, Mexican cruets, wide champagne glasses, bone-china egg cups, menorahs, chafing dishes, fondue forks.

Nora and Tibby left for the pool and were immediately seen through the window to be getting introduced by a miniature white-haired woman to two visiting high school boys. Pep called to us, "Marion Whachacall's out, per usual, and she's got a coupla gay blades."

"Good," Lainie said from the kitchen.

He called, "You could also be in the market for a young *chassen*. You in the market for a new young boyfriend?" He sounded almost relaxed, for the first time since we'd arrived.

"Don't you be flip with me," Lainie said happily.

In the afternoon, after some concentrated hours of intense and perfectionist shelf-papering, I walked to the pool myself. I lay under my hat, listening to faraway traffic and to a radio turned way down, playing salsa from Miami. I made some lists of things to order for school: visual discrimination flip books, figure-ground activity cards, Scrabble for juniors. I started rereading *Lolita* and turned happy and serene. Until the book's last page, I could see, lost self-contained Lo and godless despairing Humbert would protect me from ups and downs. Occasionally the two boys swam alone in the pool, the decorous atmosphere preventing them from splashing. They threw no Frisbees, chugged no brews—just climbed out and dropped onto their lounge chairs. The sun got low. At the far end of the concrete, Nora and Tibby, completely oiled, lay as if dead.

Our last evening. The girls wanted to eat early, so we were setting out in daylight.

I came out last, when the others were dressed and standing around the car. Nora and Tibby wore sandals and flowered dresses. All the car doors were open, and people seemed to be just on the point of getting in, arrested by sudden conversation. Walking toward them, I felt pleased with our group and purely happy to be a member of it.

Everybody looked fed up. Across the roof of the car, Lainie was glaring at Pep. She was saying, "Sweetheart, nobody is *ganging up* on you! For God's sake."

"Get in the car," Pep said, and got in himself.

Nora leaned into the car and said, "Look, Grandpa, you decide on the restaurant and the way to get there. Tibby is not involved and I am not involved."

"That's absolutely ridiculous," Lainie said. "What that signifies is, if somebody has a tantrum, then somebody gets kowtowed to." Even frowning and tossing her head, Lainie looked as beautiful as usual. She was wearing a red silk suit, red sandals, a necklace shaped like a flat collar of silver. Pep was wearing his usual food hues—butter-colored trousers and a peach-colored jacket. He tapped his two-toned shoe and smacked at the seat. "Get in the car!" he said.

Lainie lifted her skirt and, with glacial composure, settled herself on the seat. She turned to Pep and said, "I don't know what's gotten into you, sweetie, but I have *just about had it*. There is *no reason in the world* why you can't *be pleasant* to people who are trying to *be sociable and get along.* You have had *such a bee in your bonnet* all week and I *do not see why.*"

Practically grinding his teeth, Pep stared straight out over the wheel.

While Lainie was finishing her remarks, Nora and Tibby and I pretended not to hear; we busied ourselves squeezing into the back. They smelled like shampoos, oils, grasses and flowers. They had white ovals around their eyes, left by their sunglasses; otherwise, their skin was livid, giving off heat—Nora's arm against mine felt as if she were running a fever. Pep jammed the car into drive and, in a heavy silence, we jolted off.

At the restaurant, Nora waited to sit down until Pep was surrounded and already crooking his finger at the waiter. Lainie became enthusiastic about ordering soft-shell crabs and then grew demoralized because nobody cared. I tried to engage Pep in conversation, but he continued leaning into his menu as if studying Tal-mud. Quietly, next to my ear, Tibby said, "Um, do you think clams casino would be good to order?" She had never worked out how to address me. Lainie said, "They are excellent!" Tibby said to me, "Um, do you think the shrimp scampi?" Tibby got a drop of salad dressing on her dress and she and Nora went away for a long time. Pep sent back his scrod for being dry and we had to wait another half hour. The waiter brought Pep a complimentary glass of anisette, which Lainie reached for and drank at once. And we concluded with two rounds of cappuccinos and decaf cappuccinos— enough liquid to float a boat.

On the ride back, Nora and Tibby immediately started stripping off their necklaces and bracelets. The sky was glowing and navy blue. The heat wave had ended.

The whole kitchen was covered with all the stuff that should've been in the cabinets. All we could think to do was grumpily drink glasses of club soda, then get ready for bed. My bed was too narrow and the sheet was too short. I thought: I have to change my life.

The next morning, before I woke, I noticed I was on my back and it felt delicious to be still asleep. I was embracing myself: my legs were crossed, my arms pressed close, one hand holding the fingers of the other. They whispered and left, the door clicked shut, Pep stayed in his room. Great decision, Pep. Good for you. I held my own hand and sank back down.

Some time much later, I began slowly to collect the information that it was dark outside but light was blazing in the room, and finally I opened my eyes to see that some lamps were on. Lainie and Pep, in their bathrobes, were standing near the closet looking alarmed. I tried to explain this to myself: we were crossing the Atlantic, it was night on the ship because of the time zones, and Nora and Zachary were gone—they swam away.

"What time is it?"

"Oh, good, dear, you're up," Lainie said. "The girls seem to've *gone out*."

"So they're not back yet," I said.

"What do you mean! They're supposed to be sleeping!"

"It's three o'clock in the morning, darling," said Pep.

I was confused. "Oh, I don't know," I said. "I'm asleep."

"Well, *wake up*," Lainie said, quite irritated. "The girls are missing!"

I staggered into the bathroom and stood there a while. When I came out, even more lamps were on—the house was full of light—and Pep had gone out.

I stepped outside. It was pleasant—still and cool. I couldn't see Pep's flashlight, but after a few minutes he came around the pool house and walked back toward me. When he got near, he said, "Not swimming." He spoke in a low, conversational tone, and his voice carried easily. Then he walked up the walk and I saw how worried he was.

I said, "Pep, they snuck out for a small adventure—I'm sure they're right around here somewhere. Those boys are okay, aren't they?"

"I covered the whole complex, darling."

I said I thought they'd come back soon.

"Darling, this is very concerning."

"Peppy, the worst that happens is they're riding in a car. That's the *worst*." I'd been working on this stance a couple of years: a refusal to get agitated too early about ordinary things done by adolescent children. I was getting good at it, and hard to budge. I said, "In fact, now I remember Nora said those boys had 'four-wheel personalities.'"

Pep stared at me. At last he said, "Darling, what the hell're you talking about!"

I tried to put my arm around him and he shrugged me away. He switched on his light and aimed the beam off through the darkness.

Back inside, I started cutting paper for the cup and saucer cabinet. Lainie was making coffee. "I am *so annoyed with those girls*," she said. "I am fit to be tied!"

I said I was sorry—they didn't always show wonderful judgment. The paper wrapped itself around my arm and clung to me.

"I am shocked that *Nora* would be so inconsiderate!"

"They'll be back," I said, sort of clawing at the paper. "This kind of thing happens once in a while."

She said, "And I fail to understand how you can be so cavalier!"

Ferociously, I tore the paper off. I said stubbornly, "Hey look, Lainie. They'll be back."

Out the window I could see Pep on the catwalk, his light panning through black air. He aimed at the pool and caught the steam transpiring from the surface of the water. For a few moments he aimed overhead, and the light swung like a beam from a searchlight, out in old-time Hollywood.

We waited for an hour. Lainie took Pep a mug of decaf, and he got mad because it wasn't full enough. He refused to come in. After another half hour, Lainie was ready to call the police. I set all the mugs on the new paper, lining them up perfectly, as if permanently; I tried to get her to admire them. We opened our books; Humbert and Lo were zigzagging across America in the car—too nerve-racking. I was worried. I didn't want to say so. We decided to give them forty-five minutes; by then it would be starting to grow light.

Half an hour passed and Lainie said she was not waiting, she was dialing. I told her to wait, and an argument ensued—an oddly mild one, whose function was mainly to kill time. Then we sat, in the brilliant room, and, almost in passing, Lainie said, "Do you ever think you and William might get back together?"

"Not really."

"Dad and I have never understood why you two couldn't patch up your differences."

"But it's over now," I said. "We're divorced. It really seems better this way."

We were both fidgeting, glancing out the window, worrying and at the same time very annoyed. She looked at me. I said, "We really like it better this way, Lainie."

She smacked the couch cushion. She said: *"Well, you're both spoiled brats!"*

Outside, Pep suddenly cried, "Here come the girls!" Lainie leaped up and rushed out, leaving the door standing open. Pep turned back toward her, and for that moment I could see the look on his face: pure joy. Then, at top speed, he started moving forward down the walk. Nora and Tibby were coming along beside the pool, and they could hear Pep calling and see him waving his light and grinning at them as if he were the main organizer of their ticker-tape parade. Their faces looked very white, almost gleaming. They started to run toward Pep, and their hair flew behind them, and I went out and snapped their picture as they ran through the dark.

11. Poltergeists

T hree years later, I was still living "alone"—actually with two adolescent children, which is more like living simultaneously at both ends of the isolation-connectedness continuum. You can never predict that you will be unaccompanied. On the other hand, because you have virtually nothing in common with your companions, you're about as solitary as people get.

On the face of it, the kids had only grown, into tall, slender, competent people. But they were mysterious. In the mornings, things seemed normal, though with an indefinable heightened quality: supranormal, metanormal. Zack and Nora were glossily beautiful, standing in the kitchen eating breakfast in silence, conserving their deep reserves of energy, saving themselves for later. Zack's breakfast was four pieces of toast and a quart of milk; Nora's was a Diet Coke. Sometimes I squeezed oranges and carried the glasses of juice to their bedrooms where they were blow-drying their marvelous hair. *Oh thanks!* they'd call patiently, through the dryer's roar. While I watched, they'd take a sip. On my way to the training school I'd drop them off and I'd watch as they crossed the school lawn—they looked dynamic but pacific, arrayed in calculated shabby black; they looked calm. I had a persistent, strange feeling: I couldn't prove that those were not my children. The crossing guard looked like the same guy he'd always been; but the kids had been replaced by Martians, leading a Martian life.

Daytime was the Martian time. Graciously, they did many things: Nora did gymnastics and Zack played his guitar; they were both lacrosse players, student council representatives, actors, and members of the Black Literature Club. After school, at the health food cafe, Zack made sandwiches invented during the sixties; Nora helped run a theater program for tiny children, walking the kids to the bathroom, tying their masks onto their little faces, restraining the biter. If I got home late from work, the house would already be thumping, a giant heartbeat in the walls—Nora's Jane Fonda video. This was still daytime, and Nora and Zack were doing the well-known, complex adolescent impersonation of people fully engaged with the daytime things. But what was becoming clear was: Everything happened at night.

The kids were going to concerts. Every Saturday they set out in the morning and rode long distances to foreign venues. In the parking lot for hours before the show there'd be a city of cars, and packs of young people in late sun and then gathering darkness, staggering around playing music and handling each other and buying and selling and consuming loose joints, pills, the usual seductive killer drugs, and a fluid called Liquid Lady. Nora and Zack told me about these events. Did their friends drink and take drugs? I asked. Zack said amiably, "The bottles to be wary of are the ones that look like cologne."

Other Saturdays, they stayed in town. They walked

around their rooms for three hours after dinner, dressing and phoning. At ten, washed as if for surgery and artfully got up, they rushed out. At two, hoarse and depleted, they staggered home.

At parties, muscular stoic boys would kneel and take the end of a piece of tubing deeply into their mouths and tip their heads back like sword swallowers, and their friends would pour whole beers through a motor-oil funnel, straight down their throats. Girls did it too— Nora reported that when this happened she sometimes left the room. This was terribly dangerous, I said, drinking like that, those boys could get very sick. " 'Get sick'?" Zack said. "Actually, Mom, that's pretty euphemistic. They could die." I planned to call the parents of the whole-beer swallowers, to inform them. Which parents would you single out? the kids said. It happens constantly. Please, Mom. It's the least of it.

"Mom," Zack said. "Here's a funny incident, but you can't do any phoning."

"What is it?" I said.

"We can't tell you these things if you start talking about calling people."

"What is it?"

"Is it about Benjy?" Nora said to him, starting to laugh. "Oh, it's ridiculous! It's nothing, Mom."

"*What?*"

They were laughing so happily, so healthily. They pounded each other, stamped their feet, wiped their eyes. They both cried: *"Benjy drank a beer through his nose!"*

Zack's girlfriend, Bibi, looked as much like Nora as somebody else could—a sexier, ruder Nora, in muddy cowboy boots. In daytime Bibi smelled like a puppy— she was working after school for a veterinarian, planning to become one. She liked to tell long, bloody, oddly arousing stories about veterinarian life. Bibi was very beautiful and sloppy. I was jealous of her. The first time she came to our house, she immediately picked up our cat Bonky Boy, pressed him to her, and licked his fur; Zack sat down suddenly, as if to avoid swooning. Now whenever she had a chance, Bibi would come over and stay for many hours with her jeans straining to cover her strong, elegant legs. She would slip off the boots and lie down with her feet in Zack's active lap. Then she'd nuzzle and fondle the cat in truly inventive ways, and Zack would watch her.

Nora suddenly got a boyfriend too, a deep-voiced guy named Mark. He was less annoying than Bibi— not as clever, and not around much. A sophomore, he was already planning to be a surgeon. On our first meeting, I asked how he knew that for sure, and he said sonorously, "I have a special aptitude," and wiggled his fingers. He grinned. Nora blushed horribly. We all stared at Mark's jiggling, dexterous hands.

On a back road at the end of Halloween night, driving home from a party, at about ninety miles an hour, two kids rolled a car. They climbed out, stood up, vomited on their ghost costumes, and walked away in the moonlight. After that, some parents of party-givers started making all the guests sleep at their houses so they wouldn't drive home drunk—when you arrived at the party you had to surrender your car keys before you could repair to the keg or upend the bottle on your nose. Zack didn't have his driver's license yet; Bibi did. Zack and Bibi and Nora got in the habit of pretending to their hosts that they'd been driven by someone else, and in the middle of the night, after everybody had fallen down on the mattresses, they'd slip out and meet on the lawn and run for Bibi's car and make their getaway. These stories sounded like contorted fairy tales— the ghost-boys walking down the deserted road in the bright night, the tall boy and the twinlike girls escaping from the big dark crowded expensive houses. I said, "like modern-day Hansels and Gretels, leaving their trail of crumbs," and the kids looked at me sympathetically, impressed by the irrelevance of my ideas.

After they fled the party houses, the three would drive out to the diner, wash their faces and comb their smoky hair, eat platters of scrambled eggs, and, when they felt organized enough, drive on home. "Don't any of these parents happen to refuse to serve alcohol?" I asked, kind of wearily.

Zack said that the parents didn't serve marijuana and cocaine, and that that inhospitality had virtually no impact on events.

"Cocaine? Is that a *common* thing?"

He looked at me absently. He said it was a pain, because cocaine traditionally happened in the bathroom, so any time you wanted to go to the bathroom, you had to go out in the yard.

Nora laughed. "It's really true!" she said. "Julie comes with me to be lookout."

But what would happen if no alcohol were served? Would anybody go to the party?

Sure, they said. It happens. Everybody goes.

And then nobody drinks?

Zack said, "People bring vodka and drink it in cups of tea."

"I don't want you to drink and drive!"

We never do, they said. Are you crazy?

"Do you smoke joints?"

Mom, they said, kindly, holding my gaze.

"I don't want you to drink or smoke at all."

We know that, Mom. We know you don't.

Annie came over to have tea and talk about the kids. Annie's daughter was a gymnast like Nora, and her son had played Dungeons and Dragons with Zack, and worked these days alongside Zack at Tempting Treats, squeezing the carrots, massing the sprouts in the pitas, melting the Monterey Jack, killing a little of their enormous surplus of time—Annie and I had been banking on these pursuits to keep the kids safe. Now we sat in the dining room with our teapot in its ineffectual outmoded little cozy, giving each other intense looks. Zack was in his room. His door was closed, and through the closed door, instead of sound, the usual waves of sexual energy were pouring into the rest of the house, agitating the air. He was in there presumably finishing his essays for college, desperately pulling on his hair. "Probably not his hair," Annie said glumly. She said she'd used to worry that when they reached high school they'd start having lots of sex, dangerous 1950s sex, and it'd be traumatic, and now there was AIDS which was unimaginably worse; still, if they wore their condoms and chose their partners, she'd decided that on balance the safest illicit activity currently available to the kids was making love. "At least while they're having sex they can't be driving the car a hundred miles an hour," she said. Passing the dining room, Nora called pleasantly, "Why can't they?"

After an eventful New Year's Eve, when he got his butt squeezed by a beautiful girl he'd never met before, and also underwent a conversion and rededication to academic excellence, Zack devoted eighteen nights to studying for his third round of SATs, long into the night like somebody possessed. Then he and Nora stayed over with friends and came home on Saturday morning gray and staring.

Here's what they said:

We watched "The Love Connection." Then "The People's Court": a case about a beagle and some rat poison. Then the five o'clock news: Lou Gossett was on. Then "World News Tonight": We love it. Reagan was real happy down in Mexico shaking hands with the Mexican president. Then we got souvlaki and took it to the party. We left early and went back to Holly's mom's and watched almost all of *The Shining*. Then *Repo Man*. Then Robbie said, "I'm Robertson Parson Shattuck III" about forty times and then tiptoed out and tried to walk on the edge of the upper terrace with his eyes closed, and fell onto the bluestone lower terrace and broke his arm. Then we took him to the emergency room and waited for his dad, and his dad rode over in his Jaguar with his Haitian driver. Then two guys from the high school came in; they had been beaten up and their faces were meat.

Then "Tom and Jerry."

Then morning came.

Then what happened? I asked.

Nora: "The sun came up."

As the year progressed, the parties seemed to grow more intense. Shooting the Boot was introduced: each guest drank a sneakerful, out of the host's high-top sneaker. Vomiting, of course, was perennially big: the technicolor yawn; riding the porcelain bus; talking to Ralph on the big white phone. Urination was big; there was a kid named Soup who liked to go into the bathroom immediately and piss into the shampoo. One couple or another always had to have a fight and one or both of the lovers had to run out of the house, and maybe the girl would key-scratch the guy's car. There was always the abused guy. There was always the depressed girl who pulled guys seriatim into a bedroom or closet. Something valuable always had to get broken.

If, as could happen, the parents were fools enough to leave town, everybody showed up, and then there'd be the trashed house, and weird things going around in the dryer, and maybe the whole population of the high school outside on the deck, some of them mid-urination when the deck falls down.

Nora didn't drink. She reported that a boy had asked, When did you stop? I never drank, she said. Never? Unsteadily, he held out his big strong feverish hand for a crunching handshake. He nodded sagely. He said, *I'm very impressed.*

Some narcs came to school. Nora loved this. She said the narcs, a man and a woman, were wearing amazing disguises: bell-bottoms, fringed vests, *hair*. They looked about thirty-five. Nora claimed the narcs had sidled up in the hall and asked where to buy "stuff," and she'd said, "Officers, I actually have no idea."

In fact you could buy your drugs in the auditorium, in the wings. Or outside the gym, against the wall, where the regular daytime dope-smokers stood dreaming. Every Friday, a blue van pulled up behind the gym, and the dealers, three seniors—Jason, George, and Robbie—ran out, got in, and in two turns around the block bought the school's weekly supply. From Nora, their pal, I got a clear impression of the dealers: Robbie was a neglected handsome depressed rich boy, George was a deeply gentle skinny cocaine-dependent poor boy, and Jason was a hardened criminal.

I made an appointment with the principal. He was a tall fellow, as precisely decked out as one of his students, as clean-shaven as a person can be. The skin of his cheeks shone like a baby's and he had a baby's clear guiltless eyes. When I arrived, he turned this face toward me and looked pleasant. "What are you doing about the drug problem?" I said, and he held the expression. As far as the narcotics, he said—"Please sit down," he said. As far as the narcotics, the administration was aware, they were paying steadily close attention, there'd been marked improvement, hopes were high.

"A van comes every week to sell dope," I said. He said he wasn't at liberty to say publicly what was being done about that possibility. "Have you considered stopping it?" I said. "That seems pretty straightforward."

It wasn't that simple, he said amicably.

"It is that simple. You pick up the phone, you dial, you tell the cops. They drive out and they arrest the dealers."

This was a community of very concerned parents, he said. It was a community full of resources.

"I don't get it."

We gazed at each other with hatred.

He said that no parent in this community—perhaps, and he certainly thought so, myself included—would want to see the future of any local student jeopardized by what many might argue could be a very unnecessary police presence.

I said, "You mean Robbie Shattuck is too rich to bust."

He told me that the concern of parents like myself was a source of support and nourishment to the high school administration and he could only impress upon me that they were continuously at work on addressing the pressing problems facing us, not just narcotics-related, not just alcohol-related, not just violence-related, not just prejudice-related, but across the board. While saying this, he stood, and all the wrinkles fell out of his suit. He said some more. Meanwhile I imagined him studious in cruel bathroom light, scraping the razor time and again over his cowardly face. I lunged across the desk and we shook hands—our hands were wet. He promised to keep me and people like me apprised. At last we gave up and said a brief, loud, disgusted good-bye, like lovers who were sickened to recall they had ever shared a moment.

Nora wanted to go to Florida with her boyfriend. "You've got to be kidding," I said. She said, "That is *not* a nice tone." I was drawing up some flashcards for school, using basketball terms and the names of beloved players. I printed: HOOK SHOT.

Her boyfriend had two plane tickets to Fort Myers and an uncle's empty condo on Captiva Island. I said that was nice and economical but cut no ice with me.

Behind me she said, "Well, I want to go."

"Ask your father," I said. She snorted—she and Willie were mad at each other. She was secretly not talking to him; that is, technically she spoke with him, but meanwhile she knew she was only pretending to speak.

JUMP SHOT. Who else was going?

Nobody.

"Honey, please," I said. "This is silly."

"*To me* it's silly to say ask Dad all of a sudden. If I'm *with* Dad, I *ask* Dad. But actually, I'm not actually asking." While I printed FOUL LINE, FAST BREAK, TOUCH PASS, and MICHAEL RAY RICHARDSON, Nora explained my philosophy to me: that I took the position that they had to make their own decisions, always balancing their decisions against my concerns and feelings, that that's how we'd arrived at their curfews, that's how we'd arranged things for years, I trusted them, this was no different. I printed: ZONE

DEFENSE. I said, "Well, my feelings are very strong. I don't want you to go."

"Excuse me, Mom, but I think that's kind of hypocritical."

"And why is that?"

"Because Mark is already my boyfriend, and we're not going to do"—ominously—"*anything in Florida that we can't do right here.*"

That didn't matter, I said, even if true, which I doubted: what mattered was the intensity of the honeymoon-like situation, the five days alone, my feeling that although I didn't need to intervene in their inevitable sexual life, I did need to make my own statement about precisely what my hopes and, yes, I said bravely, *my expectations* were for her, and what my own values continued to be, and so on—I warmed to my topic, and, somewhat befuddled, hoping to gain the advantage, lavishly gesturing with my magic marker, jawed on.

"I'm sorry, Mommy!" she said finally, and she began to cry.

"Why are you crying?"

"You're a wonderful mother," Nora squeaked. "And I really feel bad about this!"

"There's no harm done," I said.

"I can see that you and me are going to have to have different views!"

"We certainly do."

"I feel so bad. I hate to not do what you want!"

"I'm sure you'll do the right thing," I said.

"That's why I'm upset!"

"Why?"

She said miserably, "Because I'm going!"

I took my time. I wrote DOUBLE DRIBBLE. Then OFFENSIVE REBOUND. Then I fixed her in a menacing gaze. I said: "*I hope you'll make a different decision.*"

"But that's just it!" she cried. "I feel so bad about it! Because I *won't.*" And she dried her face and went to phone her friends to borrow their many infinitesimal, iridescent G-string-based bathing costumes. I screamed after her, into the next room, "Don't you kids ever have any *real* problems?"

Nora, a week later, at dinner, apropos of nothing: "Mom, I hate to say it. But I don't know what's wrong with you. It's like you're turning into a different person."

Zack, to Nora, when he thought I was out: "It's stifling! It's so *stifling* living in this house! There's not enough air in this house to support life!"

I now had, of course, a psychiatrist. My psychiatrist was cautious, stubborn, wily, deft, like somebody whose survival in a hostile world depended on extreme cunning and vigilance. It made sense: he was a Freudian—his type was supposed to've already vanished, like the theater and Yiddish. His office contained a prominent couch which I wouldn't consider lying on should it come to that, a couple of kilims like Freud's, a card thanking the patients for not smoking, a tissue box decorated with kitty-kats entangled in their yarn balls. Early on, he had accidentally revealed that he loved Cheech and Chong, and then nothing for months. I had been talking to him all year; he appeared sometimes drowsy or faintly addled, sometimes alert; behind him the light falling through the window brightened, dimmed, brightened; the newest rug slightly faded; a humidifier joined us and the air grew moist. The most comforting thing my psychiatrist ever said to me, and it was extremely comforting, wasn't even a full sentence. He murmured: ". . . the inevitable disquietude of spirit in a house where adolescents live."

Zack was in *The Three Sisters*, a shortened version, cut by the drama teacher—three acts, fewer military men, and not so many pronouncements about life. The kids called it *2½ Sisters*. After the play's run the entire cast came for dinner, and sat at our round dining table wearing idiosyncratic and sexy clothes, flushed and attentive like a ring of children at a birthday party, and I served them a turkey, although it was February, and one bottle of California champagne for all of them, for a toast to Chekhov and themselves. When I brought in the platter, their dilated pupils shone and they all cried, "Turkey! My favorite food!" They pantomimed abject disbelief—all their lives, they'd only had turkey once a year. Vivaciously, they toasted the turkey, as if he were a pal. They all had to go to the bathroom constantly; each time, whoever left said good-bye to the turkey carcass. After dinner they all drank many cups of tea. Then they all walked to the front door and stood there and looked at Zack while he said to me, "Oh, where is it, where has it all gone, my past, when I was young, gay, clever, when I dreamed and thought with grace, when my present and my future were lighted up with hope?" Then the others took turns thanking me with lines from *2½ Sisters*, tossed their complicated hairdos, and rushed into the night. Zack went with them. I stood on the step a long time, staring out into total darkness.

At midnight, after a video outing, Nora got home, looking sensible. Nora's planned mock-honeymoon was still three weeks away; we weren't talking about it; but she had been laying low, leading a remarkably staid life. She seemed to be playing a character in an imaginary young person's novel: *Nora Green, Good High School Girl*. Now she put on her boxers, yanked back her hair, washed her face for half an hour, and went to bed.

At two, Zack's expected arrival time, he wasn't home. I decided to read.

At 2:30, he wasn't home.

At 3:00, he wasn't home.

At 3:15, the phone rang once, then stopped.

At 3:30, I heard Bibi's car approaching very slowly, coasting in—she was driving admirably carefully, and they were almost home.

But they weren't. The car paused, then moved on. When I went to look out, it was gone. Empty street, in quiet darkness.

I thought I could call Willie and wake him, to say— what now?

I could call the parents of Zack's fellow actors. Half an hour more and I'd be willing to go that far.

I waited. I could wake Nora and ask her where Zack had planned to go—of all alternatives, that seemed preferable, waking a young person instead of some

parents who, troubled, compromised, were still somehow managing in the middle of a Saturday night to
catch a few pathetic winks.

At 4:00, I tapped at Nora's door, then tiptoed in.
Her lamp was on, casting soft light on her tangled bed.
Nora was gone.

I dialed Willie, let it ring. He was out. I saw him in
an expensive Parisian hotel, moist limbs entwined with
those of a young woman in complex lingerie, while
teenagers continued to terrorize me and grind up what
remained of my hapless life. I enjoyed one moment of
resentment, very brief and rich.

I phoned the parents. They didn't sound like they
bore any resemblance to the parents I'd imagined encouraging future Ivy Leaguers to ingest beer through
gas station funnels and vomit onto their shoes.

The parents went and looked in their children's
bedrooms. Nora's boyfriend, Mark, wasn't in his bed.
Bibi wasn't. Tim, the senior class president, wasn't;
Katya, the vivacious environmentalist, wasn't; Jessica,
the mathematician, wasn't. Beebop, the boy with four
earrings, wasn't. Holly, the girl with the shredded jeans
and visible underpants, wasn't. Alan, the tall weight-
lifting boy with the velvet hat who was going into the
army, wasn't. The rest of the cast were. It was four in
the morning. Almost all the parents answered on the
first ring; struggling to awaken, they were remarkably
gracious, as if genuinely welcoming my call. None of
them was curt with me, and none sounded at all re-
sentful. One couple, whom I'd never met, whose son
was home and sleeping, offered to come over and sit

with me because I was a single parent. Two of the fathers offered to drive out and look, but we couldn't think where they should go. One of the fathers offered to go out, find them, and run them over with the car, and his wife and I laughed hysterically for a long time. We all spoke familiarly, almost tenderly. We knew we were in it together.

One of the mothers called the police, who had no information. Let's get off the phones, we said to each other. Maybe they'll call.

At six, in birdsong and rising light, they arrived. Nora slipped her key in the lock like a safecracker, slid the door open and stepped in. Her lips were rosy and puffy, prominent in her ravaged face. "Oh Mom!" she said groggily. "Oh no! You're up!"

And I was also *really disappointed,* and I was also *really mad,* I cried. How could they do this? Hadn't it occurred to them I'd be worried? What was in their minds? Half the parents in this town had been awake half the night! "—*And I cannot believe not one of you had the consideration to call! It's absolutely incredible that*—"

"One of who?" she said.

"*All of you!*" I cried, and I stamped my foot in its fuzzy slipper. "*I have had it! I can't believe you guys would betray my trust like this! You go out right now and tell Zack to send Bibi home and get in here!*"

She looked horribly confused. "What do you mean?" she said.

"What do *you* mean?"

"Isn't Zack here?" she said.

"Zack wasn't with you?" I said.

Pause. Tiny voice. "I was with Mark."

"What a surprise," I said. "But where is Zack?"

"Well, Mom," she said mildly, the way she'd said it to the hippie narcs. "I'm sorry, but I actually have no idea."

I recalled something funny the psychiatrist had said. The Kleenex box sat over near the couch. Occasionally, sitting in my chair across the room, I threatened to sniffle, and then we both half-rose and he shoved the Kleenex box toward me through the empty air. Once he muttered, in consolation, while shoving the box, that a poltergeist was like a sort of ectoplasmic manifestation of adolescent libido.

"What?" I said.

"Poltergeist," he said.

I snuffled.

"The ghost that makes noises and throws plates off the shelves," he said.

I said damply, "Please. It's really not helping. I could use some *advice*."

After a pause, he said, "Fine. Here it is: Put the babies up for adoption."

I was standing on the driveway in my bathrobe and coat, looking at the frosted lawn and the sun ascending, when Bibi's car pulled in. They both got out and walked toward me slowly. They'd both been crying. Zack's shirt sleeve was torn off and wrapped around his arm as a bandage. He dropped Bibi's hand and put his arms around me, and for a moment I laid my head on his shoulder and hugged him back. "Oh, I hope you weren't worrying," he said softly. And that the line had been busy when they'd called last night—four tries and then they had thought it was too late.

I said that was ridiculous, I was very mad at all of them, and where the hell had they been?

"Oh no. I hope you weren't up worrying," he said again.

Of course I had been, I said. What had happened?

"Gee, I'm sorry." He looked exhausted, and so disheartened that it made me feel quiet.

"Your sister has just taken all the flak for you," I said, but my heart wasn't in it. "What *happened?*"

He said to Bibi, "Will you come in with me?" When he reached to take her hand, she pulled it away—her palms were covered with little cuts. Inside, Bonky threw himself against her legs, and she looked down at him absently but then she didn't pick him up.

We sat down and they started telling their story moment by moment.

A long complicated night. Implausible, undoubtedly real events. It had taken on a life of its own—it *unfolded.* First they'd started to drive to Washington, to see the Vietnam monument, to show it to Alan, who'd been threatening for months to join the army. They were going to call me from the road. Holly, one of the girls, had a father, a doctor, in Philadelphia, and she wanted to stop at his apartment to show Alan a photograph of him, taken twenty-five years earlier—her handsome fresh-faced young dad before she was born, in green beret and full regalia, in Panama, in front of a grocery store, giving the camera a devastating look of confidence. In two cars they drove down to Philadelphia. On South Street, Bibi's car got a flat. It seemed reasonably menacing—many guys in shadowy doorways. Bibi drove Holly's car to a phone booth and called me but my line was busy—

Still in my coat, sitting at the kitchen table, I was listening hard. They were across from me, slightly leaning against each other. Zack's good hand was in Bibi's jacket pocket. Their story was oddly persuasive, told in those intense, soft voices.

Zack and Tim and Alan changed the flat; they all drove to the divorced father's apartment, he was gone for the week, couldn't find the photograph, ate some bagels out of his freezer, thought of calling me but got distracted, then it was too late, got exhausted, lay down.

"Eight of you *lay down*?"

Well yes, they said.

They slept a while. Some people were smoking recreational amounts of dope in quiet darkness on the living room rug; the others were in the father's room on the bed and in the chair, under their jackets, sleeping. Later the living room people slept, the bedroom people woke up. The apartment smelled like dusty smoke. Holly was gone. There was confusion. Much later it turned out she'd been out, wearing her father's navy blue overcoat, walking around the block: Spruce, Fifth, Pine, Fourth, over and over again. It was cold out, with a high white moon. When Bibi and Zack finally went to look for Holly, they stepped out into the street and there she was!

They reorganized themselves, turned on some lamps, brushed their teeth with the absent father's toothbrush, opened then closed the windows, patted at the cushions. Alan, the boy who was going into the service, was upset—maybe he was planning to do the wrong thing. Holly was upset—this drifting night in her father's apartment, surrounded by his furniture, was in some strange, powerful way the most intimate time she'd ever had there. Some of the group wanted to debate with Alan; others talked quietly with Holly. After a long time standing in the foyer, they went out.

They found their cars. ("Why did you have to *find* your cars?" For a moment his usual wry self, Zack said: "Suffice it to say, we had to.")

They drove to a diner. Holly was agitated and trembly and afraid people were looking at her; Alan was crying. Alan had been drinking a lot of tequila. He wore his velvet hat; while he wept, he held it on his head.

Some of them were starving for pancakes. Others couldn't eat. It was late—they gave up the Washington trip and decided to turn back. When they came out of the diner, into the huge parking lot, Alan suddenly wanted to drive—he pushed past and jumped behind the wheel of Bibi's car. They cried, Alan! You can't drive! but he started off, slowly.

To stop him, Zack stepped in front of the car. Tim and Bibi stood to the rear so he couldn't back up. ("*What?*" "Alan carries bugs outside instead of squashing them. He'd never run us down. How could a guy like that be a soldier?")

But Alan locked the doors and started calling increasingly loud frantic warnings out the almost-shut window into the freezing night. They were all jiggling around, cold and dancing, when he finally eased into second and started toward Zack.

Before Zack could jump away, Alan speeded up. When the car touched him, Zack did a strange thing:

he put his hands against the hood and tried to push it back.

Alan had the windows up now; he was calling something, his friends were running alongside yelling, he accelerated; Zack was backing up fast, pushing the car, and he could see, through the windshield, the tears shining on Alan's sad, lonely, determined face.

Alan speeded up.

Zack flung himself onto the hood. ("Like Harrison Ford," Bibi said fondly, and I blinked at her. I thought she was talking about an American president I had temporarily forgotten.)

Zack was face down across the car, and he grabbed the wipers and the edge of the hood right under the windshield and held on with his fingertips. Alan was driving almost sedately through the parking lot, two of the guys were reaching for Zack to help him off but it was too fast, and Zack was going to lose his grip and fall under the wheels. Alan speeded up. Zack laid his face on the hood, it reminded him of lying with your face against sand hearing footsteps; he thought he could hear Alan's desperate flopping heartbeat, and his quiet sobs. He thought, this is ridiculous. I'm gonna get killed. He'd be this year's high school death, in front of a gleaming diner, age sixteen.

He closed his eyes. The parking lot spun around him. Adrenaline heat rushed up through his body, as in a nightmare. He could hear Bibi's voice, feel the cold metal under his weirdly hot face. When instead of turning out onto the highway, Alan rammed a low wall sideways, and the car stopped, Zack flew off almost slowly, he thought, and he could see behind his eyes the arc being described in the black air by his body—

arms, legs, gelled hair, calm mind—before, at last, he landed.

He passed out. Under his forearm was half a wine bottle. There was glass all around on the ground like confetti, glittering, and Bibi knelt and brushed it away from Zack, making many little cuts in her hands which only showed up later after they'd pulled Alan out of the car and embraced him, and Zack had opened his eyes, and they were seated back inside the diner ordering doughnuts and many cups of coffee like long-distance truckers. They were all squeezed in one booth, pressed against each other. They were punching the buttons on the personal jukebox. They felt light and almost cheerful now. Zack laid his head back on the vinyl and tried to take Bibi's hand, and all the little cuts had started to bleed. Then Zack and Bibi both started to cry.

It was morning—outside, it was cold and sunny and still. I thought about their friend Alan, about his habit of holding the velvet hat onto his head, as if against a stiff wind. We were still sitting at the table in our coats. "Look, I know this sounds crazy," Zack said. I was about to say, it certainly does, how dangerous, how unwise, and also you passed out, you should be looked at by a doctor. Instead I said, "You seem so sad."

Zack said, "Well, we are sad. That's just it. We really are."

And after that for the rest of high school nothing much happened. Nora didn't go to Florida; five days before, she broke up with Mark and unpacked. Zack got into college in Vermont; trying to imagine him there, we drove to the mall and bought long underwear and Arctic boots. And then something seemed to drift out of the house, like the fog breaking up; or as if the kids were already gone.

Spring came. I took to spying on them. On Saturdays I'd walk past Tempting Treats and try to catch a glimpse of Zack in his green apron behind the counter. Or a couple of times on the way home from work I drove to the grade school where Nora ran the theater program; I stood in the bushes outside the window and watched Nora kneel and apply makeup to the exalted faces of five first graders. She'd stay with me one more year, a placid, celibate girl. In three months Zack would leave for college, never to return.

The week before Zack graduated, the seniors had a dance—not the prom, a dance to blow it out. Around ten o'clock I drove to the school. It was a dark spring night, warm and fragrant, and from half a block away, you could feel, then hear, the music. I went in, stepped into the crowd—it was hot and breezy in the gym, and everything was throbbing—sound and darkness and bodies moving.

I had never seen Zack dance. After walking invisibly around for twenty minutes, I finally saw him across the floor, dancing fast, Bibi moving against him, sliding away, sliding back. They were portraying, of course, their lovemaking, which looked pretty nice—intense, responsive, slippery. The music picked up. Zack started whirling so happily—he jerked his head back and his hair flew up. He danced like a cartoon character, feet jumping. I stood near him and Bibi in the lively dark for a while, watching them shimmy, watching their silver earrings flashing, their ecstatic faces. In a minute they'd see me and we'd say hi and then I'd go home; I was already imagining walking out of the shrieking music into the warm quiet night.

Bibi closed her eyes. Then for a long time I continued to stand there, just about to step forward. Over and over Zack jumped and grinned and seemed to glance my way. But he never saw me.

Part III

12. Volpone

As I walked into the lobby, William rushed up like an advance man, wild to kiss my face. Immediately, we both assumed old postures, which no amount of time passing helps us unlearn: he was bussing me and I was pushing faintly against his chest like a cat being hugged too hard. "Will you stop it a minute!" I said—my first words after not laying eyes on the guy for four months.

He didn't take offense. "So!" he cried, releasing his hold and letting me drop. "We're reconstituted!"

William's father was toddling at his side, wearing a salmon-colored sports jacket arresting in its silkiness, in which he nevertheless looked like a little leathery Florida animal. "Hi, Peppy," I said, and I leaned toward his brown cheek.

"What a pleasure, darling," he announced, and shifted his head, so that I kissed him hard on his nose.

It was March. I hadn't seen Pep in eight months; I hadn't seen William since Thanksgiving—I rarely saw him these days. Willie was beautifully dressed, in a pristine wool suit, monogrammed silk shirt, and red crêpe tie. "That's a great shirt," I said, and he grinned as if vindicated.

"It's elegant but sportive," he said. Then he flung his glance about the lobby, taking in the fieldstone fireplace, the chair rail, the rag rugs floating on the carpet. "So this is the *vrai* Vermont!"

We were here to watch Zachary play Volpone—the first time in three years that our family was gathering in one place. "Ms. Cupcake is indeed ensconced," William told me happily. He meant that Nora had cut her last class and driven up the Northway from Saratoga; so we were all here.

William was wedging himself between me and the counter, urgently inclining my way. I felt like getting to my own room to—what? Be alone with my suitcase. I touched his soft lapel lightly, as if I were a Mafia don, restrained in gesture, capable, without making a move, of menacing even those of comparable rank. I said, "Willie. Mind if I check in?"

At five in the afternoon William and Pep and I gathered in the dining room, where a guy was still vacuuming the rug. Zachary arrived, took off his coat, sat down at the table, and rewrapped his muffler around his neck as if he were getting ready to go out. We looked over the tops of our menus, out of the restaurant dining room and across to the end of the lobby, where the elevator opened to reveal a young woman already rushing forward, wearing a tiny skirt, from which thrust legs oddly mottled, or encrusted, with patches of black. It was Nora. In arrival and greeting so like her father, she plunged into the dining room crying, "Hi! Hi! Hi! Hi!" and swirled around the table, kissing us all—Pep on top of his head, me with her arms around my neck,

William as he called "Norie, Norie, here!" and thumped the chair beside him. She sat down, then immediately stood up and said to Zachary, "What do you think?" rotating her legs left, then right, like Betty Grable on ice.

I said, "Oh, you wore them. They look really lovely."

William pointed into a booklet, and the waitress peered into it at his finger.

"Zack?" Nora said, attractively shifting her weight. She told Pep, "These are black lace panty hose, Grandpa. They're very current."

"Beautiful, darling," Pep said.

William said, "Can you bring the bottle so we can see the year?" and the waitress looked at him intently, then rushed away. He said, "Let's see, Norie!" and then I was having a familiar sensation of intimacy, and he was whispering near my ear, "Is she kidding? What should we do?"

Nora was balanced with one knee bent, gazing into her brother's face. "They're good," he said to her, and for a moment everything seemed to hold still. Nora was eighteen and Zack was nineteen—now, for the first time in their lives, they lived apart.

Outside, through French doors, late sunlight was slanting past, and all the dining-room lamps now turned themselves on. "Oh, perfect!" Nora cried, and sat down and looked around at each of us—William, Zachary, Pep, and me—one by one. The guy cut off the vacuum cleaner and the roaring sank and died. "Isn't this so nice!" Nora loudly insisted, in the sudden silence.

"Well?" she said. "Well?"

———

"I saw your shacks," Nora said.

"Shanties," Zack said.

"How's that going?" William said, chewing shrimp.

Zack said, "Well, y'know, at Berkeley they *routinely* get their heads smashed. At Georgetown they build one shanty and they get arrested. Here, it can be kind of discouraging, because the school is so quietly accepting that if you're not doing violence or, you know, something disgusting, you can basically take any stand you want and they'll say 'Well, that's fine,' and it just gets sort of *instantaneously absorbed* and everybody just goes on."

Pep cleared his throat to say importantly, "I note they don't use 'Professor' here. It's pretty much on a first-name basis."

"Pep. Wait," William said, and waved at him. Then he smiled a sympathetic curving smile, and Pep looked at an asparagus tip and forked it into his mouth.

Zack said, "Well, that really is on the point, Grandpa, and unfortunately there are times when that kind of institutionalized relaxed approach isn't so much help. I mean there's such a tradition of genteel liberalism here that— Here's a great example, this is funny: The president addresses us. Hodell will come out on the chapel steps and *address the shanties*. He'll be kind of standing there grinning and, you know, he's cool, he wears hiking boots, and he looks real sincere in this sort of *arcane way*, and he says, 'Guys. Beautiful symbol. It's wonderful the way you're expressing yourselves on this crucial issue. So in the spirit of the school.' Then he goes back inside, we feel recognized, we keep building shanties, he puts *no pressure at all* on the trustees to divest, everything is defused, and nobody cares!" Zack laughed a harried laugh.

William said, to Zack but in my direction, "But for your purposes there's no question a less accepting school would not be any particular improvement."

Zack was chuckling, still telling his story. He said, "I mean, the lawnmower guy comes out with his tractor to mow around the chapel, and every week because of the shanties there's less visible lawn. The guy just says *'How ya doin'!'* and mows around us!"

"Ha! Ha!" Nora cried, and fell over onto Zack's shoulder. He looked at her, surprised, then joyful.

I asked, "Can you work in the tents?"

"If I can't work, I can't," Zack said quickly.

"But I mean . . ." I said. "Well, they wouldn't let you keep them up during exams, I guess."

He looked extremely pleasant. He said, "Hey. Y'know?"

After a pause, I said, "Well, I'm sorry you're not making more of an impression on the trustees, but, speaking as a mother, there are times when I'm really glad you're not at Berkeley, or wherever, getting your head routinely smashed."

Zack gave me a curious look, and Nora sat back and gave me an amused one. *"As a mother,"* she said. "You usually try not to say that."

I said, "Well, I mean, I'm torn. Obviously I support you and I'm proud of you, and I think it's important you stand by your convictions, and obviously I *don't* believe in trying to keep my kids from operating independently and doing what they think is right. At the same time there's a part of me that says I really don't

2 2 5

want you getting smashed in the head." Although stagy, this sounded so reasonable to me as to be unassailable. William was supportively, absently nodding. "It's a conflict I've not resolved," I said, "and—"

"It's kind of irrelevant, Mom, whether *you want* to try to keep us from 'operating' in a certain way," Zack said. "We're people. We're already 'operating.' It's nice that you make an effort to frame it in a 'liberal' way. But your idea, Mom, about whether you should *let us* do it is kind of—I don't know, not exactly germane."

"Zachary, your mother is talking about an issue of consequence to her," William said, looking personally offended. "The only point worth discussing isn't necessarily whether the president of your college should or should not stand upon the chapel steps and congratulate you people for your exemplary achievement in constructing seven plywood shanties!"

Zack looked out the window. After a while he said, "Pretty amazing."

"Uh-oh, don't start this crap," William said.

Zack said, "Well, Dad, your contribution seems to be generally that you think it's cute that we *pipe up and speak* like adults. That seems to really kind of take care of it." He said to Nora, with a sweet, helpless smile, "Great. This is great."

"You find what I said 'amazing'?" William asked, peering at him.

Zack turned his chair to face halfway away from the table, and Pep looked up, startled. Nora leaned and set her hand on Pep's forearm. She said, "Come on, guys."

There was a silence, in which Nora reached across to Zack's plate and picked up his last curled shrimp and said to him in a warm voice, "You want this?" He shook his head. Nora held the shrimp up in her fingers before popping it in her mouth, saying, "This is undeniably a Vermont shrimp." She grinned at Pep. She said, "This shrimp regrets everything."

Pep set his fork down and gazed across. He said, "If I were running this college, I'd be *proud* to have you as a student, Zackie."

"Thanks, Grandpa," Zack said, bitterly chuckling.

Pep said, "So, Zackie, you mean you sleep in the shacks?"

"What's the situation with getting enough sleep?" William added.

Nora said, "Come on, Z."

He turned his chair toward the table again. Tears stood in his eyes. He was composing his face into a bland, relaxed face and he did it pretty fast. He said to Pep, "I go to class all morning. I rehearse most afternoons. After dinner, either I build or I make a wood run, and then I either work on lines or study—the last few nights I've had performances—and then I go to sleep." He looked at William. "I sleep fine in there, Dad. I've got my futon and my sleeping bag. There aren't many people—it's totally comfortable. I fall asleep right away, and in the morning I get up and I walk straight across to Talbot for Baroque." By the end of these remarks he was talking to all of us again, looking cheerful to signal his eagerness not to quarrel. When William said, "When do you get time to study?" he grinned intently and cried, in a tone so affable and energetic it was like pleading, "Dad! Dad! I study all the time!"

———

At the end of the dining room, a pale man in a woodsman's shirt set up a music stand and began to play a dulcimer, and while its silvery notes floated over to us we made our reports. It was family dinner, the first in years.

William told about a recent law case full of what he called "involutions and human interest."

Pep told about Florida, where for four years, since Lainie's death, he had been living alone, eating bowls of ice cream, attending meetings of his recreational-facilities committee, and playing cards with his cronies, three ancient women.

Before us was the wreckage of our dinners—on Nora's plate the julienne of vegetables, on Pep's the center of his roast-beef slab, and in the middle of the table half the miniature bread loaf with the knife still protruding from its side. Outside, the light was fading, and the obligatory distant mountains were starting to turn lavender, then dark. Nora told about playing lacrosse back at her own school, defensive wing, with William lobbing in questions drawn from several sports, both amateur and pro. Pep burped, faintly popping. "And against Colgate?" William asked.

She said placidly, "They ate us for lunch."

Before I got to make my report, Zack suddenly had to leave. He was telling about his roommate, a lively Zionist. "He doesn't even think I'm a Jew. I mean, he thinks at best I'm a misguided assimilated Jew of the Diaspora, which—well, I guess I agree with. He can be quite a pain in the ass about it. But I respect that opinion, I think that—"

Those who know William well can invariably see him formulating his sentences long in advance. Now his eyebrows lifted and he flicked his fingers. Zack shoved back his chair and stood up. Wild look. He pulled at his muffler, then at his hair. "I'm freaking out from stagefright!" he cried. "I'm getting over the edge!

While we waited to go to the theater, I told the rest of them about my new project, the book I'd started working on with Michael Roseman, the developmental psychologist. Michael had made videotapes of sixty children at the dinner table with their families, starting when the children were three. I had told him about a childhood friend whose dad used to hang his belt over the dining-room chandelier. Together Michael and I were writing *Crystal and Leather: The American Family at Dinner.* "For example," I told them now, "we're probably all kind of aware that we automatically—perhaps you'd say naturally—sat down in this constellation. We didn't discuss it, and we probably didn't think about it. We all just knew where to sit, in the places appropriate to our relationships or to our relative status or power."

On my placemat I drew a diagram:

"William saved a place at his right. I saved the one on my left. And Zack sat right between them to leave room for Nora—it didn't matter to him which side she took, as long as he was buffered by empty space on one side and Nora sat next to him on the other. By the way, I think Nora would've sat next to me if William hadn't skewed the results by yelling, 'Sit here!' "

"*Oh, Mom,*" Nora said sadly, in a thrilling warm, low voice.

"No, it's just interesting," I said. "It's just that in families these alignments have long since sorted themselves out, and every family member finds what everybody agrees is the 'right' seat without conscious thought on anybody's part. It doesn't mean there's a reason to be insulted—it's just that the family kind of automatically arranges itself in the way that feels correct."

Nora gazed at me sympathetically.

William said, "I assume this material is all prefatory? Because I suspect most people are already rather aware of this sort of patterning when they sit down at a table. Most people are often quite intensely conscious of who they want to sit with, I would think. And who they wish to avoid, for that matter." Pep coughed at his ice cream, and Nora looked at him. "No?" William said to me.

Nora said, "I'm sure there's a lot more to the book."

"This is general scene-setting. This is not even *in* the book," I said.

William said, "In any case, I can also imagine the seating pattern that emerges here might be informed by precisely the fact that we *don't* eat together anymore. It clearly expresses something about *that* reality as well."

"Which doesn't contradict my point at all," I said.

Nora said cheerily, "And also Daddy is not Michael Roseman's biggest fan of all time."

William signed the check. Then a waitress in a leather waistcoat brought the dulcimer player a plate of meatballs and rolls, and we pushed back our chairs and walked across the lobby, heading out into the cool night to see our Zachary on the stage. The carpet was plaid. Nora bent to link her arm through Pep's and pulled him along, saying, "The family after dinner, walking on checked wool!"

Ninety people sat on folding chairs and watched their friends and relatives play *Volpone* in aerobics clothes. Instead of a stage, there was a space cleared on the floor, with lights shining on the tape marks. Zachary wore a sweatsuit and a rakish scarf. Several pretty young women, expansively gesturing, played roles written for men: Corvino the Raven was a tiny, wild-eyed girl in a black leotard. Between scenes, we sat in blackness and felt ourselves shift position near each other while we listened to props thumping and John Coltrane.

Backstage afterward, Zack was standing close behind the young woman who played Mosca the Fly, the sidekick to his Volpone. He had his arms around her and was resting his chin on her head and grinning at everybody. His friends were with him: Corbaccio the Crow and Voltore the Vulture.

Corbaccio squeezed our hands. "Your son is a nice young man," he said loudly, grinning at William, Nora, Pep, and me. "Yes, that's how we talk about him: *'Isn't he a nice young man?'* "

2 3 1

Mosca had a red rose, which she held up by its long stem under William's nose. He flushed and looked proud. "You were awfully persuasive," he said to her.

"You were great. You were very greedy," Nora said.

A couple rushed in—two small people, one white-haired, one bald, who pushed through the crowd to get to Zack, squeezing in front of Pep. Zack introduced us; these were the Didis.

Mrs. Didi cried, "See Zachary, we got here! We couldn't miss it!" while her husband reached around Mosca and pumped Zack's hand.

Then for a while longer the audience stood around and told the cast some more about how wonderful their performances had been. Zack told us that right before he steps onto any stage he says to himself, *"Sant' Antonio della barba bianca, fammi trovare cio che mi manca."*

Nora looked excited. She said, " 'Saint Anthony of the white beard . . . help me to find . . . that which I've lost'! Oh my God, I can translate!"

"And then I don't forget my lines," Zack said, and kissed the top of smiling Mosca's head.

Mrs. Didi was standing beside William, who gave her a look of collusion. He said, "These modern kids grow up without much in the way of religion, I'm afraid, and they are forced to find their prayers where they can."

"He's our adopted son!" Mrs. Didi said.

"We like to see this guy every day of the week," her husband said. Pep following his every move, he shook Zachary's hand again. He was almost exactly Pep's height. "Welp! Back to the salt mines!" he told Pep.

"We'll be there soon," Zack said, and we all watched the very small couple turn and go out the door.

"Who *were* they?" Nora asked.

"The Didis?" Zack said happily. "They own the Pizza Solution, where I live the rest of my life."

Zack went off with the cast, and we walked back to the inn. On the way, Nora showed Pep some stars and William walked with me, holding my arm hard the whole time, as if he were pulling me aside for consultation. He whispered, "He's sleeping with Mosca or she's a pal?"

I laughed. But I was remembering Zack in the play, moving in white light and crying out his lines, plotting with his sidekick, feigning vivid death and flashily rising again. Zack, whom I hadn't talked to or listened to in so long, looked happy—he looked like himself.

At four I woke up, thinking, Don't wake up. In the other bed, Nora lay slantwise, with her blankets rolled around her as if she were camping, with the clock flipping numbers near her head. I got up and went down to the lobby, where two lamps were on and an old man sat behind the counter looking at a television set the size of a dinner roll. When I got outside, it was quite light. The moon was out and high clouds were scudding, and I thought I would just walk around and see some things in the rustling, bright night.

I walked toward the college chapel, which looked from far away like a big seated animal attended by trees. As I approached, I could see set out on the grass some cardboard boxes patched with wood scraps—the shanties—and I stopped thinking my walk was aimless. I wanted to see Zachary.

Taped to the side of his shanty was a square of cardboard, the shutter for his window. I lifted it and looked in, but the room was empty. I looked into all of them; sometimes they were black inside and sometimes when I lifted the cardboard the moon streamed in, but nobody was sleeping there. I stood still on the lawn.

Far away, a couple were coming toward me down the walk, and I thought I might ask them why the shanty people weren't asleep in the shanties. But when they were nearer I saw they were a young man and woman wearing only sneakers. These were two famous students, the Nude Strollers. Every time they stepped under a light, their bodies looked very roundly modeled and shiny; they were deep into a friendly chat. I thought, Well, I won't ask a naked couple—they wouldn't know. And I started following the paths back toward the inn.

Ahead, at the far edge of the campus, the inn was sitting in the dark like a ship, pouring light into the black air and out over the grass. All the lights were on. Fire trucks were outside, with red lights pulsing but no sirens, and firemen were stamping in through the front door.

In the lobby, a few people were standing around wearing windbreakers and coats and robes with pajamas and nightgowns sticking out the bottoms, among them Pep in his seventy-fifth-birthday robe. Nora stood wrapped in her blanket, listening on the house phone.

"Dad doesn't answer. Oh, here he is!" she said, and handed me the receiver.

William's voice was rough and stiff, but even half asleep he was vivacious. "What is this!" he cried. "You're phoning? There's somebody smashing on the door at the same time! JUST A MINUTE!"

"It's the firemen," I said.

"WAIT A MINUTE, I'M ON THE PHONE!" he cried.

"They're the firemen, Willie. Open the door and come down to the lobby right away. Don't use the elevator, okay?"

"Oh—firemen?" William said, and hung up.

"Just what I need," he said in greeting. He was wearing a maroon warm-up suit—silver stripes on the sleeves and ironed sweatpants. I said, "Did you bring that in case of a fire?" and he smiled grimly and turned to walk away. He called back to us, "I'm getting drinks. Don't bother giving me your orders. I know what I'm doing."

More people arrived in the lobby. The manager announced that we could stay inside because it was undoubtedly a false alarm. Nora got sleepy. We were on a high-backed couch, Pep balanced on the arm, Nora far down in the cushions with me, still wearing her blanket.

"Grandpa, in Florida do you go to Disney World?"

"Not yet, darling."

"You should go," she said. "You'd dig it." She looked dreamy. "I went," she said. "Remember that, Mom? I went last year, with my two roommates, Susan and Suzanne. They invited me, and they said it's not expensive and it's great. But everything cost just so much more than they said. When we got to the ticket window, they said, 'It's twenty-five dollars.' " When Nora had told me this the year before, she'd cried; now she only said, "Mom, I worked so hard for that money."

I was thinking about what I had thought as I ran toward the lighted inn—the craziness of reassembling a family in one building just so the family could burn up together. Nora said, "When we were little, we used to play fire alarm. David Beecham would set a fire with twigs and Zack and I would start running." She stopped and looked out over the lobby. "I remember Zachary's sneaks! He had Keds! His legs stuck out like brown sticks!"

"Rest your eyes," Pep said.

"It's five hours till checkout," Nora said. "I'm talking about a long time ago, Grandpa," she went on, fuzzily, in a cottony voice, as if he had just arrived and she could fill him in without having to wake up again. "When Zack and I were little."

Pep said, "Here comes your soda, darling." Nora let her eyes fall shut, and at that instant the glass door swung open and Zachary came into the lobby, smiling in our direction.

I waved. Then I looked to see what Pep was talking about, and saw William. He was wobbling toward us, maroon and silver, holding against his chest some huge paper cups. Across the lobby we could see him threading his way through families standing in circles with their backs to the circles of other families, and we could already hear the ice clicking against the curved waxed sides of the cups and imagine the cold, sweet flavors, although he still had a long distance to go to get to us across the rug. Outside the window, the black sky was fading. Pep was tapping his pajama leg and gazing off. Nora was asleep. Nobody but me saw Zachary walking toward us, though he would reach us in a minute. I could see that Willie and Zack were going to reach us at precisely the same moment, and I couldn't wait.

13. Some Evenings

Evenings found me in a family restaurant, talking with a family. Initially when I approached, they'd be wary; soon they'd turn forthcoming, sometimes irrepressibly so. Occasionally the whole family would be mobilized by my honest interest in their dinner hour and they'd end up telling me huge numbers of extraneous details, cutting away to faintly related topics, drifting back in time to beloved mythic early family days. They looked like immutable groups, smoothly traveling together, easily reassembled at a new table, nothing to hide. As soon as the children could speak, it appeared, they could tell all. Chomping their burgers, passing the fries, the family was an open book.

Michael Roseman and I were nearing a deadline on our book about the families eating dinner, and all I did was work. I still taught at the training school, twice a week now, to pretend I hadn't left. I'd stayed there years longer than I should've, I realized—it was turning out I was the kind of person who'll try any contortion to avoid saying good-bye.

Apropos of that, on Saturday night I still often went to New York with Steven, the handsome lawyer. On the turnpike in his beautiful, powerful car with its un-

derutilized turbo capabilities, then at the ballet or a restaurant, then later in his redwood tub, we'd sit placidly
side by side; late at night, we'd make love for a reasonable length of time, amicably, facing each other at last.
Steven had made a will for me and I had cooked him
some dinners. Sometimes we had dates with other
people, which were too strenuous or didn't pan out.
In the mirror from the restaurant banquette, we occasionally noticed we were growing older.

The kids would finish college soon. I was keeping
their stuff—Frisbees, fuzzy animals, jewelry from babyhood, sweatshirts, Dungeons and Dragons equip-
ment, drum sets, copies of *Lord of the Flies* and SAT
study manuals, commemorative beer steins—things
they needed and which they'd never come back to claim.
The stuff was eternal: all over the country, parents were
keeping it; we were supposed to keep the stuff forever.
The stuff and I and Bonky Boy had been living together for four years when my own forgotten adoles-
cence came back for a reprise.

At the bar at a wedding, I was standing next to the
best-sounding man on my old friend Sam's short list.
Just do it, I thought, and I touched his gray sleeve,
through which his forearm was radiating ordinary human warmth. I said, "Okay, the groom says we should
meet." The man looked at me. Then he held his glass
out and down, for me to sip at its edge.

"This is what?" I said. "Cranberry juice?"

"Are you kiddin'? Don't you recognize it?" He had
the remnants of a Southern voice, blurry and soft. Like
the families at dinner, one question and he spilled cru-

cial data at length. He said, "This is a great day; I've been experiencin' some truly surprisin' things. I've just been talkin' with Lucy, my former wife, about our kids, and we found ourselves sayin' how glad we are that we got to be married to each other. It's odd, isn't it, the way somethin' like that can suddenly happen?"

"Well, it sounds wonderful," I said. The voice was amazing.

"But overdone, huh?" He smiled down at me, ironic, pale, tall. I gazed up. I did not want this man to go back to Lucy. I wanted him to stay here with me for life—for our few remaining years. At night the recessed lights would dim, we would stretch out on this *faux* malachite bar; we would rest our heads on the stack of cocktail napkins, eat maraschino cherries for breakfast, chew on the slices of lemon and lime. "When did you stop drinking?" I said.

"January first, six years ago."

"And you go to AA?"

"Sure," he said—sipping, smiling. "I see you're not too partial to just lettin' things unfold."

I was confused. "Is that right? I guess that's right," I said.

He said, "Boy, you're a lovely-lookin' woman."

While I was getting oriented, he asked me out. He wanted to hear a gospel chorus and then he wanted to stay up all night. "It might be kinda Southern for you."

I said, "I can't on Saturday."

"No, me either. I meant Friday."

"I work early Saturday mornings."

"So do I."

"I'm pretty busy generally."

He grinned. "Me too, sister. Would you be more comfortable forgettin' it?"

I looked at him. I said, "I'm nervous talking to you."

"You do look somewhat alarmed."

I said, "Look. Are you the type of man who has intense and voluptuous occasional dates, and works all the rest of the time, and never gets really involved, and won't let the woman move in, and starts again with another new relationship when she finally gets fed up and leaves you?"

I blushed, and we laughed. We smiled at each other tenderly for a while. "Yes," he said finally "Regrettably, darlin', I am."

Ewing was a psychiatrist; he did some kind of tedious-sounding, all-consuming, not immediately comprehensible medical research. He said he had recently visited my town, to give a colloquium for some psychologists, and gone out to dinner with Michael Roseman—already we shared a social life. Ewing's talk that day had been called "Inhibition as the Organizing Principle of Behavior: the hormonal design of postprandial satiety." "Yikes," I said. He said it meant you spent your life watching rats and thinking about the idea that we're probably organized to do everything— eat, sleep, have sex—all the time; he was apparently looking day and night for the thing that makes us stop. Smiling, he said, "I'm an expert in satiety, not appetite. That fact hasn't escaped my notice."

"I don't know what you're talking about," I said. "If that's a come-on, it's not a good one."

We kept shaking our heads at the hors d'oeuvres trays, sending them away. He reminded me a little of Willie's law partner from years ago, David Grieves— same height, and the luminous smile; I reminded myself of myself as a high school girl—addled, weirdly focused. I got drunk on white wine, standing there gazing up at him, and had to leave the reception early.

The day before our date, I saw I wasn't going to make my chapter deadline unless I worked all weekend, and I called Ewing at his lab. He kept covering the phone and yelling to people in the background. I heard him yawn. In the moment before we said goodbye, he asked me out for the next Friday instead, as if compelled by his ingrained Southern politeness. Okay, I said glumly—we understood that we were being courteous and the week might pass but we'd never really see each other again.

On Thursday, Nora drove home from school for the weekend, running a fever. When she arrived, her face was gorgeously red and hot, and she was carrying Lambie from childhood in the pocket of her leather jacket. Coming in the front door, she stopped and yanked off her cowboy boots. She immediately got into bed. "I'm staying home," I said.

"Mom, I'm fine," she murmured from her bed.

"No, I can see this man any time."

"Thank you a lot, Mom," she said sweetly. "But I don't really need my mommy to sit with me."

"Nope, I want to stay."

"I just need to sleep."

"I've already decided to stay."

"Mom, I hate to say it. But I'm twenty."

"Nope."

"*Mom,*" Nora said. "*Please. Have your nice date.*"

I called and told Ewing's secretary I couldn't meet him. When he called back, he said, "I know your child is sick, and we'll get another chance. But are you a little scared?"

"Not at all," I said cheerily. "By a prospective date? Not at all."

"Okay."

There was a long, companionable, rather dreamy silence, in which I felt encouraged to think a while. "Maybe I am," I said finally. "I guess it's possible. I might be a little apprehensive."

"Scared?"

"It's possible."

He said, "You should be."

Early on Easter, while I was working on the exuberant Lewis family, four people who inordinately enjoyed dining out, Ewing phoned to try again. Then he had to hang up to go to church with his former wife and the three splendid children they were so happy to have raised together.

He wanted to take me to someplace that sounded like a Brazilian nightclub. I left my desk and closed the door and spent the morning thinking about dancing with him, and trying on many pairs of shoes—three times I tried my newest, tan suede which matched my foot, and bent my knees, and studied my looks, and turned this way and that. I thought, No. People might step on my feet and scratch the suede. Anyway, I wanted something narrow, pointy-toed, black silk. I imagined sambas, the elegant crowd in Spanish evening clothes, the front of my body, all down its length, rhythmically grazing Ewing's tall beautiful front.

The kids were home for the week. Zack was playing his electric guitar without the amp—for hours, I tried various unlikely outfits, listening to his bare foot mournfully patting the floor, the guitar strings pinging.

Three times, Nora came into my room and watched me for a minute; said nothing; went away. The fourth time, I said: *"What?"*

"I'm worried about you. You seem strange."

"I *am* strange!" I grinned. She frowned. The next time she looked in, I pretended not to see her.

I was busy giving the mirror a mirror face I now recalled from an earlier life—lovely, steady, intent. This took half the day.

The club was a glowing black room, the music was deafening, and everybody looked intense in the roiling darkness. Sweating men—bulky young blonds in T-shirts—were staggering around daintily carrying long-necked beers by their necks. The woman in the band wore a G-string made of pearls: when she turned, satiny buttocks with a pearl necklace between. Her mouth gleamed white as she grinned into the pulsating crowd. She jiggled. Plumes sprouted from her head. I whispered to Ewing, "Are we the oldest people here?" "Sure," he whispered.

The tables were tiny and close. We slid in alongside a small sturdy-looking couple, remarkably well dressed, she in red silk, he in a black suit and a bracelet of gold links. A waiter brought them a platter of meats—chicken legs, hunks of bloody steak—and bowls of rice and beans. Sweet-faced and self-contained, she watched her plate as he spooned food onto it—mounds of black beans, glistening. He said, "When I like somebody, I like to see them eat." He set her fork into her hand.

Automatically, I imagined interviewing the couple for the book—maybe they were a family: *When I like somebody, I like to see them eat.*

Instead I laid my head against the wall and closed my eyes. Ewing turned his chair to sit next to me, and for a while he seemed to be taking my pulse, which started to race embarrassingly; then he held my wrist. I ate some bits of Spanish sausage and got grease on my fingertips—he wiped my hands, pulling the napkin hard along each finger. I was aware of the beautiful little couple nearby, filled with meats, dabbing their lips, looking so continuously into each other's dark eyes. I felt faintly ill with desire for Ewing.

The Brazilian band was going crazy, the room trembling and roaring. I opened my eyes. I leaned and kissed Ewing's mouth. He didn't look surprised, though I was.

Our food came—platters carrying whole baby salmons swimming through lettuce leaves. I leaned my head back and swallowed a bone, and the bone turned sideways and lodged in my throat.

Carrying the bread basket, I ran out into the street. In the cab I swallowed hunks of bread, which caught on the bone, terrifying me every time. Streets rushed by, lights, buildings. I said crazily, "Can't you *fix this?*"

"I'm not a real doctor, y'know." He held my hand. Getting out his wallet to pay the driver, he tucked my hand under his arm and pinned it there.

The emergency room was filled with white light. The doctors were young men and women who hadn't slept in years, steadily running back and forth, hour after hour all the long night, calling to each other. A man was wheeled in, fast, with blood seeping from his mouth. A man was carried in thickly screaming, his eyes blurry. Sad mothers with skinny, beaten children. Street people talking to their hands. After two hours thinking about their lives, I started to cry.

Ewing came closer. He smiled hard at me. He said, "Come on, little sister. You're gonna live now," and wiped away my tears with his thumb. "That's not the point," I said irritably.

I stood for another hour in a complicated situation: holding my folder with its red triage sticker; worrying about the people in the emergency room; afraid I was just about to die; and thinking, this is embarrassing— I'm falling in love with my date. I could feel him standing near me, as if we were already touching. His body was protecting me—he stood between me and the death that otherwise would've claimed me hours ago, back there with the music and pearl G-string and meats. I wanted to live long enough to get to know that body.

Bitterly snuffling: "What the hell was I doing, going to a *nightclub!*"

"Sugar, let's just try to press on a while."

The X ray showed the bone, a vertical sliver of white inside my cloudy gray throat. The youngest doctor took a moment to stare at the picture—gee, it was quite a bone. He ran his hands through his hair. Finally he said, "I haven't been inside a real restaurant in years."

I could be admitted, or I could go home and give it a chance to slide down. I looked at Ewing. "We can give it the night," he said.

I lay on my back holding perfectly still, planning my imminent return to a sensible life.

Ewing had other plans. He lay near me and talked— absurd, classic American things we would do after the bone slipped down. We'd ride all night south to Charleston and sit with his aunt, Miss Jane, on the piazza. We'd drink strong coffee filled with brown sugar, Jane's gray hair would be piled under her hat, and a strand would fall into her cup and she wouldn't notice. First we'd get ready, select a pickup truck for maximal hauling power, try the radio and kick the tires. The truck would need warming up—we'd hit the starter and butter her a while.

Another time, we'd drive straight west, we'd cross prairies, grasslands, desert, hot day and freezing night. He'd pack my bag, wash my hair, shave my legs—the bone dug at my throat. "Stop saying this stuff," I said.

"Women shave their legs again now, don't they? Hasn't anybody ever shaved your legs for you?"

"You have a stupid bedside manner," I said unhappily.

So he talked about that. "With men, it's like with pets—you put your hands on them. Bein' touched alarms men, and they sorta lose their bearings. It makes them think you're sayin' somethin' profound."

I tried to laugh, carefully.

He leaned over me and ran his hands down my arms, and I shivered.

"I'm not a man," I said.

"I see that."

"I'm not alarmed."

The moon was out and the room full of shadows. "Lie still," he whispered.

"You think I was planning to move?"

He drew nearer, set his mouth against my hair.

"Don't kiss me."

He smiled sympathetically.

"Don't kiss my neck."

"Hush now."

I let my eyes close.

"I want you to be grateful, now, for all I'm doin' here," he said after a while.

I said, after another while, "I'm grateful."

It would be almost light when Ewing finished making love to me. I held still. His tongue on my nipples, under my arms, along my thighs, between my legs. Later he held me down and I still hardly moved, under him. Much later he smoothed back my hair and whispered me to sleep. In the morning the fish bone was gone.

On Saturday night, Steven was away, but Ewing wasn't free. I worked on the Conway, Reiser, and Powitz families, who loved their own cooking. I went to Deenie and Michael's to play backgammon and discuss life; I didn't mention Ewing.

On Monday, at the boys' training school, I moved as through clouds. Jamal and Robert came to their lesson wearing snakeskin caps, shouting at each other about Peugeots and Audis and Saabs. We were going to read the phone book, some newspaper headlines, a U.S. armed forces recruitment brochure, comic strips, *TV Guide, Road and Track,* and a driver's manual—"in case one of you ever wants to drive a car legally," I said, and they grinned and jumped in place.

Jamal to Robert: "Nothin' stand out like black and white. Beige ragtop. Canary yellow with black strip. Burgundy ragtop, burgundy interior."

"You guys want to sit down?"

Jamal, jiggling slightly to inaudible music: "My niece's boyfriend, Sweet? Got twenty year. Sweet he talkin' about $60,000 bail, lower sixties. Come up $80,000. I'm telling you, man, the way these niggers bust your behind."

I opened the Yellow Pages.

"There was powder burns all over my pants. They try to take my pants for evidence. They blocked the projects off, they blocked off Parnell Street. I just want to live quiet in the city."

I turned to "Automobile Repair." Pages rustling.

Robert said, "Trenton's all right, but Trenton go to sleep at two o'clock. Come down my way, boy, you might like it. As far as seein' chicks and like that."

Jamal said: "I don't have no destination right now. I'm lookin' for a destination."

I peered into one of my manuals. It said, "Teachers

cannot be phonies. Young adult students can detect a phoney."

Softly, Jamal danced a couple of steps. He said some more things—my little sister, my baby brother, my 300-pound uncle, my niece, my niece's boyfriend, come to my place sometime, I got a cousin look after you.

"Could I interrupt?" I said. "And maybe we could actually read something—"

They looked at me.

Lots of people at the training school got their information from Jamal and Robert; they were two extremely smart boys, dependably quick to see and understand.

"Okay?" I asked.

They stared.

She not here, they said to each other.

She lost.

She gone.

14. Zack's Graduation

On the plane on the way to Zack's graduation, I told Mom about Ewing—I called him "the new man." Mom was perched in the seat near the window, wearing a black silk dinner dress with her shapely little knees sticking out, black stockings, Chanel pumps for a Barbie.

Mom should do airline ads. While the rest of us were wedged between the armrests, straining up to adjust the air blasts, buckling in and starting to sweat, she was just sitting there humming along with an instrumental version of "Penny Lane." She was enjoying a Lifesaver. She was interested in the activity on the tarmac. She didn't take up two-thirds of her seat.

"Nice, he's tall," she said. "I like that for you."

Before the bone had slid out of my throat I had become captivated, and of course I'd spent the subsequent days in time-consuming, tiring, ordinary oscillation between two ideas: (1) We are not coupled and never could be. (2) We will begin, together, a new life. "He has a Southern accent," I now reported, as if it were an endowed chair.

"Get an unlisted number," Mom said, and her eyes delicately rolled. She was recalling her own five-month love affair with a fertilizer entrepreneur from Georgia.

Mom looked straight ahead, the plane roared, and we rushed forward. An hour later, aloft, she was looking at me politely as the soft tones of some fictitious, fully imagined South Carolina continued to slide from my mouth. I talked on, my mint julep at my elbow, the veranda around me, catfish jumping.

I might want to go a little slowish, Mom said.

Of course, I said. There was something wrong with the guy. Had to be.

But I turned my head, to enjoy a private moment. I was feverish and exhausted. Ewing and I had stayed up all the night before. At dawn we'd gone downstairs and put on my new disk—Chet Baker, "She Was Too Good for Me"—and slowly danced in an ironic embrace in the kitchen, then carried our mugs into the yard while it was getting light and strolled around on the wet grass. Birds piping, sun rising. It had been a classic situation, almost too pleasant to bear, which had left me slightly sickened.

Mom was looking at me as if I were convalescent. In other circumstances, my mother had remarked that there is one way and one way only to find an acceptable man in America: watch the obits and rush over with a casserole. She buckled in, right before being told to, and we suddenly landed.

Vermont was having a heat wave. It was ninety degrees, bright and hazy, blue-gray mountains in the haze. My mother waved once, economically, from the door of the airplane, then descended and stepped neatly onto the tarmac and through the roar of noise and heat and blazing light with perfect equanimity, as if heading across the Aubusson toward the chaise.

Behind the wheel of Zachary's car was a woman—a small brown muscled arm leaning out the window, a pretty tuft of hair under the arm, and a line of white paint describing her hairline: Cynthia. Zack was smiling, watching us approach, standing beside the car holding her pinkie. Early in the morning, a week from today, Zachary and Cynthia were going to get in this car and set off toward California so they could begin, together, to live. "So great you're here," he said now, looking at me and Mom with apparently genuine pleasure.

We had been about two years late making our reservations, and couldn't stay in town at the inn. We rode for thirty miles, into town, once around the campus—past the arch, past the bandstand strung with flags, past the guys setting up 3,000 chairs on expanses of lawn under thick leafy trees—then fifteen miles out the other side of town. Cynthia drove, wisps of hair flipping out the window. Zack turned and talked into the back seat, moving rapidly from things of general interest to esoterica. He told us about San Francisco; jobs they might get; his band; Salsa, congas, timbales, vibes; Zouk Machine, M'bilia Bel, and Zaiko Langa Langa. Mom and I paid close attention, grappling with deeply unfamiliar information.

Zack said, "Dad wants to know how Cynthia and I and members of our 'cohort' are 'conceptualizing things these days.' I didn't know what to tell him. Basically, we're terrified."

They planned to drive west, through Albuquerque

and Needles and Barstow. I said, "Your trip sounds great. You might have to unroll your futons and settle in Santa Fe."

Zack said distractedly, yeah, they'd love that, if that day ever comes. "But, Gran, what's new with you?"

She waggled her fingers at him. Mom said, "My cohort is hobbling to the Safeway for a single chop."

Our motel was a combination motel and cocktail lounge, with the lounge easily asserting dominance over the modest rooms lined up alongside it. It was set back at the edge of a vast parking lot, in which were parked two enormous semis. Pine-covered mountains in the background—but somehow the parking lot and the trucks seemed to dwarf the mountains, rather than the other way around. Mom selected the room at the end of the row, off near the tall weeds, and went in fast, Zack following with her little bag.

When I got to my room, William was already in it, sitting on the edge of a bed. He had the curtains closed and he was sitting in air-conditioner wind and television light, watching the Bulls chip away at the Pistons. The fans were going insane, and Willie with them.

"If I exit, that'd enhance your ability to settle in," he said, and he stood up and smacked off the television. This reminded me that in old days he'd used to call me Special Handling.

He picked up my key and left, through a rectangle of white glare, and the room fell dark again. I got into bed, under the flowered, quilted bedspread. The sheets were a lovely, even, cool temperature, and the bedspread weighed about as much as a Honda hatchback, a very pleasant weight in the cold, humming room.

Years went by, and then William was back sitting on the other bed again, talking to me as I started to notice him and to know we were together far from home. I swam back, already sleepily chatting. We were in the dark, but not in New Jersey, I now understood, and not at night. It had to do with our son. Heavy curtains, Willie's warm voice full of color, his fingers stroking the end table's wood-grain laminate. My chest and arms and feet were nicely hot. I had a new lover, and I hadn't yet admitted it wasn't going to work out. Deeply comfortable and starting to feel obscurely in the wrong, I came to.

"The situation is nutty," he was saying.

"I need to get up," I said. The clock radio blinked: 6:16.

"Dad brought a woman," he said.

"What are you saying?"

"Pep is here. He just checked in. He brought a woman with him from Florida. They checked into one room. Now they're in it." He smiled and glared at me.

Had he known she was coming?

"Do I look like I knew she was coming? I didn't know she existed on this earth! He says I did, of course: 'Willie, I told you. You forgot.' "

"You didn't happen to bring any cream rinse, did you?"

"*Cream rinse?*" he said. "What do I look like? Yes. I also brought a manicurist."

The door knocked, William opened it, and Pep was standing out there in the fading light. He looked surprised. "Hello, darling," he said.

William gave Pep a powerful look: half-irritated, half-inconsolable. *"Step in,* Dad."

Pep was Mom's size, tiny; in the last few years, he had settled into being about half the size he used to be. Willie went over and took Pep by his elbow. Then they shuffled across the indoor-outdoor carpeting to my bed, William still holding the small bent arm. I had never before noticed how alike they looked; they were big and little, dancing an obscure dance. Behind them, through the open door, a man jumped and plummeted and water splashed up. The haze was blowing away; the mountains, still compact and small, were coming into view. I was thinking about sex with Ewing.

Weightlessly, Pep sat on my bed. "You're not under the weather, are you, darling?" he said. "It's time for the festivities. I want to introduce Lorraine. I brought her with me."

"So I heard." I smiled rather stupidly.

"So she heard," William said. "But, Dad, nobody heard until about ten minutes ago."

Lorraine was back in the room, Pep said to me, so he was going. I kept smiling.

"But why did you knock?" William asked. He followed Pep back toward the door. "What did you want? Was there something you wanted to tell us? Or tell Joey, actually, since this is her room?"

Cheerfully, Pep said, "To be frank, I knocked on the wrong door."

When I came out later, night was falling and the sky was deep gray shot with rose. Pep and Mom were standing on the far side of the lot, and from this distance, next to a mammoth rear tire of one of the trucks, they looked about a foot tall. They were talking intently like the old friends they were, with their heads close together in the dark pink glow.

This was the evening before graduation, on the grass with the other families—poems and songs, lights strung on wires, night coming on. Up on the bandstand far across the lawn, Zack was playing congas with his band. I missed Nora—she wouldn't arrive until the morning. Cynthia was in whiteface, one of the mimes. Mom and William and I were on a blanket with Lorraine, Pep's companion, drinking plastic glasses of wine and eating fried chicken out of white paper boxes. Pep had his camera, and he was rushing around making it flash in the dark. The light, the taste of the food, the voices of my family—meanwhile I was with Ewing, who had become inordinately brilliant and large; his hands on the wheel, his toes, the beautiful arch of his foot, his cock, his breath in my hair—real events paled.

Trucks: Lorraine said to my mother that the trucks in the motel parking lot were not comparable to what she and Pep had recently seen. They had been driving somewhere and had stopped in Reading, Pennsylvania, at a truck exhibition and the trucks had been outfitted in such various ways it was rather surprising.

Mom was interested. "What did they have, fuzzy leopard seats and little fancy kitchenettes?"

"Well, that's right. They had tiger fur. They had hot plates. They had built-in coffeemakers. They had

2 5 7

special radios. They had *beds*. They had everything you can imagine in your wildest dreams. Pep marveled at it."

"I like this!" Mom said.

"C.D. players playing Johnny Cash?" William said jovially. "Portable plaque detection kits? Tufted tweed ceilings? Quilted banquettes?"

"What are you doing?" I said to him.

"How did you happen to visit this truck demo in the first place?" he said.

"Oh, you know your father," Lorraine said.

"His long-standing interest in eighteen-wheelers?" William said, and laughed.

"Hey, Willie," I said.

He said, "Actually, I thought Dad stopped doing this long-distance stuff. I'm surprised he decided to drive the car all the way from Royal Palm Beach to Reading, Pennsylvania."

"Well, I drive," Lorraine said. "You know how your father doesn't care for being behind the wheel."

William set his chicken leg down and gazed at Lorraine, who didn't notice. Mom stopped eating and looked at William. William's head swung and he looked at me. In the forty-one years of his marriage to Lainie, Pep had never permitted her to drive him so far as down the street. If they traveled for eight hours, Pep drove for eight hours. Now, six years after Lainie's death, he was known as a man who didn't care for being behind the wheel. Not far away, Pep's flashbulb started going wild, sending out bursts of glare, and Cynthia danced by with the other mimes, her white face shining, her small arms thrusting. Her group was enacting—what?

At the end of the evening, Zack said he was getting a cold, and he and Cynthia left to go back to his house so he could eat vitamin C and barbecue thousands of pieces of broccoli and zucchini for a hundred friends. We all stood and watched them go. Walking away, Zack bent and kissed Cynthia's face, and when he turned to wave, his mouth and nose were white.

Much later, in the cinder-block hallway next to the canned-soda machine, I dialed Ewing and left a message on his machine. He had said to call, he'd be home. I had been hoping for phone sex.

Turned on Johnny Carson, where Ed McMahon was honking and fawning so persuasively, as if his excitement were genuinely irrepressible. A man wearing a beautiful hairdo and Italian clothes sang in bluish light, strings swelling behind him. "And you belong to me! I'm yours exclusive-lee!" he sang. His eyes fell closed, his head tipped back, the mike obscured his chin.

Back in the hall, I called Ewing. His machine was off and he didn't answer. I bought two cans of Classic Coke and went outside and down to the end and knocked on Mom's door, and we yelled back and forth for a while until she was sure it was me.

"What was that song?" I said, when she finally let me in.

" 'On the Wings of Love,' " she said, and tears came to her eyes. "Wait a minute." She was wearing pale-green satin pajamas with a designer's monogram on the pocket, and an angora beret against the air conditioner's chill. She went into the bathroom and immediately came out again and got back into bed and snapped open her Coke. "Oh don't you spit at me," she said.

"What's the matter?"

"Absolutely nothing," she said. "Weren't there so many bugs out there around the light?"

"I crushed them all while I was waiting to get in here."

Mom blew her nose. She said, "Okay. You tell me. How does a woman like this Lorraine manage to find a boyfriend? She's a nice person, I'm not saying that. But you just tell me how a woman like that goes *out there*, and somehow *looks around*, and just *hooks up with* one of these codgers! I really want to know and then I'll be quiet."

"First of all, Ma, I think she probably thinks differently than you do about what she wants in a relationship."

"And than *you do!*"

"No, my life is perfect. I know exactly what I'm doing and I'm doing everything perfectly," I said.

"I am going to learn from her example! When I get home, I am absolutely going to *extend myself* and look around."

"You do extend yourself—"

She cried, "And there's a *dearth!*"

We laughed a while and then I said, "But realistically, Ma, it's not as if you and somebody like Pep would ever end up getting together."

"Don't put him down," she said. "He has his attractions. He's never unkind."

"*Ma.*"

"Yeah, you're right," she said.

She turned and looked at the set, where David Let-

2 6 0

terman was making fun of his guest, an elderly keeper of parakeets. Then she ripped off her hat and threw it on the rug. She decided to throw her crumpled Kleenex down after it. When she spoke, her voice was husky and small. She said, "Wouldn't I just wish I could find a reasonably intelligent old gentleman."

All through the night, I could feel the music from the cocktail lounge. I hadn't reached Ewing, and I was nervous. I woke early—too early to make a phone call—and opened the curtains on brightness and visible heat. I thought I'd walk across the parking lot, out to the road, and down half a block to the diner, and sitting there drinking juice out of a plastic glass and reading the jukebox, I'd feel better—"less unsettled" or "more myself."

When I came out, it was already hot and the air was milky and glaring. William was standing next to the pool, stripes of aquamarine light on his face, looking toward my room.

I called, "You look like you're waiting for me, but how did you know I was up?"

"Not everything refers to you," he called back. "I could be poolside for myriad reasons." He strolled over, and we turned as one and set off toward the diner. "I've been out here since six," William said, "immersed in Americana. You would've loved it. Believe it or not, at six o'clock there were already people out, stuffing their wood-sides, or whatever you call those, full of cylindrical sport-sacks."

"Why are you up?"

There was a pause. "I feel lousy," he said.

"What's wrong?"

He said he didn't want Zack to go all the way to San Francisco, it made him feel we'd never see the kid again, and he'd been finding Zack inaccessible lately anyway, and thought Zack's remoteness had to do with the influence of his girlfriend, Cynthia, "whom I must say I don't join the dazzled multitudes in particularly cottoning to—brilliantly accomplished though she may be—and who, on the contrary, I think is quietly high-handed, rather dominating, defiant underneath the much-ballyhooed reticence, and *rather steely*."

I laughed. I said, "How about 'accomplished though she may be, black leotard though she may wear, French though she may speak'?" I hadn't heard him make one of these speeches in years, and I was suddenly so pleased to be here in this Vermont parking lot, listening.

Meanwhile, he looked furious. "You can't resist coming in from the outside, in lieu of engaging," he said.

"*I'm joking.*"

"I'm not in the mood."

"No, come on. I might even sort of agree with you."

"I'm sure you do," he said resentfully.

"But we don't really know Cynthia."

"We know Cynthia fine," he said.

"And we couldn't do anything anyway." I had time to think, If Ewing goes, he goes. I barely know the man. "What else is happening?"

William said, "What else. At the moment I'm having to add several unanticipated expenses to my already *mannered* financial situation. In the background is always the reality that I'd like to explore getting remarried to you. And Pep has arrived at a point where he's totally out to lunch."

He certainly did not want to remarry me, I said.

"I know what you mean," he said.

"You don't have any interest in remarrying me."

"I know," he said. "But actually, on balance, you may possibly be wrong. Anyway, Pep—"

"William," I said. *"You want to remarry me? Since when?"*

"We never talk about it and this is not the forum," he said unhappily.

"Willie, this is not serious. You're saying it because we're at the graduation now. It's not a real thing. Even while you're talking about it, you're annoyed with me."

"Your interpretation. I'm fine with you."

What I'd seen recently, looking back, and it'd truly taken me years to notice it—what I'd seen was that in our whole long interesting spirited marriage Willie and I had almost never shared one peaceful moment. I thought, well, I'll say this, and I did.

"What?" he said.

"Peace," I said. "Peaceful."

He stopped. He looked both bewildered and preoccupied; he stood still for a moment, a victim of a psychological ministroke. Then his energy sort of flowed back in. He said, "Believe me, I have no trouble grasping realities here. That doesn't mean they aren't deplorable. Let's can *this* now."

The diner was huge. We stopped in front of its bulk and stood on the macadam next to the steep steps. Occasionally a car zoomed by, blowing up dust: Vermont rush hour.

William said: "Pep is hanging out with an inappropriate woman, with whom, amiable and aquiescent though she undoubtedly is, he has nothing in common. This is a perfectly pleasant woman of no special intelligence, no special grace, and no dynamism. He just appears to have undergone some sort of bizarre geriatric metamorphosis from which I can only hope he *has to rebound*."

"I don't get it."

He looked at me.

He might not find me much help on this, I said.

"Why not?"

I said, "Gee. No woman in the world is good enough for these sterling guys."

"Uh-oh," he sang.

So I told him that Pep liked her, they seemed happy, and I didn't know what more we should want for him. I said I loved Pep but he wasn't the world's most dynamic person himself. I began enjoying the sensible tone of my remarks, so realistic and accepting and direct. I said, "Pep has been very lonely. And Lorraine is very nice to him. What she isn't, of course, is your mother."

"Oh good," William said. "Nice clarification of formerly abstruse issues."

"Well, what the hell do you want me to say? She's not Lainie and she's not beautiful and energetic and smart like Lainie, so *you're not comfortable:* that's what I *think*."

"Great," he said miserably. "I love it. Joey to the rescue, with some pronouncements with which, if I had a subway token, I could make my misguided way uptown." We climbed the steps. "You treat me like I'm just a windbag," he said. "You humor me. But really I'm lonely because I already miss my son." He looked relieved—we both knew he was right. He held the glass door for me, and we entered, past the cigarette machine, into swirling, blinding cold.

Three hours later, we were assembled at the graduation—expanses of lawn, hot wind blowing. We dragged our chairs back and lined them up in two small rows under a tree. William sat behind me, very close, set his hands on my shoulders. Zachary was leaving us, and now I saw it surprised me too that he hadn't already gone: just then, amazingly enough, in procession with the other graduates, he strolled by. He looked urbane, as he always did when nervous, and he was holding Cynthia's hand. She was bopping along beside him, wearing her whiteface with her cap and gown. She had to reach to tickle his closely shaven cheek.

"Rights, privileges, and honors thereunto . . . given unstintingly of themselves . . . commitment and vision." Back here under the trees, the voices of the speakers were small, like voices from a radio tuned low. Far away, we could see the striped awning shading the orchestra, tiny graduates mounting then descending the platform, and a skirmish between the people who were taking pictures and the people who wanted them down in front. There were some dogs, and kids running silently around. Nearby, three louts in bermuda shorts yelled at a friend, as his hand reached for his diploma. "*Just say no!*" they bellowed, and blindly whistled and stamped. William whispered, "Dad! We're here now!

Stop with the arranging! You're not gonna get stranded in Vermont!" Nora leaned against me. Mom, on the other side, held my hand.

After a long time in the heat and emotion, at last the band played again, and the graduates stood, and we stood to watch them go. Since we couldn't reverse time and go back, I wanted us all to keep standing here for a long time: just not go forward. In a few moments, in fact, our family would walk to Zack's house to eat lunch, and Zack would be staggering around happy and sad and exhausted, still sick from charcoal-grill fumes and with his hands hurting from playing congas all night. Zack would fold Cynthia in his arms; he'd tell William, "Dad, I think Grandpa feels about Lorraine the way Billy Joel feels about Christie Brinkley." Pep would worry about his broken camera case, and William would cry, "Dad, it's just the case! It's not a working part in the innards of the camera!" Nora would give Zack a graduation present: his own stuffed bison from babyhood, which he had thrown away four years ago and which she had saved from the trash. Zack would greet the bison with real cries of joy.

Mom would sit with Lorraine and talk about categories of airplanes and tell her which ones were the safest. Pep would snap Zack's picture, the same pose five times. I'd try Ewing again, five times, and by the time he wasn't there five times I'd begin to get the idea.

On the wall of Zack's room would be a big map of the United States with the southern route outlined. The room would be full of dust and suitcases and stereo speakers and boxes, and William and I would find a spot to stand and we'd stand there together and look at the map. We would not be talking. We would be looking. We would be imagining the two of them crossing the country, tiny figures in a tiny car, drinking Gatorade, passing into California, making a right turn and heading north again, starting up the coast: first time they will have driven north since dropping us off at the airport today.

15. My Companions All My Life

W here have you been all this long night?"
"In what sense?" I said.

"Where'd you sleep!" This was Mom, from her hospital bed, in the remains of a morphine haze. She had just had a hysterectomy and been saved from death by cancer. I'd been staying all week in a hotel across the street: Mom had forgotten. But in deeper sleep than this, she'd remember she's my mother.

Mom's twenty-two sampled nodes were clear, her tumor had been demure and well-behaved—instead of wasting horror she was to have tiresome convalescence. I wanted her now to feel safe, and happy; maybe I could make it happen; here in the hospital, I thought I might be getting a last chance. But I'd been doing something quite insupportable and strange: helping her recover by laughing at her.

I laughed. "Ma, the night's not over! Last night is still going on." Actually, I'd spent it with Willie—a lost night, eventful and long. As it was ending, I was living in a floating city, far out on a glassy sea; all these years after childhood, my mother might still be able to see the events of the night and the dreams in my head.

Every morning at 5:30 when I crossed the street,

the air was already hot and thick, and cars were rushing through Boston with their headlights on, beaming light out into the blackness. I'd lean near my mother's tiny face to hear her. She'd glance around, jiggling her nasal tube. She'd whisper: "Is it me or is it the personnel?"

Here was today's report: the nurses are callous, she calls and nobody comes, that's why she needs me here. They never come! They don't turn her, she'll get pneumonia! Her throat hurts, the nurse said she'd bring a spray to fix it, but of course she never deigned to keep her promise. Cohen was in for ten seconds, that little peanut resident: another wise guy. "Did you see any doctors?" she asked.

Her surgeon would make rounds in half an hour, I told her. She shook her head briskly, and her haircut rippled. "*Other* doctors!"

I looked at her, already insistently chuckling.

"*For you.*"

"Ma, I don't want more doctors. I've got too many doctors already."

I didn't want to tell her Ewing had probably decided—not to leave, he was cagier than that; to fade out. Anyway, Ewing was too charming for Mom. *And an Episcopalian.* And what's with the constant trips to St. John the Divine? she liked to cry. And what's with him and the dog? What's the brouhaha about a pet? Meanwhile, here in the hospital elevator at six o'clock in the morning were packs of harried Jewish interns twenty years my junior—Mom pretended to imagine I'd select a last husband from among them.

I thought about it. I'd remove the boy's stethoscope, his shirt and tie; kiss his narrow chest, his desperate face, his mayonnaisey lips; then march him before the rabbi and legalize our love. Ewing would like this fantasy. If I remembered to tell him, he'd say, "Come here, little sister. Show me things I didn't learn in medical school."

Mom had some potential cardiac problem so she had spent the first day in Intensive Care. When I first visited her there, her pain was so vivid you could almost see it. Specks of brilliance floated in the air, blocking my vision. Her teeth were gone, in a plastic box, and her eyes were shut and she was weeping. Such a glamorous, buoyant little woman only a moment ago! I sat down fast to avoid fainting, and took her hand.

Stuck on her thumb was a rubber cup, measuring the oxygen in her blood. "Don't touch that," she said with her eyes closed.

My mother's hand was surprising—so cold. Her eyes opened and tried to see me. "What am I going to do?" she said—directly to me, as if I could really answer.

They couldn't get her comfortable and would have to wake a doc to prescribe more morphine; nobody was crazy about the idea of waking a doc. Across Mom's body, the nurse and I looked at each other hard. "I can give her a little more," she murmured. Mom said: "Stop discussing me."

Nurses were running back and forth, talking about men, trying on each other's sunglasses, pushing people around and keeping them alive. Across from Mom was Donald, a strong young-looking man steadily yelling for a blanket. His face was too white, as if the blood had run out of it; his pillow was splotched with watery stains. He had flown off his skateboard, straight up in sunny air, and bashed his skull on the pavement. He rolled his big injured head. "I don't want people looking at my privates!"

Nobody's interested, a nurse said pleasantly.

Other nurses: "Don, we don't care about seeing what you've got!"

I muttered, to cheer myself up, "I do. *I* want to see your privates, Donald." I could feel my face looking weirdly amiable, stiffening.

Donald passed out. A nurse ran over and shook his shoulder. She called his name until his eyes fell open and he smiled a baby's smile.

Mom woke too and looked at me.

"Take a rest," I said.

She said, "What about your dinner?"

"I'll eat."

"How will you get time, if you spend all your time in this crummy place?"

"I'll have time."

"You should get a nice dinner," she said miserably.

The nurse sent me away. I slipped my fingers out of Mom's grip and walked out into night air cooling like soup.

In the morning darkness, to cross the street I dressed up: expensive trousers and a linen jacket. I wanted my mother to be impressed.

Donald was gone. I missed him. While she slept, Mom's tears slipped out of her eyes. She was holding a piece of cotton tight in one hand, close to her chest.

When she woke, she looked amazed. She said, "I was waiting for you. I was hoping you'd come."

I was staying in the hotel instead of in her house in Union Square so that I could come in moments. We were trying to avoid Mom's having to wait and hope. "I'm here all the time," I said.

"Everything is filthy and ugly! They have to wash me! I can't keep myself clean!"

"Well, they can—"

"I'm afraid I'm going to die if you leave me here alone."

"I'm not leaving, Ma. I'm sitting here."

She said reasonably, "But you'll leave sometime."

Mom got moved, to a private room high above Boston, and her condition wildly improved. Many bouquets lined up on the windowsill—I rushed over and changed the water and threw out the dead petals and rearranged the whole display. I phoned the many friends and thanked them; I said Mom couldn't talk, which they found striking.

Then I began: Ma, when you get out you *have to* start exercising! You *have to* have a regular walking program, and you cannot allow yourself to skip one day, you *cannot flag!* and so on.

She said, "Look! the i.v. runs into this wrist, but, see, the pole is on the wrong side. I need it changed— see, that's the kind of person I am."

I got up and moved the pole around the bed, sat down and again took up my mother's hand.

"Pieces of my lip are coming off! The skin is peeling!"

"Nina will give you some Vaseline."

"I doubt it," Mom said.

"I'll ask her."

"That Nina's not really nice. She's pretty but very withholding."

I said, "She's not likely to withhold the Vaseline," and I laughed. Mom's face reddened and she turned away. After a while she said, "I did not have the concept of the nursing care here. I expected it to be more sympathetic and . . . fulsome."

She was having a good day. She said, "When I came for tests, on the other floor, I was the most popular one."

I smiled.

"Stop it. I mean I could be nice then. I wasn't *so sick*."

Mom had had two older sisters, who had raised her after their mother died; she had already spent most of her life as the most popular one. All her family dead now, and the baby darling left behind. Crazily, I grinned on.

After a long silence, she said, "I need to ask you, because you are the only one who will answer: is there something they didn't tell me?"

"Nope!" I said affably, "absolutely not," feeling as if I were lying.

The nurses were young and swift, wearing street clothes, sweats and hightops—they looked like athletes whose team color was white. Stepping out of the elevator, I could already hear them cheering *That's good, you're doin' good! you're doin' fine!*

They had got Mom into her gray cashmere sweat suit and sitting in her chair. Draped about her neck was a silk scarf she had dyed and overpainted—sky blue strewn with lilac clouds.

"You walked to your chair! That's great!"

"I hate that Nina."

"Did she walk you?"

"Some deal," Mom said. "Now I have to be worried for the rest of my life if something else should come up."

What an opportunity for levity. "Ma, that's the nature of life in our world! We're all worrying, all our lives, that something might come up!" I was high on caffeine, excessively jolly and fierce.

Nina, the nurse, walked in and reached for Mom: "Ready to get back?"

"Don't start pulling me!"

Nina crossed her arms and sneaked a look at her watch. Mom struggled to stand, rose two inches, and sat down. She cried, "I can't do this all by myself!"

Nina, dragging Mom across the room—chiffon scarf floating: "You could have your painkiller now."

"It makes me too groggy! It would make it worse!"

Silence. Mom gaining on the bed.

"The morphine makes it worse!"

Nina, almost inaudibly: "I think it makes it better."

"I think it makes it worse!"

Nina dropped a thermal blanket over Mom's legs, then left the room fast. I was smiling—pained and all smiles. Mom said, "If this is so funny, you should leave."

"*Oh ma, it's not funny.*"

"You're not a help to me. Either you're sullen or

you make fun. You just wiseass all around, at the expense of an old woman who is very sick."

I said, "I'm not laughing at you." If true, what was I doing?

She looked ready to stamp her foot, though she was lying on her back perfectly still. She said, "You do not understand what it is to be old."

Well, that was true.

"You don't even try!"

I said, "Look, I'm here to help you. Don't start bashing me."

"Do you think it's bashing somebody to be laughed at all the time!"

"Well, I'm sorry if I've been laughing—"

She began to weep, hoarse loud sobs. She cried, "What do you *want*? Do you want your childhood to have been different? Then you're a *baby*. It's too late for that! Do you want me to not have been such a *crummy mother to you*? I can't do that now!"

She cried, "What did I do to you that you're so impatient? So I'm an imperfect person! I'm an old woman. And I'm all alone and you are *an ungrateful child*."

That was precisely what I was beginning to feel like—a unbalanced and ungrateful forty-five-year-old child. "This is so sad," I said. "I know you feel terrible. I'm trying to—"

"You—sorry-for-yourself person!"

"*Hey look, lady*. I'm doing my best here. You're making it tough."

"You look down on everybody!"

"Nice," I said. I stood up.

"You think I didn't love you. I *did* love you! You think I was a mean mother and you harbor your complaints like a . . . squirrel! I don't know what you think I did to you! I didn't kick you, I didn't steal your cookies! What is it, because I went to my studio and didn't stay tied to a house sewing bows on your blouse? I had you and your sister around my neck! Your father was *an absent man. And then he just died.* I'm an old person! I did my best! When do I get out on parole, Joey, in the martyred daughter's eyes? What kind of a doddering husk will the old villain be, when the forgiveness finally comes?"

"I'll be back in a while." I started to walk out, backward.

"All you want to do is get away!"

"I'll just be back."

"I have to pretend," she said. "If I tell you how bad I feel, you'll go away."

"Mom. That's certainly not true."

She said, "There's *something* very true about it!"

She was right—there was something. I reached to touch her crumpled stylish hair. She swatted at my hand. I noticed how tiny she was: I could easily lift her and drop her onto the linoleum.

"I want you to go out of my room."

I looked at the door, surprised—I was halfway there.

She swabbed at her eyes. "Call the nurse," she said. "Send in that little Nancy, the good one."

In the smoking lounge was Rae, her hair scrambled, plumes of white smoke rising around her. Rae slept here nightly on a cot on the floor, next to her own mother's bed. Her mother was ninety; Rae was a fairly elderly woman herself, a remarkably pretty one, her mother's only child.

She sucked in smoke like air and smiled with her saint's eyes. "How's Mother, dear?"

"Making a tremendous effort," I said, impersonating a daughter as stalwart and lovely as Rae.

"I'm keeping my eye on that lady. She's very, very sweet."

"Thank you."

The lounge was full of the cold hazy residue of years of chain-smoking visitors; the slats of the blinds were edged in black; the copies of *Woman's Day* and *Sports Illustrated* had been thumbed until their pages were fuzzy. "You look tired," I said.

Rae said, "My mother loves me. She wants to talk to me all night. I say, 'I love you too, Mother. But I'm going to sleep now.' She says, 'That's good, dear,' but she forgets to stay quiet."

I thought of walking across the room through the cold air and laying my head in Rae's lap. I looked over. She said, "I know. It's your only mother."

Later Nina came and tapped my shoulder. Mom had had painkiller and wanted me back. "She should've had morphine earlier in life," I said, and Nina grinned—I had betrayed my mother.

She was floating, awake enough to say she was sorry, she had just felt so bad.

"It's okay."

"But I *feel very sorry!*"

"I know. It's okay."

We sat.

She said dreamily, "I'm thinking about a shrimp

scampi while I'm falling asleep." After a while, eyes closed, chuckling: "I didn't forget 'scampi' is redundant. I'm not that far gone."

Outside, it was hot, a humming September summer night. I crossed the street, rose fast in the elevator, stood in the middle of my room on deep, glimmering shag, looked toward the windows. The city of Boston stretched away, glowing blue and full of lights. I thought, she's dying, and I wondered how I could possibly live without her. I imagined calling Ewing, telling him, "My old friend and antagonist is dead."

I dialed him at home and got no answer. In San Francisco, Zack and the band would be setting up. At school, Nora would be asleep or out for the evening. My sister and Tom went to bed early—she would come from Vermont soon enough, next week, to take care of Mom. Deenie and Michael and Annie were all away. Down in New Jersey, Willie picked up the phone on the first ring. He said promptly, "I have to go to Boston anyway. I can do it tomorrow."

"That's crazy," I said, and he laughed.

A storm was going to pass through fast. High up were stationary clouds with moonlight shining on them, and, much lower, sheets of lacy gray rushing past. I wanted to go out and see the complicated sky reflected in the Prudential Building, the mist flying across its face. But, dressed, I grew afraid to walk out into the night city.

Instead I walked back and forth on a diagonal across

my room, waiting for morning so I could go back and keep my mother company and try to do a better job of protecting her from terrors. I got sleepy, turned off the lamps, walked until I walked into the wall. My father's death seemed to be following us now, a constant shadow—some familiar mystery returning, about where he had gone. It had been nothing like this—suddenly he had been disappeared, leaving behind his car, his face in some photographs, his socks in the drawer. Now I recalled I had imagined that the money he left came directly out of his wallet.

Early, just before the sun came up, I sat at the window watching Boston fade back in. To the east behind the buildings, gold light started to blaze, and my spirits rose with the light: I was counting the money I would get when she died.

I saw my new beach house with its sky-colored ceiling, my new BMW convertible, myself strolling on the pine needles of my new wooded acreage, myself mailing an enormous check to provide thousands of sandwiches and cartons of milk and bananas and pears for homeless people for years to come. Myself absorbing the cost of a dialysis machine or CAT scan for this very hospital, pointing to a burnished plaque bearing my little lost mother's name. I was getting weirdly cheerful, with utterly false but convincing cheer. I saw myself at the funeral—pale, saddened forever, rich, finally free.

I pressed my face to the glass and looked straight down. Fifteen floors below, the flowers in the planters looked tropical in the strong new light. I had to get out.

Outside, boys were still walking in groups, packing

nine-irons, but they didn't mug me, just strolled on home. I went into the park and sat on a bench under the low sky that presses down above the guilty. At last I lay on the bench, and fell asleep. Slept on the bench until the commuters started.

The phone was blinking. Ewing had finally left a message, that he was driving south. In Charleston, his hometown, people were waiting for Hurricane Hugo, afraid the landfall would came on the high tide. He would meet his Aunt Jane, and when it was over take her home again—

"Did he leave a number?"

The desk clerk said, "It also says: 'I ate hominy at a truck stop called Mama's.' "

I crossed the street, got my pass, rode up.

Every day contained more hours than the one before. After the long afternoon, Rae and I descended. A sign in the elevator said: "Hospital staff are reminded that patient information should not be discussed in public areas." The hospital staff didn't look old enough to know the names of the conditions they were forbidden to mention in our hearing. I said this to Rae, but she was intent on preparing to debark, and ignored me.

The doors opened, and William was standing there.

When he saw Rae, he cast her a fervent smile. She patted me, then pepped off down the hall.

"Speak to me," he said.

"I guess she's okay."

"You're not okay."

"I'm fine. She goes home tomorrow. But she's still confused, and she's very scared, and I think—"

"You look very—"

"—maybe she could stay another day, but she wants—"

"You look rather like a puppy who's been—"

"Willie!" I cried. "I'm not the patient!"

He lunged and folded me in his arms. He pressed my head down so it lay on his Italian raw-silk shoulder, and tenderly held it there. William had never liked Mom, nor she him. After resenting him for twenty years, she had begun to modify her opinion when Ewing came along. Retroactively, she claimed to admire William. I'd said, "Ma, he's been Jewish the whole time and never kept a dog. How come you've changed your mind?" She had turned from the sink and thrown the dish towel into the garbage, saying, "Poo! Get off my case!"

My neck ached, bent like this. I struggled out of William's consoling grip, hurting his feelings.

I wanted to eat at McDonald's, where I had eaten six nights running and was known as a regular. Willie went crazy with alarm. He led me four blocks to a restaurant, to another planet, by the elbow.

It was a series of low-ceilinged rooms attached to a bar, art gallery, and greenhouse. At every table people were ordering raw fish and salads of flower petals; sipping wines made at minuscule California vineyards; selecting goat cheeses from a bed of leaves, pointing with marvelous fluency at the little lumps rolled in ashes. I was disoriented. My eyes and knees and back hurt. I felt as if I'd been crossing borders and time zones, finally to arrive at this table where across from me a man, brother and stranger, was looking at the bottom of his glazed pottery plate as if it were a Vermeer.

At the next table three extremely white men removed their jackets and discussed how to microwave a pizza slice. One of them had been to a club in New York City where the two genders had shared a rest room! A girl had entered, wearing essentially nothing. "She did her business," he said, "I did mine." His friends grinned—broad, uneasy grins.

The waitress was slim, with high breasts under a butcher's apron, seed pearls hanging in every one of her many yellow braids like beads of sweat. She leaned to pour Willie's taste of wine, her head faintly clicking. He thrust his nose into the glass. The waitress held the bottle to her lovely chest and looked off in a dream, time stood still, Willie sipped and finally nodded, and she came alive and poured some Spottswood cabernet onto his hand. He looked at it. He said, "This ain't too auspicious."

"I'm sorry, sir."

"That's perfectly all right," he said, flashing white teeth as she mopped at him. At the next table, one of the men winked at me. I thought about Donald, his head leaking blood. I thought about Mom saying, You don't know what it is to be old. I started to cry.

"*Oh Joey.*" Willie looked quietly thrilled. He rushed around the table and embraced my shoulders.

"It's okay," I said.

"You're understandably very agitated!"

I blew my nose on my napkin. I said I hadn't realized how hard it would be, I'd been alone here too long, and my mother was unlike herself; she was so pained, so afraid she was about to die, and I was starting to be almost afraid she was right. She was diminished, poignant, heartbreaking. "And also frankly she's impossible, and I'm going nuts."

"You're not by any means alone, Joey. This dinner, for example, is not a solitary activity."

"And I hate her!" I said. Better than anybody except Mom, Willie brought out the child in me.

"You don't hate her."

"I hate that person in the hospital bed."

"No no."

"I almost do," I said stubbornly.

"There's a sense in which you resent your mother, but you don't hate your mother," he said. "Don't make this an addendum to the list of self-flagellations." He was leaning over me, starting to kiss at the top of my head.

"It's not Mom. That's not Mom," I said, sniffing. "And, Willie, I don't think I'm helping."

"You're doing fine. You're acquitting yourself in stellar fashion."

I said, "The first day, I was already acting like a hardbitten i.c.u. nurse—you know, fleeing into vulgarity to escape the grim awareness of death? I was in there spontaneously offering to fuck a guy who got creamed falling off his skateboard."

Up close, he looked offended. He leaned, too close for us to see each other, trying to smile in my face. His tie grazed my cheek, smooth silk, creamy yellow.

I pushed at the tie. I said, "Thank you but will you please sit down!"

After dinner, we drank obscure grappas as the restaurant emptied. On their way out, the three men passed our table. One of them, the man who had bravely urinated with an unknown woman in the room, squeezed my shoulder. He said, "Hang in." I immediately imagined going home with him in a cozy sedan, to a house with cans of soup in the cabinets and a quilted spread on the bed.

Walking back, I realized the most disorienting thing about the week and I told him: that every time I came into her room, I was astonished to see Mom alive. As if, back at the hotel, I always assumed I was in town for the funeral.

Why was I in the hotel anyway? he asked. Instead of my mother's house? Until the surgery, she had stayed out at the Cape. She had said the Boston house was still closed up—sheets over the furniture, the rugs rolled up, or something. Mom had reserved my hotel room and put her own credit card on it. Finally I said, "So I can be available every fucking moment," and then felt ashamed. And we continued walking slowly through the steamy dangerous-looking night.

In Mom's room, the television was on and she was dreaming. She opened her eyes. "Did they let you in so late?"

"I sneak, through the emergency room."

She looked proud.

"Willie's here. Should he come in for a minute?"

"Not right now," Mom said.

"He could just say hello."

"Not now."

"He has to go back tonight."

Mom stared at the television: people boarding up houses and gas stations and grocery stores, high waves crashing.

"He came pretty far," I said.

"Well, he *came* to see *you*," she said, quite correctly. "Isn't that accurate?"

"She says no, she's too exhausted."

"I'm not suggesting a panel discussion," he said. "How about a two-minute cameo?"

"She can't."

"If she can't, she can't." He colored slightly.

"Don't put me in the middle."

Willie pressed me to his warm shirtfront. *"You're not in the middle, you're not in the middle,"* he intoned. So I had another thing to thank him for before we said good-bye.

I tiptoed in and kissed her forehead. A doctor came in and stood at the side of the bed. "How things going?" he said.

Mom looked at him without moving her head. She said, "Things hurt."

"Uh huh."

She said, "Things are lousy beyond description."

He said, "You kind of have to keep a Talmudic balance. Enough morphine to kill the pain but not enough to knock you for a loop."

"You think I'm not knocked for a loop?" she inquired pleasantly.

Back in the hotel, I tried to call Ewing at Aunt Jane's, but the lines were down.

I lay on the bed and turned on the sex movie. If I watched for more than five minutes, it would automatically register on my bill, I hoped not with a triple X. The movie was softcore and dated: a woman knelt and made as if to suck the front of a man's bell-bottoms. The curtains were open and mauve light was pouring up into the room from the city spread out below. I lay there watching, all the while imagining the hotel lobby, the Charles, the swan boats, the uneven brick sidewalks of Cambridge, the bright streets and squares, my mother across the way in her bed breathing quietly in half-light, her private duty nurse, if she'd had one, knitting under the lamp. The fictitious nurse in the early morning going home to her little apartment, starting to cook some breakfast, her thoughts turning to the edge of the city, the suburbs with their stretches of lawn where she planned on taking her grandchildren to live, Massachusetts fanning out and beginning to become rolling, then hilly, then mountainous, and stopping short as the view was taken over by New Hampshire and Vermont.

On the screen in misty vivid colors, the locale shifted from a strobe-lit bar to a bed with black sheets, where two people were doing some simulated fucking. She had blond cornsilk hair, two white sections on her body describing her bikini. He had a remarkably compact body surmounted by a large head, with gigantic sideburns, and a peace-sign necklace which bobbed against his chest. They pumped on, screaming about their transported state.

I lifted my nightdress, up to my chin. I scrubbed at myself without much hope. I was upset—even just a few years ago, I thought, even a film like this could've aroused me. He flipped her onto the other end of the bed and jumped on again, midstroke; she cried out rhythmically, as if hooked to a metronome. My hands fell still. I had utterly forgotten Chomper, my childhood dog! Now I remembered him: eager, matted, steamy, given to doing things, like these two people, suddenly: suddenly licking himself, suddenly plopping down and falling asleep.

At last I got up, dressed, and went down to the lobby, where freezing air was blowing as if through a giant corridor. The place had a feeling of being hushed, although swelling from the speakers was an instrumental version of "Stone Soul Picnic"—like the sex movie, the lobby seemed a sort of homage to aesthetic landmarks of the sixties.

Alone in the bar, in almost total blackness, were the bartender and a Japanese man wearing an expensive suit. I climbed onto the next barstool. He ordered more scotch. William came out of the men's room.

"What are you still doing here!"

While pulling up a stool, he palmed the back of my neck with a hot hand. "Sticking around a bit," he said. "I wasn't getting closure. Have you met Mr. Tahashi?"

The man turned and handed me his card, which was so impressively complex that I understood he was high up in the corporation without getting any sense of his line of work. He stared at me a while, with the disappointment of not receiving my card in return. Intelligence and tenacity shone in his eyes. Finally he said, "Your husband has been speaking with me. I told him the best way is to take care of the most helpless things first: First the plants. Then the animals. Then the children. Then . . . the wife!" He was smiling. Into my other ear, Willie whispered, "Your mother would take him down with one punch."

The bartender was standing before me. I hadn't had a cocktail in years, I told him, and, silently, economically, he feigned amazed interest. Much later, my tropical drink came. Mr. Tahashi picked up a miniature paper parasol and waved it around. He said, "This may be a surprise: this is a Taiwanese product!" Willie set his hand at the back of my waist as if to guide me across a complicated intersection.

Mr. Tahashi said that when he had first arrived in Boston he had fallen clinically depressed.

"Many do," Willie said genially.

"Stop it," I said to him, and we both turned to listen.

His wife had given up and returned to Tokyo. Mr. Tahashi had an acquaintance at the Mass Mental, and at last he had become part of a clinical trial of a new antidepressant: fewer side effects, he said almost regretfully; the way he said it, it sounded like some side effects would've made good companions. It had been years of recovery. He was not sure of recovery yet. Intently, he smiled. I imagined Mr. Tahashi left behind in a Union Park house, down the square from Mom, with some small jade trees, perhaps a little dog — for company, only the most helpless remained. "It's a tough story," Willie said. He was quite sincere. I was so sorry for Mr. Tahashi and so grateful for Willie's being here I could hardly speak. He tossed back his martini and the bartender approached like a shoplifter.

Above us was a ceiling of upside-down glasses, ahead were bottles massed against a mirror speckled with metallic colors, in the mirror were the three customers side by side. Hours went by. More drinks came. I felt enormously cheered. I sat between Mr. Tahashi and Willie, seeing them flanking me behind the swimming copper flecks, feeling them beside me like my companions all my life, hearing the three of us speaking as one.

I woke with a hangover. Willie had dressed in early-morning gloom. I remembered his soft footfalls, the door clicking shut. When I pulled the dark curtains, it was noon of a glaring bright day. Charleston had been blasted. On the front page was a photograph of pleasure boats piled up like peanuts in a bowl.

I was across the street, in Mom's room, and full of coffee before I recalled meeting Mr. Tahashi, and Mr. Tahashi vividly parting with us under an awning in the middle of the night, shaking my hand until my drunken arm flapped.

Mom said, "See, whatever his faults, and flawless he's not, William Green is terrific in a crisis."

I said, "As he would say, he acquitted himself in stellar fashion." He had touched my skin lightly and mindfully, as if we were sober and bent on orchestrating our ascent. Then our shared mood had deepened until we were drenched and thudding like the sex actors, before we suddenly dropped unconscious like Chomper, our fingers entwined. I felt genuinely rested by his visit—hung over, certainly sad and uncertain, but *emptied*. And at the same time I almost might've imagined it: it had been the most silent evening Willie and I had ever spent.

Mom said cheerily, "Takahashi sounds like a superannuated yuppie."

I turned her way, delighted at her tone; through hung-over ears, I heard her changing her tune. My mother's mood was picking up. Soon enough we might be walking together to the closet, taking out her Ungaro suit, then getting a pass and dancing out to the Ritz Carlton Grill. She glanced all around, looking for an object for witticisms. She was pale and calm as a little angel. She said sweetly, "Yuppies don't get anything done. They can do little things, but nothing big. That's why I brag I do not have any yuppie daughters."

I laughed. Laughing made my head hum.

Mom laughed too—a silvery laugh, her first in months. She said, "You're a wonderful girl. You're my favorite girl. You always have been. Thank you so much for coming to see me!" and her face grew radiant, with real gratitude.

I was so happy to see my mother feeling better that I almost felt physically well myself. At the same moment I remembered there had been another reconciliation: the three of us under the hotel awning in the shining city night, and now I recalled that Tahashi and Willie and I had embraced. Spontaneously, we'd rushed at each other like triplets separated at birth—two big triplets, one small one, uniformly bowled over by re-union feeling. We'd stood back to regard one another a last time. Mr. Tahashi had suddenly said, "And the funny thing is: I still love my old wife!"

I had looked at Willie, who didn't return my gaze. Willie had said, "Don't give it a thought, man. I still love mine."

My mother was an orphan. Late in the day, that's what she told me: although she had a father, and a mother for eight years, she feels it inside her, orphan-ness. If you asked, the information would fly out of her mouth, that's how close to the surface her alone-ness lives.

When her own mother died, my mother told me, she died too. Her life ended. She was eight and her mother was gone and her life never started again. For months she walked through the house looking in the corners and behind the doors, like a cat whose kittens have been taken. She pulled her own hair, to punish herself for losing track of her mother. She sat in the sun and smelled her own arm, sniffing for her mother. She went to school early, to steal the pencils of other girls; and to draw private pictures of her mother, wear-ing rubies in her hair and a velvet cloak. She stood in the road to be the first to see her mother coming home.

When her ninth birthday arrived, her sisters picked some peaches and baked a cake, and my mother would not share it. Cut your cake, her father said. But she lifted the whole cake on its china plate and carried it to her room and they let her go. She shut the door. For two days she ate only peach cake, sitting on the rug, feeding bites of it to her mother, chewing and swallowing the bites for her mother because her mother, dead, could no longer eat.

After high school when she suddenly left home to become a painter, her life still did not begin. Even years later when my father came and took her out of Greenwich Village, and married her and made her rich, her life did not begin. "It's a common story, isn't it?" my mother said. "But not the part about the cake."

"No," I said. "It's not common."

At the end of that summer of her ninth birthday, 1928, she was sent away from her little Pennsylvania town to Philadelphia, to her mother's sister, an aunt she had never met. In Philadelphia, she could barely eat; she removed bits of food from her mouth and dropped them out the window. She lived there in the city a year and she doesn't know why.

Once each season, her sisters came, bringing ribbons or a sweater or sugar lumps wrapped in paper. They had gotten jobs as teachers and they still lived at home; her father lived on, too, and why was she sent? "Maybe to become more Jewish," she said now, as if, even this late, the explanation might appear. But it didn't make sense: her family went to *shul* only on High Holy Days, and in other respects lived like everybody else.

"Maybe to be with a woman. Maybe to be with Herschel." Here behind the house was a little walled garden, and here was her cousin Herschel making her roll with him in the spring mud. She imagined killing Herschel, burying him in the garden, raking the leaves over—sending him to visit her mother and bring back news. In the night, she stood in the hall and listened.

At home at night, before her mother had gone, she had been able to hear all the family breathing in their beds.

She began to think: Aunt Rhoda looks familiar! In Philadelphia, after half a year in this narrow house on a short narrow street, my mother started to feel two things: Her Aunt Rhoda *was* her mother, returned in secret, incompletely disguised. And Aunt Rhoda was just about to be leaving.

She was just on the point of setting out on a trip that would continue forever. My mother imagined her aunt, upstairs in the evening after a supper of potato and cold soup, laying her hat into an oval box, folding her black Yom Kippur dress, lost in quiet concentration, rehearsing, quietly packing and repacking her bags. Aunt Rhoda walking out in the night, letting the door fall shut, carrying her two bags to a waiting cab. In the early mornings when the milk wagon bumped along the cobblestones, my mother thought it was the carriage arriving to carry her aunt away.

All afternoon she talked to me, in and out of sleep. She said, "I am in this private room because your father married me and gave me the money."

I imagined the hospital bed with my mother not in it, and finally thought a simple thing: I still have my mother with me.

Evening arrived and we never turned on the lights; night fell, and my mother talked on, in the expensive, darkening room. "And then when you came," she said, "another life started."

———

The doctor came in, stood at her bed in the dark, and looked at me and said, "How 'bout we take Mother home tomorrow?"

She cast me a brief but searching look: *is this guy nuts?* "You gotta be nuts," she said. "But okay."

"You've got the gear for it," he said. He moved to pat her hand. Mom snatched it away and stuck it under the blanket.

After he left, I said, "He seems smart."

"Oh he's *bright*," Mom said. *"Infallible* I doubt."

In the hotel in the morning, I folded my clothes, gathered the miniature bottles of shampoo and the soaps in boxes. I turned on the radio and it started blasting out a soaring love duet depicting the ineluctable femaleness of woman meeting the inevitable manliness of man on a mountaintop of emotion. I turned it loud. Jovially I thought, It's an American right, to listen to your radio as loud as you want in your own hotel room!

I remembered the sound of radio music, in bright air, in California, decades ago. As I was zipping my suitcase now, what fell into my head was a picture of my young mother, with her hair rolled, smoking. It was my earliest memory of her; of being with her. We were outside—glazed blue above us, diamond cinders under our feet. She wore stockings; she was seated; I stood near her silken leg. There had been other times I was so in love with her I could hardly remember the world outside.

Now my mother was just about to amaze us: to return to her life. My head was filled with stories from many years past, and we were just about to be released from a hospital room and a hotel room, respectively, and meanwhile my rented radio was blaring nice loud American rock-and-roll love songs, about me and my mom.

16. After Ewing

For a while after Ewing left, I couldn't hear what anybody was saying. I went around town interviewing men: their family dinners past and now. I'm the responsible party, they said, to a man. My life is not my own.

Annie wanted to cheer me up. She had gone to high school with a man who had become a movie star, and she got him to say he'd talk to me about dinner.

Outside his hotel, fall was well along, and yellow was overtaking the green of Central Park. He looked surprisingly natural—flushed and dreamy—while he talked about some foods served by his mother around 1958. Then he wanted to know if I was always this rigid and tense. "You gotta be an amazing stiff around the house," he said. He yawned and his eyes got watery. He stared out his hotel room window, over the tops of the yellowing trees. Slowly, reflectively, he slipped off his lizard shoes. "Relax, the important little machine is still running," he said. "It's got a bunch of shit on it you'll twist into fascinating data. So what else are you dying to know?"

I said: "Just don't tell me anything further about *me*."

Here on a high floor, in this padded suite with heavy curtains and a velvet carpet, we talked about the movie star's meteoric rise, artistic plans, admiration for his co-workers, and motion picture philosophy, as well as the nightly seating plan and holiday variations of his family of origin, until an agreeable silence fell. The traffic noise was faint, as if coming from New Jersey. He removed his silk socks and felt the rug with his toes. He was tremendously fed up with his life.

After a while in the silence, I said: "No, I am not always this stiff. I am this stiff right after my son moves to California, my mother gets cancer, and a man I started to love dumps me. You'd be 'stiff.' "

"He's got somebody else," he said.

"That's not true, actually. Don't you think I could tell something like that?"

"He *wants* somebody else. You interested in uncle's advice?"

"Probably not," I said. "I think I'm older than uncle."

"Here it is: This guy died. Go out, have lunch with your girlfriends, get yourself a tiny bit screwed as soon as humanly possible. Drink. Dance," he said gloomily. I gazed at him, my adviser. He had had his incipient baldness repaired at several dollars an individual follicle. With his palm he felt the top of his velvety, beautiful head.

I walked down Fifth Avenue in the sun and wind, through clouds of souvlaki smoke. To wait for the phone to ring, I was going to stay away from home all day. In a midtown atrium, among the potted ficus trees, under a soaring artificial sky, there was a lunchtime piano concert, a young guy in striped shirt and arm bands playing songs popular from 1850 to 1905. At the end, an old man joined another old man at his table. He peeled open a package and gave his friend half the sandwich. "Well, Samuel," he cried, "he really tore at your heartstrings, didn't he? He really belted out the old standards, didn't he? He really wailed out the old songs, didn't he? He really wailed 'em out."

The old men were so small and careful they were breaking my heart. I went to the booth and dialed Ewing at his lab. When his secretary answered, I hung up.

I called Mom in Boston. She was doing fine. Rhody had stayed with her, then gone back to Vermont. Hilary had moved in for the month, and Raymond was constantly present, wielding his Dustbuster, returning videos, and serving vegetarian paté to the many guests. "Raymond is being wonderful. And *you* were *too*."

"You've told me many times," I said.

"Oh poo. Then cover your ears."

I called Michael Roseman, who had known Ewing before I did. He said, "Honey, you already know how sorry I am, but the guy's a well-known isolate."

"Then why did you encourage me?"

"Hey. He's ambulatory. He's employed. No, forgive me—this is no time to kid. He's a good guy. I thought it might work out. How was the actor? Did he always sit at Mama's right hand?"

"He was fine," I said. "Insulated and discouraged. Michael, can I ask you? Don't you think Ewing really cared about me?"

"Yup," he said. "Two minutes," he whispered to

his secretary—an intimate tone, which hurt my heart. I could hear him hold up two fingers.

"I think I got closer to him than anybody," I said.

"Could be true."

"I asked him what went wrong in his marriage. He was very honest. He said, 'I couldn't do it right.' "

"Well, sweetheart, I'm really sorry."

"I think I was dangerous for him. He did feel threatened."

Michael said, "Honey, he studies rats? People are *like* rats. They flee anxiety."

"I think he took a risk with me."

"Maybe you got him ready for the next girl," Michael said, chuckling darkly. "But we better talk tonight."

"I'm hardly a *girl*," I said. "Jesus. Your research assistants must knock your block off."

I called both Deenie and Annie. "The prick," Deenie said. "He was a professional. He just finally stopped doing his shtick."

To each of them I said, *I hope he'll be alone for a long time.* After the two calls, I conflated their answers, to create a powerful supportive chorus crying, *He will! He will!*

While I was there, I called my machine. Rustling silence and then my sister's voice: "Say hello." Then the sound of a little kid breathing. Then the phone slammed down.

I stood in the booth, which smelled of sweat and new and old urine, and ran through all the messages, going back weeks, hearing Ewing's voice five times. I'd been hogging the phone for an hour—enraged citizens had come and gone. The receiver was greasy and hot, as if, after relieving themselves, everybody in the city had just talked into it today.

I walked twenty blocks up Madison Avenue, to purchase some caresses. At the salon, my scalp was scrubbed with velvet soap by Jean-Baptiste, a boy wearing nail polish and plaid pumps. He kept the water always slightly too hot, a delicate sadistic note. But this was what I'd come for: my head tipped back, my face in clouds of perfumed steam, Jean-Baptiste's fragrant shirtfront against my hungry cheek.

I found myself telling Arlo in the mirror that Ewing had left. Behind me, Arlo stood snipping the air with scissors, considering; in front of me, our eyes briefly locked. "This person will return," he said absently, while cold water laid itself drop by drop onto the back of my neck.

"He won't," I said, "I know him," though I actually still thought it possible.

"Well, who is this person who doesn't want a sensational woman? What is the name of this dumbo?"

"Ewing."

"You're saying 'Ewing,' as a first name? And Ewing is what, a plantation owner?"

"Psychiatrist."

"Oh this is not so good." Arlo stood back to see if I looked like a maniac yet.

"I think it was my fault," I said—I did think maybe it was and I could fix it. "I pushed him around. He was nice about it—he's always nice. He said, 'Gosh, you work your raw material pretty hard.' "

"Nope," he said. "Keeping perspective, this person

is a shrink. They simply cannot place themselves in anybody's hands.''

Arlo rushed at me and dug his fingers into my hair and stirred it up, then spun me around and dusted me off. Before I turned to go, he came up close to me and mimed empathy at me, into my damp eyes.

Saturday, I got up at six and drove to Vermont. I needed to go home. Dark October morning, and the road was treacherously curving, demanding too much attention, and the new tape player was broken. Gray clouds like watermarks in the sky. Heart broken by the indifference of the turnpike toll-taker. My tears refusing to come down.

Originally, I recalled, I had resisted him because he made love like a womanizer: he was so fluent, so steadily ardent, it seemed generic. He had a straight gaze, pale-blue eyes with black edges. As a child visiting in Mississippi, he'd been babysat by Eudora Welty. The week after the fish bone, he'd admitted he feared commitment and then sucked my tongue out of my head.

My sister and Tom lived in a handyman's special, on a country road, next to a river. There were no front steps, just a door suspended in air: to enter, you had to dive up. When I pulled in, I could see them inside, standing together on the living-room rug: Tom, Rhoda with the new baby, and Nicholas in his pajamas. Rhody kept talking to Tom, while she pointed for me to walk around to the back. They stood there framed in their window, an ordinary family, safe from harm.

To be spunky, I was wearing running shorts. In the

kitchen, Nicholas embraced my legs and laid his face against them. My remaining bravado lifted away. I felt suddenly very shaky, smelling sawdust and paint, looking at my family, feeling Nips's hot breath around my knees.

Tom grabbed the sleeping baby and started to dance a kind of samba, holding her tiny arm straight out. She curled against him and slept on. He sang—Latin rhythm: "Happy little baby! Happy little baby! Even her own family drives her crazy! Just a little baby is what I am! Maybe Mom and Dad will fry me some Spam!"

"How's it going?" I said.

Tom said, "Nothing that fifteen milligrams of Xanax and a week in Ocho Rios wouldn't cure."

"Active," Rhody said.

Tom said, "I've discovered why humans don't hear as well as, say, dogs. Early on, they damage their own hearing by screaming. So, for millennia we haven't been able to hear as well as the beasts."

"Did you talk to Mom today?" Rhody asked.

"She's fine; it's a magic recovery."

"And did he call?" she asked. I shook my head.

Tom, still dancing: "The misbegotten slug. There's a sense in which you probably don't need further advice. You've probably already considered disembowelment. We're still enjoying reflecting on the early tongue incident." My tongue had turned black. Ewing had chuckled and said, almost inaudibly, "Darlin', I could say I'm sorry but it seems it'd be so very inadequate."

Sabina, the baby, had wet brown hair. Rhody said, "She's all sweaty all the time because I'm always hugging her." Rhody had been up since four, when she had walked the baby out in the yard to let her see the moon and hear the small night birds.

Tom and I stayed up late together and got in the truck and drove down the river road and out to the highway to the all-night convenience store. The patrons, moving around in AM radio and bluish white light, looked as if they lived in the store, like plants thriving all night in the basement under a grow-light. It was two in the morning. Tom and I stood in a long line. We were suddenly very short. Set out in a former potato field nearby was a junior college. Young basketball players were in here, staring and standing around carrying gallons of milk and enormous boxes of doughnuts.

I said, "Ewing used to buy dark brown sugar for his coffee."

Tom whispered, "Calm yourself, honeycat, these people don't want to hear about your tragedy. They don't have the emotional wherewithal to absorb the news." He was stoned. He stood with one hand pressing the front of his chartreuse bowling shirt, as if holding it in place on his chest. He rattled our potato chip bag as a rhythm section, accompanying some music only he could hear.

After a long time in the line, Tom said slowly, "Here's a story for you. A guy's worst faults were as follows: (1) Broiled and ate a T-bone. (2) Thought Reagan was fun to watch on television. (3) Used maps to get places."

"Is this you?" But he let his eyes fall shut and showed me his palms.

In the back of his landscaping truck, two small trees were standing in balls of earth wrapped in burlap. On the ride back, he drove frantically fast in the moonlight, the pickup shuddering around the curves, the river rushing nearby, as I told him things: Dogs are not allowed to run free, but Ewing would let his labrador out at night, because the dog was black. His tenderness with the dog when it was sick. The way he picked the dog up in his arms and carried him downstairs so the dog could pee; the way he slept at night with his arm hanging, his hand on the dog's hot back.

Tom, wildly steering: "No no. I do not think so. The maudlin is not your proper refuge."

How Ewing had once wanted to be a composer and music was always pouring through his elegant shabby house. How Ewing went to a ball game with some colleagues in satiety research, and when they got tired of cheering for the Yankees they cheered for parts of the brain. How maybe Ewing and I were not finished yet.

"No no," Tom said. He accelerated. The little treetops rustled at the window behind our heads. He wheeled into the driveway and slammed to a stop. He sang, "Get out of my truck! Get into my home!" I followed him across the front yard, through tall grass like deep fur. He climbed up, balanced on the door jamb, pushed open the front door. Then he reached down and pulled me out of the yard, up into the dark house.

The next morning, early, I half-woke making love with Ewing, in some unknown house at the beach, during a black cold night. As I took off my nightdress in the dark, sparks crackled around my torso. There was a penlight on the table, and when he turned it on a dot of light jiggled on the wallpaper. He pointed the penlight and ran it over my body, describing a line of light like a brilliant thread running all over me. He shined the light once straight into my eyes. I tried to look, and when I couldn't, he set his hand over my closed eyelids. Later he switched it off and dropped it on the blanket, but until then the point of light showed his fingers touching my arms, my breasts, my belly— the light trembling, eventually, when he did. He leaned over me and licked my body, starting from the edge of my hair, like a cat. The cold and the sparks were inventions—we hadn't known each other long enough to go through a winter.

Sunny, quiet morning. In the kitchen, looking down through trees at the river, I dialed, and when I heard his voice I said, "I feel like punching you, through the phone."

He laughed.

I insisted on knowing: what actually had gone wrong, what was in his mind? Until this moment, I said, I'd been too alarmed to ask. "Are you happy?"

"I'm not feelin' particularly happy. But I didn't expect to."

"Then why are you doing this?"

"You know it's not perfectly apparent to me why. You know I'd like to think it'd be temporary. But you need to be goin' on with your life."

"I'm not really going on with it," I said.

"Well, that's not right."

"I can't break through to feeling that I want to go forward."

"Well, that's what you've got to think about now: how to proceed for yourself."

"I don't admit it," I said, "and sometimes I don't even notice it. But I'm waiting for you."

There was quiet on the line. Then he said softly, "Don't do that."

I had called to affirm my confidence in both our continuing connection and my ability to let him go. Instead I said would he please ride up here for the night and we could talk?

"Joey, I don't think we wanta be havin' talks right now."

I asked again.

"It's hours away. I'm writin' all weekend."

There was a pause, and then, typically, he suddenly reversed position, and said, okay, he'd do it; he'd drive up today.

My spirits lifted so radically that the air looked different. When I came down after my shower, the house smelled like coffee and they were all in the kitchen. Nicholas patted my leg with a moist hand. Rhoda and Tom were discussing a funny couple they knew, a brand-new feminist coming to it late in the century, and her formerly dominating, guilt-ridden husband. Tom said, "She just has to say the word 'patriarch' and the poor palooka hands over the money."

Rhody laughed and tried to bend her nipple into Sabina's mouth. Tom leaned down and said, "Right, little baby? Right, little baby? *Right, little tiny beautiful baby darling?* Right, would you beat a fellow up for his cultural conditioning? Would you raise a fellow to shoot big guns and defend your honor and then change your mind and mop up the floor with him? Would you? Would you? Well, what *is* it? What *is* it?"

"She can't eat if you do that," Rhoda said.

"Dad has been dispensed with, little baby," Tom said into the baby's bright black eyes. "Dad was a sexually besotted fool. By donating his sperm, Dad rendered himself irrelevant."

"See? She looks at you," Rhoda said.

Tom walked me out into the warm fall morning, through the weeds to where the garden would be established next spring, and for a while we tramped around describing giant beefsteak tomato plants, a glut of zucchinis, melon vines entwined with fancy trellises. From behind his back Tom produced a small tomato grown in Israel under artificial rain, and, as if he had just picked it from the fictitious garden, set it into my hand. It was pink, too round, fake-looking, and still cold from the refrigerator. He said, "I'm illustrating the vast gulf between the imagined and the real." "I know all about it," I said irritably. "Then cut this jerk loose," he said. He jumped in his truck and drove away.

Back inside, the baby was asleep and Rhoda was in her studio. Nicholas was watching kung fu. I found some more vegetables, chopped them up, and started a soup cooking. We'd serve it to Ewing tonight when the temperature dropped.

Mom phoned. She said, "We're putting together a rock group here. We're calling it The Grateful Living."

I heard a car in the driveway and I stepped out to look but of course there was no car.

I came back in and told Nicholas I would do anything he wanted. So we lay down on a rug shaped like a bear. The animal had pearly fangs and a synthetic fur, everything fuzzy or shiny, and we lay on his chest and pulled his paws around us. Babar and Celeste were visiting another planet, whose pacific inhabitants welcomed them with a combination of irony and joy. I held the book up and lay with Nips's hair tickling my face, and we were comfortable for a long time in the bear's embrace.

Rhoda came down. She had been working in pastel; her hands were lavender, and there were marks on her forearms like bruises. "Is he really coming?" she said. For a moment, I realized he might not. But Ewing was far too nice for that.

I set up my typewriter at the window and transcribed some tape. Long hours later, as Ewing's car pulled in, the movie star was saying, "You need this advice real bad: you gotta *lighten up.*"

The day had cleared. He was standing on the driveway, contemplating the brilliant light. White clouds were lifting out of the sky, leaving trails in a new field of blue. I said, "My brother-in-law gave me a single tomato. He thinks that's an appropriate gift for me now." Ewing grinned.

We sat in the kitchen. I affected an attractive facial expression: accepting, strong, calm. But then I said how bewildering it was to feel like this, so young and fragile again—and to feel that the only person who might understand is the one who's gone.

"It's odd-feeling, isn't it?" he said. "I know that feeling."

"Why can't we talk about negotiating something?" I said.

"I'm not much of a negotiator, y'know."

"We love each other. Why are we throwing it out?"

He gazed at me.

"I don't understand," I said.

He said, "This is so hard."

"Are you involved with somebody? I mean, I don't think you are but I've thought about it."

He smiled. He said, "You sound like a little girl."

"I know. It feels awful. It shouldn't be this bad—you and I haven't even been together that long. I don't really remember, but I think it felt like this when I *was* young—when my father died."

"I wondered about that."

"Well, look, answer my question."

He said, "There's nobody else."

"Well, I don't understand."

"Joey. This is hard for me too. I don't know why my feelings have changed so dramatically. I was feelin' so very intense and positive. And it just finally sorta evaporated on me."

"What does it mean! What does it *mean,* evaporated? There's fluctuation in everybody's feelings for everybody!"

"I know."

"I don't understand," I said. "Don't you love me?"

"You're wonderfully generous to even want to talk about it this long," he said. "It's so—"

"Do you not love me?"

"There're other things—"

"Oh man. Just say yes or no."

He looked at me softly. "Then no," he said finally. "Not right now."

I tipped my head back, just to breathe. Late sunlight was slanting into the room, making everything rosy. Ewing's hands were glowing, lying on the glowing table. Tom had made me laugh, half a year before, saying, "Are we sure we want this fellow awash in continual celestial light?"

I could smell the soup. I stood up and walked over and lifted the pot, lugged it to the sink, leaned it on the edge, and poured the soup down the drain. Steam billowed up and I stood in it.

He came and stood behind me and put his arms around me. "Please don't go," I said.

"You know I have to. At least for a while."

"It won't be for a while. If you go now, you won't come back."

He stood with his chin resting on my head. After a minute, he said, "You're so smart."

Tom and Nips came in, and Ewing said to me, "Walk me out."

In the living room I said, "I don't want my sister and brother-in-law to hear me. Don't make this be final."

"Nothing's final to me, darlin'. I've got such a long view of the future."

3 1 0

"Wait a minute," I said.

"I've got to go now. It's gettin' so much harder."

He started toward the door, and while he was taking one step, I changed my mind about something.

I touched his sleeve, and he turned. I swung like a batter and hit him in the head. His hair bounced! I hit him again, fast, and again. Instead of backing away, Ewing stepped forward—that was interesting to see—and I just kept hitting. A familiar feeling rising: I was starting to enjoy myself.

We rushed to the door. I pulled on the handle, the door swung in, Ewing moved, and I shoved. He fell easily, *nicely*, backward, out into the end of the weird summery day, looking as surprised as I'd seen him look in the short time I thought I knew the man. His feet flew up, he landed, and his head dipped into the long grass, just before I smashed the door shut. The sound of the door slamming continued to ring pleasantly in the room. I could hear Tom calling, "Everything okay?"

"Fine, fine!" I yelled.

I was about to turn and rush into the kitchen and start making lists: plans for Michael's and my next book, things to buy for the house, calls to make, possible men, and the longest list—stuff to throw out. I was out of breath. I stood a moment with my pulse settling down. Almost dreamily, almost cheerfully, I stood there, already imagining myself returning to the world and turning recognizable again. At the same time I was seeing Ewing, his sweet face staring and his arm flung back, as he lifted off the edge of the house and out into bright air. He didn't surprise me. He flew the way I always knew that Ewing had to fly.

17. The Tap Dancer's Bride

Here's a story I've told myself:

Summer 1973. The new neighbors in back have five baby huskies, the children of Samantha the Siberian husky and her full-bred husky boyfriend. The baby huskies make no sound, except twice a day for a few minutes when they yelp in concert, and then the sound is watery, modulated almost as human voices are, and shrill. Next the puppies are fed and fall silent for eight hours. In the daytime I imagine them steamy, whimpering, dreaming, coiled in sleep.

While I've been putting the kids to bed, William has been talking with the neighbors. Through the window I watch him turning away from the fence, crossing the lawn. Night is falling, he is wearing his bathing suit. In silhouette—all that hair—he looks like a creature with an enormous, burdensome head. His limbs are white, moving through darkness.

"I dealt with them," he says, slipping in past the glass door. "What's wrong with this screen?" he says, alarmed.

"What did you tell them?"

"I told them, either feed the dogs later in the morning or—I *just told them*." He tries to wrestle the sliding screen door back onto its track. William hates the initial shock of discovering something is broken, and during that first moment he always tries to force the broken thing intact. He especially likes things to open easily and to move smoothly on tracks, and he has large supplies of 3-in-1 oil for making kitchen drawers glide, and graphite for the car doors. We have three new ladders of graduated sizes—one so tall we're afraid to use it. We are new homeowners, crazily well prepared.

William snaps the door in, slides it four times, pats his bathing suit. "They're quite intriguing people," he says. "She's an attractive middle-aged woman, about forty. He's an obsessive-seeming, nice guy. He used to have komondors, apparently a huge moplike Hungarian dog, and Bouviers. He has a bathtub in the basement for bathing them, and he showed me how he used to command the komondors to jump into the tub."

The upshot is that William told the neighbors that once feeding time arrives and they step inside the pen, the faster they could get the food to the little huskies the happier we as neighbors would be.

" 'We as neighbors'?" I ask.

He looks sly. "I told them that we wanted them out, this town wasn't big enough for all of us, I'd give them five minutes to split. I fired at their shoes and made them dance." He jiggles the screen door. I feel comfortable, happy, attentive. "My gun smoked, they pleaded and slobbered and fell all over themselves, while I hummed 'Slow Boat to China' and shot at their feet. The huskies cheered! My parting shot was verbal, I told them: Five huskies make bad neighbors."

Later, the night is warm and dark. William is bent over the liquor cabinet in his bathing suit pouring a brandy. We've started learning to drink cognacs and we drink them in every season. Willie and I have a project together: growing into our life.

I step over a Big Wheel and three plush piglets to get to him. I pat his naked back, which is hot and moist. "Are the baby huskies adorable?"

He is voluptuously dipping his nose into his snifter. "I didn't look," William says. "I didn't want to know."

William is in the bathroom, in clouds of steam, briskly toweling. I follow him into the bedroom where I observe his activities: the arraying of the suit and tie on the bed, the search for collar stays, the slow buttoning of the crisp shirt. I watch closely, as often. Meanwhile I continue the interview. I have been interviewing him for possible poetry, but also with an eye to getting to know him better, or something like: becoming entangled in his interior life in a deeper, more poignant way.

Q: These rituals of men dressing have always held some fascination for me. When I was very young, I remember, I was always thrusting my hand into the pocket of my father's shirt to open it. It had been sealed by starch and could be opened only by me—I was small and determined enough for the job, and perhaps otherwise justifiably favored over the others. Do you have similar memories of your participation in or of watching your father at his toilette?

A: I don't recall any. [Willie is standing in his socks and shirt, regarding his image in the mirror, struggling to knot his tie.] Why are you talking like that?

Q: I'm finding a voice. This is a formal interview. Actually [surprised] maybe I'm imitating your formal style! We know that you were often permitted into the parents' bedroom, perhaps even encouraged to enter while they were dressing and undressing.

A: I don't think that's true. You always say that, but I don't know where you get it.

Q: Remember Janet and Theo's wedding, when we went in the car with your parents and all stayed in the motel, and they were always inviting you into their room? They were always standing around in stages of seemingly intentional or self-conscious *deshabille* having conversations with you about road maps. You were always all standing with your heads touching over maps of Pennsylvania. It appeared very natural to you.

A: [Dignified] I don't remember it that way. Not at all. I went in one or two times to check directions with my father when he was wearing his shorts and garters, and my mother was in her slip in the bathroom. Their stage of undress *was* intentional, although not self-conscious: they were getting dressed.

Q: You talked to your mother all through the reception.

A: That may be, Kittiekattie, but that was four years ago and we discussed it already. The interview is deteriorating.

Q: Do you dream in color?

A: You know I do. We all do.

Q: Does one color predominate? As a former film student, you probably have a favorite.

A: Midnight blue, as you know. In my dreams, aquamarine, or, weirdly enough, powder or baby.

Q: Have you recalled any dreams?

A: [William is sitting on the bed now, dressed, fondling the corner of his briefcase.] I have one which I'll tell you later.

Q: Stay for two minutes. I have a short battery of somewhat related questions: Do you dream about me? Do you have fantasies about me with other men? With other women? When you decide not to go jogging with me, are you ever sorry after I've left?

A: Yes. Yes. Yes. No.

Q: This is a tripartite question. When my mother took us to St. Moritz, did you think about me in the mornings while you were at the pool? As you swam along did you start to experience a sensory deprivation and did your thoughts begin to drift and wander freely? If so, did they drift to me in any unusual way, and did you experience visual images of me?

A: I took a longish dip. Each day I tried to significantly increase my speed and number of laps. I thought about my increments in muscle tone and stamina. Afterward I went into the shower room, and on the first day after my shower I stood under the blow dryer next to a young man from West Germany. He was a young furrier, and he asked me with an attitude of great alertness about nightspots around town and about the relative stylishness and enthusiasm for fur coats of American and European women. He seemed taken with American women generally and interested in their being persuaded to clothe themselves more often in furs; and—to address more directly your own area of interest—perhaps was angling for an introduction to you. He had seen you at the pool the day before. He asked my marital status.

Q: Why didn't you ever tell me this?

A: Until the formal interview I was unaware of your interest. You usually ask me not to tell my longer stories.

Q: When the German man saw me, was I wearing my black maillot?

A: I'd like to add that the young German was a Jew. He immediately told me I didn't look "American." He said I looked "European"—like him. About your bathing suit, I don't know, of course. Although the interview is over for today, I can tell you this: you looked fine the whole time in St. Moritz.

Many Saturdays, of course, some effort we're making breaks down, and we stay up all night in our bedroom enjoying some of the nostalgia available to young people, looking back a couple of years—listening to Beatles and Dylan and "Music from Big Pink," smoking grass Willie buys from the guy who works on his moribund Saab. The night grows velvety, darker, thicker. It seems original to us to make love in the velvet dark. At dawn, we can feel the day starting—our eyes closed, music sliding through our heads.

But mainly, we're trying to be citizens and heads of household, grown up, settled and calm—a suburban couple.

On Friday when the local newspaper comes out, Willie reads me the real estate ads. After dinner he sits in our favorite and beloved possession, the new leather chair, and holds the paper close to his eyes while deciding whether to make a fictitious offer. He peers at smudged and ambiguous photos depicting blurry branches framing or obscuring the dwellings. He doesn't seem to recall that when we looked for our house, the houses were unrecognizable from their pictures. Even standing in front of the house itself with the paper open, you couldn't invariably match them up.

He calls out prices, shifts in his chair looking restless and amused: he *is* a little amused, and very restless. As when I interview him, I affect a voice: something almost normal. I ask if he remembers that the houses are always unrecognizable from their pictures.

"That's the way I like it," he says.

Long years ago, Willie's dad owned a lumber yard; Pep spent his days hanging out surrounded by two-by-fours stacked to the ceiling, breathing the beautiful smell of new wood, schmoozing with his many cronies. Willie and his father share an interest in being what they both call an entity in the community. This year, 1974, William has made a first try at becoming a crony himself, with Roger, who owns the liquor store. I have told Willie my feeling that his hanging out at the liquor store is a signal of his deep love for his own father and his wish to be united with him in a more overt and dependable way.

"The subject doesn't hang out there," William says, *sotto voce.* "He just looks at the new wines."

William is becoming ever less capable of interrupting any long jovial conversation, so he talks as long as Roger the liquor store owner likes. (In my opinion Willie is in conflict. Certainly he longs for escape—he's too young for this life. But he is too gratified at having got to the point where he has three pals in one shop; when other customers enter, he becomes proprietary and starts to show off, helplessly shouting into the back to Dave and Don in a hale and pushy manner.)

"Are you aware of your facial expression when you talk to Roger?" I ask him. "Roger ignores women, so I have time to notice. Your eyes glaze over, but you wear an expression of curious, tense animation."

He tells me, "It's *so hard won*."

"You mean being a successful crony."

"It means something to my life. I can't explain it. I can't just turn the guy off."

"Do you let your mind wander?"

He says, "While Roger talks, I think about forms of self-discipline, situations of rigor I've heard about. I'm like a prisoner in my little personal, solitary cell!—always moving, running in place."

"*You* put *yourself* in the jail," I say. "It's not a political prisoner. It's just you."

William says cheerfully: "More and more your message: 'Oh, it's only you.' "

The Saturday after this conversation the kids and I are walking past Towne Wines, and through the window I see Roger chortling over the headlines. My husband is also standing there, croaking out a pained croak of a laugh. Even through glass I can see him straining, hacking the laugh out onto the counter.

Q: Are you happy?
A: Often, yes. Are you?
Q: I'm the interviewer. And are you often restless?

A: Fairly frequently. [Smiles, looks charming] Somewhat depends on the Knicks.

Q: When we ate dinner with the Rosemans, why didn't you let me tell my funny story about the kids? I'm with the kids all the time, at least you could let me talk about it. Deenie Roseman told *her* story about *her* kids and everybody listened. It makes me feel better to be witty and entertaining, and I don't have that many chances—

A: Frame a question.

Q: As an only child you have never experienced sibling rivalry. Can you be experiencing it for the first time, now, with me?

A: I want you to tell your stories, I don't know what happens, I get nervous. I feel responsible for forestalling conversational lag.

Q: Can't you give a more useful answer?

A: I don't subscribe to the notion that my answers have to be of use. Anyway, you introduced it irritatingly. It's an irritating subject.

Q: Many of them seem to be.

A: Well, sue me, Kittiekattie. Most of them are.

Willie and I are in the bedroom talking about making our wills. It seems responsible, yet it's easy: we'll never die. When we come out, Zack and Nora are lying on the rug in the hall looking miserable—abandoned and resigned.

"Were you eavesdropping?" I say.

Nora says, "I couldn't understand you."

Zack says, "I heard a mumble."

So we tell them at length how young and healthy we are, causing them to look incredulous and then to humor us—little guys patronizing slightly bigger ones.

Central Park, May 1975, the celebration of the end of the war. William and I get up at six to make the lunch, and we drive to New York City and leave the car miles from the park and walk through hazy sunny streets with crowds of people all going one way. Willie lugs two shopping bags stuffed with still-warm roasted chickens, sliced beets in oil, bottles of Beaujolais, Oreos, curls of butter in a little dish. At the edge of the Sheep Meadow, he spreads our blanket with a flourish, in the dust, on sprigs of grass, and pins two corners down with his sneakers. "Eat at once," he says, and starts ripping the bags open and thrusting food into Nora and Zack's hands. The kids are excited, because we are, and because Joan Baez is their hero. People swirl around us. Balloons fly up. Willie slices off chicken legs and hurls them around. He spoons out heaps of salad onto plastic plates. When the kids walk a few steps away, he says to me, I do love you and more importantly I want to love you. In equable silence, we smoke a joint. When the kids come back, he grins and croons at them, *All we are sayyy-innng. Is give beets a chance.* The loudspeaker, from miles away, talks and sings to us half the long afternoon.

At night I walk past the kitchen and Willie's in there, on gleaming vinyl, wearing his suit, one arm out of one sleeve with the jacket hanging. He's tap-dancing. He's humming and grunting "The Sidewalks of New York," and twirling side to side. He makes a half-turn and back again, taps, nods to the toaster, taps, throws the refrigerator a confiding smile. The kitchen is full of light. I pass again and see flashes of him and listen to the slaps of his shoes. He lowers his head, tips his hat, and sings: "Tumptumpadump side. Tump pump pump side. All a-round the bump bump bump PAH!"

I go upstairs and get into bed and do the crossword puzzle while I wait for him.

After a long time, he comes into the bedroom carrying his suit jacket slung over one shoulder and moving with a sliding step like Fred Astaire. His face is flushed, his aspect serene.

He takes his shoes off and stands there. He says, "I do it because you want to think of me as a darling tap dancer, and yourself as the tap dancer's bride."

Willie and I really like talking about things, like tap-dancing and the liquor store and the huskies, that are up on the surface of the life we're imagining.

"You do it for me?" I say, filling in "liaison."

"Sure."

"That's ridiculous. You tap-dance for me?" "Eternal," then "err."

"The only remaining reason." *Remaining*, he says—as if he were near the end of his life, instead of just a few steps from the beginning.

We feel things will work out. We'll try, and we can probably do it: raise the kids, grow up ourselves, and stay together—be a family. People do this all the time; it can't be beyond Willie and me.

He stands and looks at me as my fingers continue

3 2 2

to make time over the puzzle. When I've filled in all the words, which if I concentrate should be manageable, I will have a whole completed thing that will not change. This is a story about us when we were young, more plausible than most.